I0646906

SPEAKING TIGER PUBLISHING PVT. LTD
4381/4, Ansari Road, Daryaganj
New Delhi 110002

Original copyright © Ratnottama Sengupta 2018
Translations copyright © Ratnottama Sengupta 2018

Published by Speaking Tiger 2018

ISBN: 978-93-87693-61-6
eISBN: 978-93-87164-93-2

10 9 8 7 6 5 4 3 2 1

The moral right of the author has been asserted.

Typeset in Adobe Caslon Pro by SÜRYA, New Delhi
Printed at Sanat Printers, Kundli

Contents

Nabendu Ghosh (1917-2007) was a dancer, novelist, short-story writer, film director, actor and screenwriter. His oeuvre of work includes thirty novels and fifteen collections of short stories. As scriptwriter, he penned cinematic classics such as *Devdas, Bandini, Sujata, Parineeti, Majhli Didi* and *Abhimaan.* And, as part of a team of iconic film directors and actors, he was instrumental in shaping an entire age of Indian cinema. He was the recipient of numerous literary and film awards, including the Bankim Puraskar, the Bibhuti Bhushan Sahitya Arghya, the Filmfare Best Screenplay Award and the National Film Award for Best First Film of a Director.

Ratnottama Sengupta, formerly Arts Editor of *The Times of India*, teaches mass communication and film appreciation, curates film festivals and art exhibitions, and writes books. The daughter of Nabendu Ghosh, she has written *Krishna's Cosmos*, a biography of the pioneering printmaker Krishna Reddy, and also entries on Hindi films for *Encyclopedia Britannica*. She has been a member of the Central Board of Film Certification, served on the jury of the National Film Awards, and has herself won a National Film Award.

In 2017, she directed *And They Made Classics*, a documentary about Nabendu Ghosh.

That Bird Called Happiness

~ Stories ~

NABENDU GHOSH

Edited by RATNOTTAMA SENGUPTA

Foreword by GULZAR

SPEAKING
TIGER

Foreword

Nabendu-da's film scripts clearly reveal his literary side. The warp and weft of his characters and plots are perfectly natural, logical and rooted. It is obvious that they have been written by someone who was raised in literature, and not merely in films. Those who come to screenwriting by watching films alone concoct from scenes and situations they've seen—it is as if the same food is being poured from one vessel to another. But whenever Dada wrote a scene, we got a fresh perspective, a totally new feel and flavour. That was because he was a writer before he came into the film world, and he continued to write novels and short stories even as he scripted films. The tragedy of film-writing today is that none of the writers have experienced cinema along with literature.

I remember those days when he was teaching students of direction at the Film and Television Institute of India. At that time, let alone film academies, not even books on screenplay-writing were available. Vikas Desai, one of Dada's early students who directed the thriller *Shaque* (1976), once told me, 'When Sir took classes, it was like he was holding our hand and leading us up the stairs of screenwriting, step by step.' What a contribution to Indian cinema that was!

I also vividly remember reading 'Kooda', in translation in Hindi. It is one of the best-woven stories I have ever read. Dada was writing from life experience, not from observation. That, to me, is the khaas baat about Dada's writing. And this is clear to those who have read his stories and seen the films he scripted. Nabendu-da's stories visualize action in terms of characters, and his characters always spring from the action. That is the most beautiful aspect of his writing, and that is what I have learnt from him.

And these qualities which went into his writing—whether film scripts or novels and short stories—gave Nabendu-da the confidence to hold his own with a director of the stature of Bimal Roy.

I remember a day during the making of *Bandini* (1963).

While finalizing a scene that had been discussed before, Bimal-da said, 'Iss ko iss tarah se likh do… Rewrite this scene like that…'

Nabendu-da said, 'Aami paarbo na. I can't do that.'

When Bimal-da insisted, Dada got up and said in his usual soft voice, 'I am a writer, not a kerani…' This was the unassailable dignity of a writer speaking.

When we were leaving in the evening, Dada asked, 'Kaal kakhon? When do we meet tomorrow?'

Bimal-da replied, 'But you don't agree with my visualization of the scene. Toh kaal ki hobey? What will we do tomorrow?'

Dada said in his usual unflappable manner, 'Shey kaal dekha jaabe. We'll see about that tomorrow.'

He 'saw' his stories like he did the films he scripted. That is why they will continue to see tomorrows and tomorrows…

April 2018　　　　　　　　　　　　　　　　　GULZAR

Lights!

The window to the west opens out on to the vastness that is the Arabian Sea. Small fishing boats crisscross the horizon over ceaseless waves, their white sails fluttering like seagulls in flight. The setting sun, about to announce nightfall, is setting ablaze with its sleepy embers the white, grey and purple clouds floating in the blue sky. A mystical light engulfs the world. A light that sets the heart aflutter and compels one to face one's unfulfilled desires and longings.

Salma enters the room.

'Do you hear me, Bibiji? He's here!'

'Who?' Umrao Mahal, standing next to the bay window, was startled. Umrao Mahal, who reigned as the superstar Roop Kumari in the world of Indian films. The brightest of the stars on the silver screen. Whose unmatched beauty, grace and acting prowess fetched her three lakh rupees per film.

'Who's here, Salma?'

'Him: Shaukat-mian. Did you not hear the car?' Salma said with a hint of smile.

At this, Umrao's arched eyebrows—which Shaukat once likened to a falcon's wings—arched even more.

'Why? What does the man want?' Irritation dripped from Umrao's voice.

'How should I know, Bibiji? I'm just the maid.'

'Hmm!'

Umrao left her room in a flash. Her brocaded slippers slid over the marble floor and crossed the verandah to reach a room where a manservant was giving her father, Hamidul Haq, a foot massage.

'Abbajaan!'

'Yes, my child?' Hamidul Haq turned towards his daughter with a smile. But the foreboding of a storm on Umrao's face turned the smile into a frown. 'What's wrong, Roopa?'

'He's here,' Umrao said through gritted teeth.

'Who?'

'That shameless man, Shaukat!'

'Really!' Hamidul Haq sat up. 'How shameless! Don't worry, I'll check the cheat. I know how to foil his tricks.'

Hamidul stood up.

'Tell him, no compromise is possible in this lifetime,' said Umrao.

'Yes beta, that's exactly what I'll say.'

Hamidul Haq left the room, his face reflecting his resolve.

Umrao stood still for a moment, then drew her dupatta around herself and followed her father to the drawing room downstairs.

She crossed the hall and stood behind one of the drawing-room doors. Hamidul Haq had entered the room by then. Umrao drew the curtains aside slightly to see Shaukat rise with his back to the door. He was dressed in a Lucknowi chikan-embroidered mulmul kurta paired with loose pyjamas—his trademark attire.

Umrao dropped the curtain. Just the sight of him raised her hackles.

'Salaam walekum,' Shaukat greeted the senior warmly. A ring of humility layered his voice.

'Walaikum salaam,' Hamidul returned the greeting rather gruffly. 'Take a seat. Tell me, what brings you here?' Hamidul tried to match the Lucknowi gentility of Shaukat's speech.

'Sir, I would like to meet Roopa,' Shaukat said as he took a seat.

'Why?' Hamidul raised his thick eyebrows as if he was talking to a stranger. 'What for?'

'I want to say a few things to her and ask her some things too.'

'She will not meet you.'

'Is that her decision or yours?'

'It is hers and mine.'

'Both of you are being unjust to me, janaab.'

'No Shaukat-mian, you were the one who was unjust.' Hamidul's voice was firm. 'You took undue advantage of my simple girl and tried to harm her...'

'But we are married...' Shaukat did not forget his manners.

'And we intend to break that marriage,' Hamidul replied.

Shaukat remained silent for a while, then said, 'What if I don't agree to do so?'

'We don't depend on you to agree—the law of the land is with us.'

'Will that be honourable?'

'Perhaps not. Still, it will be more desirable than damaging her life. Heed me, Shaukat-mian, these are my last words. You are well-educated, you have a reputation as a lyricist, you aspire to be a director. You will scale the heights of fame. That has been your intention all along and that was why you charmed my daughter, hoping to use her as the ladder for your ascent. I realized that long ago, but my only daughter's happiness mattered a lot more.

'You were halfway down the road to the success of your plan when you married my daughter. You have spent four lakhs of my daughter's hard-earned money towards making a film. Of course, my name is included as your partner. But that is a mere formality. I am merely a supplier of your expenses. God is truly merciful, and so we learnt of your reality well in time. Now the story will go thus: Roopa will give you a khula because even though you were married, you hid the fact from her and deceived her. If you agree to her divorcing you, we will help you finish the film you're directing. In simpler words, Roopa will continue to act in it and we will fulfil our financial commitment too. But if you decline the khula, we will be forced to knock on the doors of the courts.'

Hamidul rested his voice. He was pleased to have put things before Shaukat clearly. Standing behind the curtains, Umrao, too, felt an unnatural sense of satisfaction. She listened intently so that she could hear what Shaukat had to say.

It was a while before he responded. Did his rising from his seat mean: 'Okay Sir, I'll take your leave'?

'But you have yet to give me an answer, Shaukat-mian!'

'It is difficult for me to say anything right away. Allow me to take leave today. Aadaab.'

'Goodbye, but do remember, you have only seven days to respond.'

Shaukat's voice was heard no more. Instead, Umrao could hear his nagra shoes leave a faint sigh on the thick carpets covering the drawing-room floor.

Umrao had been learning English from fifty-year-old Ms Sheridan for two years. So she chose the international tongue to call Shaukat a name: 'Swine!'

Outside the building, Shaukat's second-hand Fiat protested loudly as he drove off. 'An old cur yelps as it retreats with its tail between its legs'—the metaphor crossed her mind. 'Dog! Bulldog! Street dog! Cur!' Umrao explored the vocabulary of expletives she could draw on for Shaukat.

Hamidul came out of the drawing room. On finding Umrao there, he asked, 'Did you hear it all, Beta?'

'Yes. You spoke well. You're right, Abbajaan.' She turned around and headed for her bedroom.

The sea was spread out under the sky outside the window. The sun had gone to bed under the ocean. All through the night it would paint the coral red and breathe life into the pearls growing in the wombs of seashells. The sky and the waves were coloured by the mystery that is night.

Umrao switched on the radiogram and lay herself down on the bed.

Salma came into the room. 'He has left, Bibiji.'

'I'm aware of that.'

'He looked pulled down.'

'Let him go to hell! What's that to you?'

'No. I was just blabbering.'

'Why? What's your interest? Do you want to have a nikah with him?'

'Hai Allah!' Salma almost fainted.

'You go now, and leave me alone.'

'Would you like me to fetch some letters from your fans?'

'No. Give them to my secretary.'

'Ji.'

Salma left to finish her errands. Umrao turned over to lie face down on her bed. She bit a corner of her pillow to arrest the words that spilled out of her: 'Monster. Bastard...'

The radiogram was playing a sitar recital—a soulful raga that churned up the memories of Umrao's lived years. It was high tide and the waves were noisily crashing against the boulders lining the shore. Their regular beats combined with the notes of the sitar to create a befitting background score for the drama that was playing out in her memory.

Umrao Mahal had travelled a long way indeed from that single room in a dilapidated chawl on a dingy lane in Parel—where she'd go to bed, alone, after a meal of salted rice, and wonder what the darkness ahead held in store for her—to 'Happy Nook', this mansion on the sea, bought for a lakh-and-a-half rupees.

Hamidul was the unlettered son of a farmer from a village in Uttar Pradesh. The village once hosted a performance by a nautanki company. Hamidul was, in those days, a hot-blooded, hot-bodied young man. He was besotted by a girl named Noorbanu who sang and danced in that company and played bit roles. He followed her out of the village, leaving his indigent father behind with his older brother, and headed out to an uncertain future. He was employed as the gatekeeper of the nautanki group, then promoted to the post of booking-clerk, and married Noorbanu. Four or five years went by and Umrao came along. Noor was getting past her prime. The nautanki group also dispersed. Faced with adversity, Hamidul moved from place to place, city to city until he reached Bombay. By then Umrao was about seven.

Noorbanu's health declined. Hamidul, at his wit's end about how to feed his family, started doing the round of studios along with his daughter. She got bit roles here and there. But her earnings evaporated faster than a drop of water in the desert sand. When Umrao turned twelve, her mother succumbed to tuberculosis. This flung Hamidul into a crisis. Noorbanu had thus far been with Hamidul like a shadow. She had words of encouragement for him and she would caution her daughter about the pitfalls in the life of an actress. Now Umrao started wilting under the pressures of poverty. But Hamidul was intoxicated by the dazzle of floodlights. He could not stay away from the studios. But how was he to keep the kitchen fires aglow? He took to working as a house-agent—strictly for the inhabitants of filmdom. It brought hardly enough to keep his dignity aloft. Unable to pay rent, he would use the cover of night to flee from one tenement to another, one slum to the next. He travelled on and on, like a gypsy household, with a trunk, two bedrolls and three or four bundles of clothing. The tramcar of his life chugged on from stop to stop until, one day, seventeen-year-old Umrao discovered that all the hardships of life in the slums had failed to rob her of a glowing, youthful body. The goddess of beauty had emptied her own bowl to fill Umrao's life with grace and charm.

Hamidul started haunting the studios once again along with his daughter, dressed in the only presentable attire she possessed. She finally landed a role; a small one with three or four scenes. Director Jamna Prasad was known for his stunt films. By the time the film was complete, he'd imparted the lesson that, to be a star actress, Umrao must use her body more than her histrionic abilities. Hamidul was desperate by then. He did not care to know anything beyond how much his daughter earned.

That very stunt film earned Umrao a foothold in films. She got a bigger role and created an impact. Its director, Mehta, christened her Roop Kumari. The life of wants and deprivations had failed to crush Umrao's sensitivity; the artiste within her had gritted its teeth and survived every odd. That artiste was not unwilling to use her body as steps to stardom and doggedly ignored every humiliation. She eventually attained stardom when her fourth film turned out to be a super hit. Before the year was over, her market price soared from mere thousands to a lakh. With four hits in four subsequent years, her going rate had risen to three lakhs.

Now, looking out at the Arabian Sea from the window to the west of her bedroom in Happy Nook, that past seemed hazy. No, none of that past would be lost in oblivion; Umrao was not so heady with success. She would not trash her memories because of her mother.

Umrao had met Shaukat somewhere during her ascent from one lakh to three lakhs per film. He had come to be recognized as a promising writer. He was the writer, dialogue-writer and lyricist of a film for which Umrao was being considered. Shaukat came down one day to narrate the script. He was charmed by her observations and her casual comments. Umrao was floored by Shaukat's narrative skill, his fertile imagination and his humility. The mutual attraction did not end there. Shaukat would find any number of pretexts to see Umrao. He would talk to her for hours, quoting from literature, history and philosophy. And Umrao started avenging herself against those directors who saw nothing beyond her seductive body. These days, they would come to Umrao with folded hands, they would offer her her current rate and Roop Kumari would turn down their offers with no qualms. If not directly, through her father. Each one of them was a swine, a street dog...

Meanwhile, her fame kept growing exponentially. Roop Kumari was always surrounded by producers, directors, journalists and fans. Shaukat stood out amongst them all. In his eyes she could see ambition, dreams of rising as a writer, and a light, a glow that she had never encountered in the likes of a Jamna Prasad or a Mehta.

Two years of interaction led to love. Hamidul Haq got wind of it and was not pleased. He opposed it. Since Umrao had become Roop Kumari, Hamidul had transformed too. The gatekeeper of a now-forgotten nautanki company in Uttar Pradesh, who was once forced to live a gypsy existence, was today 'Mr Haq'. If his daughter travelled in an Impala, he rode a Plymouth. Every week, he would be seen in one or the other film magazine, either next to or right behind his daughter. He was also a familiar face to the countless admirers and fans of Roop Kumari. Seven years after Noorbanu's passing, when he was in the lap of luxury, Hamidul woke up to the fact that, as a wife, Noor had been desirable only for a few fleeting years. After that, thanks to her ailments, she had become a burden in the physical sense. After all these years, when he was approaching fifty and had come to wear the sobriquet of 'Janaab', he was greedy to enjoy life. He expressed a desire for holy matrimony to a couple of matrimonial agents.

Umrao got wind of this and kept her counsel. But when Hamidul tried to seduce Salma, she flared up. That was the day Hamidul lost control of his daughter's life. Consequently, Shaukat had easy access to Umrao's heart and, one morning, Bombay's film world got to know that Shaukat and Umrao had had a nikah and become man and wife.

Hamidul Haq was shattered by this news. Umrao completely ignored him and started driving down to Marine Drive to spend nights in Shaukat's apartment. Her days would be spent in her own mansion, the nights in her husband's home.

All of this had happened over the previous year. When she'd gauged Shaukat's desire, she had entrusted him with the responsibility of directing a film. It was titled *Roshni*, The Light. On paper, Hamidul was to be a sleeping partner. The film would be financed by Roop Kumari. *Roshni* took off with much fanfare and was halfway done when something went wrong. A dashing young man named Rahmat joined Shaukat as his assistant. He was bold, and he must have been quite desperate too; why else would he betray Shaukat and express his love, even if indirectly, to Umrao? She was amused, initially. Yes, she loved only one man, but the whole world loved her. The last was something she had become habituated to since she had become a star. So she'd laugh and say, 'Rahmat-mian, one day, I'll be so angry, I will blast you!' But her laughter got to Rahmat and crazed him. One day, when he went up to Umrao's make-up room to give her the dialogue for the scene, he saw fire in her eyes. Rahmat promptly took a measure to put out the fire. He told her that Shaukat was a married man who had deceived Umrao to marry her.

'Impossible!' Umrao rose up in arms and struck Rahmat. The indignant youth gathered two or three witnesses from Shaukat's village to prove the truth of his claim. Rahmat was right. Shaukat had married—as desired by his parents—when he was just twenty. His wife was a rustic simpleton; she had borne him two sons who were then about twelve and eight. They stayed with their maternal uncle in some town in Uttar Pradesh and Shaukat provided for their schooling.

The conversation with the villagers left no room for any doubt. Umrao then summoned Rahmat and forbade him to come anywhere near her shadow. Then she drove back to Happy Nook and that was that. Not once did she go back to Marine Drive.

Shaukat had raced up to Umrao. 'What's the matter, Roopa?' As if on cue, Hamidul had entered the room. He'd cornered Shaukat with an onslaught of question after question. Shaukat admitted that the fear of rejection had led him to hide the truth about his earlier marriage. He apologized for that. Besides, the Quran permits a faithful to marry up to four wives, so…

Umrao had shot out of the room. *Bastard. Swine. He cites the Quran in defence of a deception! The gall! The Quran does not teach you to lie. To deceive. So?*

Umrao had a sharp sense of self-preservation. She was not willing to let go of an inch of what was hers—her house, her room, her clothes, her shoes, her money; so too her husband. She could not share what was hers, certainly not her conjugal happiness.

A husband who had deceived her? He might be talented; he could recite shers; he might be unmatched in his confessions of love; and the mesmerizing dreams he nursed in his eyes did not matter—he was Satan incarnate. He had one and only one reason to hide his past and trap Umrao in marriage: to use her wealth to become a film director and taste success. *The swine! That cheat! A Bluebeard!*

That was when the phone rang.

'Salma!' Umrao was in no mood to leave her bed.

Salma came in and picked up the receiver. 'Hello. Who? Oh, Narendra Kumar-ji! Aadaab. Roopa-ji? No, she's not in the room at this moment. Kindly hold on, I'll find her.'

She covered the mouthpiece with her hand and chuckled as she looked at Umrao.

'Tell him I'm in the bath,' Umrao whispered.

'Hello Narendra Kumar-ji, Roopa-ji is in the bath. Ji? You'll wait? Okay...'

She covered the mouthpiece with her hand once again and chuckled.

Umrao lowered her voice to say, 'I'll take at least ten minutes in the bath, Salma!'

'It should, at the very least...' Salma giggled.

Narendra Kumar had reached the two-lakh-rupees bracket in two years. He was the most reputed among the young heroes. He was married, and also had a child. But money and fame had powered him into becoming an unrestrained flirt. Of late, he had been besotted by Roop Kumari. Umrao enjoyed his infatuation. He was quite handsome, Narendra Kumar, and in all likelihood he was younger to Umrao by two years. He had travelled to Europe even before he joined the film industry and so he courted her in undiluted Western style. This was what Umrao most enjoyed. Shaukat had courted her with literature, in Arabic and Persian, with Urdu ghazals; Narendra Kumar expressed his love in English and French, with orchestra and American jazz, the foxtrot and the twist. After her marriage with Shaukat, she had been cast with Narendra Kumar in two films. This 'two-lakh' had been chasing Umrao since then. But he had not been able to gain her favour until only the other day. Umrao had herself encouraged him ever since she had stopped living with Shaukat—three months had passed by then.

Salma spoke to Umrao, 'He's rocking the other end of the line with his hello-hellos!'

'Tell him I'm getting dressed...'

'Hello Narendra Kumar-ji, pardon me, madam is getting dressed... Another five minutes, at most? Well, all right then, stay on the line.'

This time Salma started giggling as she spoke, with her hand on the mouthpiece, 'Hai Allah, you can't but admire the gentleman's patience.'

'An impatient person just shouldn't fall in love, Salma Rani.'

The 'hello-hellos' started all over again in no time.

'Tell him I'm getting my hair set.'

'Hello Narendra Kumar-ji, I beg your pardon once more. Bibiji is almost done; she's combing her hair. She'll be on the line with you any moment now. Sure, hold on.'

Umrao yawned. 'I'm sleepy, Salma.'

'Just two minutes. A brief chat with Narendra Kumar-ji will help you sleep well.'

Umrao kept Narendra Kumar waiting at the counter of some star hotel for two more minutes. She took the call after testing his patience for almost twenty minutes in all.

'Hello, Narendra Kumar-ji? Aadaab! I'm really sorry you had to wait so long. I apologize profusely! Issh! Really? You're willing to give up your life for me? What will happen to all these producers then? Ji? Of course, we'll meet... Day after tomorrow, on the sets... Don't fret, patience always begets the sweetest fruit. You don't believe that? But I do.'

Salma chortled, standing by her bedside. And, on the ocean outside the window, countless stars shimmered in that dark moonless night.

Hamidul Haq had given Shaukat seven days' time. He and his daughter started the countdown. An inexplicable restlessness possessed them; when would they be free from the clutches of that deceiver?

But seven days passed by uneventfully. They did not hear from Shaukat. All they got to hear from the grapevine was that Shaukat-mian was not doing any work. He was simply whiling away the daylight hours and, as soon as the sun set in the ocean, he would shut himself up in his room, bring out the bottle and start reciting shers.

Charlatan! Umrao would repeat to herself whenever she heard these stories. She had no doubt in her mind that Shaukat Hossain was putting on an act only to win public sympathy. She asked her father to knock on the gates of the court.

Consequently, the seasoned and invincible lawyer Mr Patel entered the scene. He punched the table and asserted that he would ensure that Shaukat Hossain lamented his misdeed as long as he lived. They—father and daughter—could rest assured on that count.

Filmdom in Bombay was already abuzz with stories about Umrao and Shaukat. Everyone was happy with the development, especially the producers and directors. Who the hell was this Shaukat? It didn't matter how good the songs he penned were; how dare he marry a top star like Roop Kumari! A heroine is, all said and done, public property. Once she gets married, she ceases to be the public's. Once married, heroines lose themselves in the complexity of domestic life, they lose their figure, their glamour and their sex appeal. Even if they don't, the average viewer has trouble fantasizing about somebody else's wife. Viewers want an actress to remain public property.

But there was a handful who rested their faith in Shaukat Hossain's talents. They tried to persuade Hamidul Haq to dissuade Umrao Mahal. But in vain. On the contrary, their efforts steeled Umrao's resolve. Naturally, Hamidul had to be firm. Just imagine how shameless the imbecile cast-off was!

The fraud! That cheat! The swindler! A criminal!

Ten days were at an end. Then, twelve days.

Mr Patel went through the law books and armed himself with case references to prove that Shaukat had been faithless. But, before the fortnight was over, a friend of Shaukat's came to meet them—Shamsuddin. He had been appointed in place of Rahmat, who had been shown the door. He came with the news that Shaukat had agreed to terminate the wedlock with a khula. That was good news.

Now Hamidul, on the advice of Mr Patel, sent word that unless Shaukat left the film's rights entirely to Hamidul and Umrao, they would stay on course with the court case because they were no longer worried about adverse publicity. He and his daughter were the ones who had invested money in the film, they were its true owners. Of course Shaukat, as the director, would receive a generous amount of money as well.

Two hours later, they heard that Shaukat was agreeable. How could he not accept? What good would it do for him to object to those terms? He had trapped Umrao only to rise in life. Hamidul laughed a hearty laugh and Umrao Mahal chatted with Narendra Kumar for a full thirty minutes.

The business angle was thus sorted out and documents readied. During this period Shaukat came over to the office only once to sign some papers in the office. With his signature on the dotted lines, he handed over the rights to Hamidul and Umrao and immediately left. All that remained to be dealt with now was the divorce.

A date was set. That day, two elderly gentlemen selected by Hamidul—Enayatullah and Mohammed Bashir—came in to bear witness. Shaukat did not propose to bring any witness on his behalf, nor did Hamidul bother to ask him.

But the two witnesses appointed by Hamidul did not take their role lightly. On the set day they arrived at 10 a.m. sharp. Shaukat arrived, along with Shamsuddin, and sat gravely in the drawing room facing Hamidul. Umrao sat with Salma and Phufi, a distant old aunt in the adjacent room. The entire proceedings had a bitter after-taste.

The two witnesses forgot that Hamidul had asked them to be as brief as possible. They requested Shaukat to come to an understanding with Umrao.

'Why get into such meaningless discussions?' Shaukat responded.

The witnesses then proceeded to advise Umrao. It was a holy alliance, they tried to convince her, she should not tear it asunder in the heat of momentary anger.

'Excuse me, but it seems to me that you are advocating on behalf of Shaukat-mian,' Umrao grumbled.

'Tauba, tauba!' The witnesses gave up their efforts to resolve the couple's differences.

Shaukat was asked to join Umrao in her room. The curtains were all drawn. The soft light seemed laden with melancholy. Shaukat looked pulled down in that light. Umrao laughed to herself. *He wears the crestfallen look of a tragic hero! But no, I will no longer be taken in by his chicanery. Everything ends today. Deliverance!*

Shaukat did not cast a glance at Umrao. He sat down, head lowered.

Enayatullah said, 'Shaukat Hossain deceived Umrao Mahal by concealing that he was already married. That is why he must accept khula. Umrao, dear child, proceed to give him khula.'

Umrao Mahal spoke distinctly. 'From this day on, I take khula from Shaukat Hossain.'

He continued to sit just the way he was sitting, with his head hanging low. The khulanama agreement had been drafted already. Umrao Mahal signed it, as did Shaukat Hossain, as well as on a copy that had been prepared for him. Then he greeted everyone with an 'Aadaab!' and left the room, his head still lowered.

Umrao began to sense liberty in her veins and blood cells. The satisfaction which prevails when a wrong has been avenged, that painful joy was flapping its wings within her ribcage. She went back to her room, stood next to the bay window, and looked out at the ocean. The bottomless blue of the salty waves was glistening in the sunlight. The fishing boats on the distant horizon looked like wild ducks turning hither and thither. A nameless bird was flapping away inside Umrao's heart too. Was it the ecstasy of liberty? She was free now, free of her bond with a liar, a cheat, a deceiver. She would no longer be trapped by the rhythm, metre and cadences of mere words. Enough. No more would anyone play with her heart. From now onwards, she was the one who would play with feelings.

The game commenced.

Narendra Kumar would call from a hotel at another end of the city and chat late into the night. Umrao would sit inside her room with the table lamp spreading a soft, romantic glow as she smiled into the phone.

'Roopa.'

'Tell me.'

'Umrao.'

'Go on.'

'Do you know what my condition is since I've met you?'

'Tell me.'

'Jabse teri nazar padi hai jhalak

Tabse lagti nahin palak se palak'

(Ever since my eyes glimpsed you

One eyelid has not met the other)

'Really? That must be so painful. Haai!'

'What is this "haai"? Is it a sigh?'

'Kya jaane yeh sach hai ki aah hai

Kuch aag si aayi hai zubaan par...'

(Who knows if this is the truth or a sigh?

Something like fire singes my lips...)

'So you've taken to shayari these days?'

'I can see that shayari goes a long way with you.'

'You must have also seen that it doesn't take you to a happy ending?'

'Umrao...'

'Go on.'

'Come over tomorrow.'

'Let me think over it today. I'll let you know tomorrow.'

She put down the receiver, walked to her bed, and lay down.
Salma came in to caress her hair.

'Salma...'

'Ji?'

'What's life all about?'

'Hai Allah, why are you agonized? What's there to brood
over? You are a famous person, a celebrity, by God's grace. When
He showers you with His mercy, what's there to worry about?
You will marry again.'

'Marry? Again? No Salma, never.'

Word spread through the film world like wildfire. The magazines
started carrying juicy stories about the khula. Hamidul lavished
some currency upon the editors to blunt the sharpness of the
critic's pen, but Umrao was unaffected. All of a sudden, she
became carefree and flirtatious. She had tasted freedom. This
delighted the devious creatures of tinseltown. They discovered
a turn-on in her 'come hither' looks. It was an invitation they
could not ignore. And it was only with great difficulty that they
could contain themselves.

Three weeks had gone by after the divorce and Shaukat had
not made any move. The grapevine had it that he had gone off
the scene. Someone reported that he had been spotted in a hotel
in Mahabaleshwar, sleeping the better part of the day. When
Salma surreptitiously reported this to Umrao, she flew off the
handle. She needed to know nothing about Shaukat! How did
it matter to her whether he lived or died?

But, at the end of three weeks, Shamsuddin showed up in
Hamidul Haq's office. It was now important to resume shooting

Roshni. Hamidul reserved four dates in the following month's calendar, when Umrao would shoot for the film.

Shaukat got busy trying to ready everything for the shoot. A set was put together and was waiting when Umrao declined to go ahead. She had been unwell—suffering from palpitation—for the last two days, she said. The truth lay elsewhere. She had rediscovered that this man, Shaukat, had married her only to use her as a stepping stone to fame, as his ladder to success, as fodder for his ambition. *He wants to shoot the film despite so much humiliation! Is he born with a rhino's skin? Any normal human would have fled, but Shaukat? No, I will not shoot. I am the proprietor; I own the film.* Umrao wanted Shaukat to realize that it was due to her good nature that he had not been dumped along with the canned reels.

Hamidul got worried. Umrao, unwell? Send for Dr Desai, he ordered. Before the doctor could examine the Most Luminescent Star of Bombay, Umrao declared nothing was wrong with her. Dr Desai laughed loud, chatted with her over tea, pocketed a hefty fee for his visit, advised her rest for three days, and left.

So the schedule was cancelled. The set was dismantled. Loss of money; that was all it meant for Umrao. She told Hamidul that she would shoot the following month. Let Shaukat squirm for a month. *The cheat! The scoundrel! Fiend! That infernal creature!*

Umrao honoured her dates with other producers. She shone bright like a diamond. She was always surrounded by directors and producers, press photographers and reporters, fans and admirers. Umrao basked in their admiration. Life is strange, and stranger still is the life of a star. The heady infatuation of so many lovers!

She would speak over the telephone now and then. The conversations connected Happy Nook with an undeclared star hotel in Juhu.

'You want to grill me alive!' Narendra Kumar would complain to Roopa.

'Is that why poets liken women to fire and men to fireflies?'

'Roopa.'

'Tell me.'

'Umrao.'

'Go on.'

'Shall I?'

'No.'

'Aage hi bin kahe tu kahe, nahin nahin...

Abhi to hum vey baatein kahi nahin...'

(Even before I speak you say 'No'

How can I utter those precious words yet?)

'No, you don't need to speak them, Poet Laureate!'

'Why not?'

'No.'

'When a woman protests too much, she means "Yes", right!'

'No.'

'I beg of you, Umrao, take heart!'

'Okay, let me think it over today...'

A dim blue light would stay on all night near her bed. When Umrao suddenly woke up, her own room would seem like a dreamland to her. It had happened again that night, in the small hours. Had some good angel transported her to this fairyland? Perhaps, like the protagonist of the *Arabian Nights*, she would find a Prince Charming by her side. They might exchange rings. And then... But who might Prince Charming resemble? Narendra Kumar? Forget it! So then? Who?

Umrao sat bolt upright on her soft bed. A soothing breeze was blowing in through the window on the west. The ceaseless waves were creating a crescendo. The crescent moon accentuated the darkness of the ocean, despite the foam that glistened upon its surface. A longing troubled Umrao's aching body. The loneliness was killing her.

Umrao sat still for a long time, thinking. She decided to

meet Narendra Kumar the following day and let him play with her fingers. And she would play her own game with him.

Which was how Narendra Kumar got to touch Umrao. Her fingers.

Now, very often, Umrao would tell Hamidul to go home, for she must meet a friend before returning. Hamidul would return all by himself, and Umrao would come home at 10, perhaps 11 p.m. She would be accompanied only by Salma and the driver, Abbas. Hamidul would interrogate Salma separately, but could figure out nothing. Thanks to his daughter's support, this Salma had no regard for him. He even summoned Abbas and grilled him. Abbas was young, and a fan of his employer; he had hidden a signed photograph of Umrao in his bedroom. But Hamidul was wise enough to read between the lines and gauge the truth from a few careless, contradictory statements. He held his peace, and accelerated the secret search for a bride for himself. Elderly and old-fashioned matrimonial agents started frequenting the house again. And the film world buzzed once more with juicy stories about Roop Kumari.

Shamsuddin came to meet Hamidul a few days later. Could the shooting resume now? Hamidul explained to his daughter that it was effectively their money which was stuck; they ought to wrap up *Roshni*. Five days were finally worked out for a schedule by shaving off a day from this team and two from that.

But as soon as she landed on the sets for the shoot, and her eyes fell upon Shaukat, Umrao was piqued.

'Aadaab!' Shaukat humbly greeted her when they met.

Umrao turned her face away as she returned the greeting and proceeded towards the make-up room. How on earth could she take his directing and live with his bidding for another thirty or forty days?

She'd just completed her make-up when there was a knock

on the door. Salma opened it to find Shaukat Hossain waiting outside.

Umrao felt the blood rise up to her head. 'What does he want?'

'He says he wants to discuss something important,' Salma whispered.

Umrao thought for a moment, then said, 'Let him come in.'

Shaukat stepped in. 'I want to say two things but only to you, dearest.'

Umrao looked away and said. 'I'll be delighted if you don't try to get intimate...'

'I apologize if I have offended you. There will be no further lapse in the use of any term of endearment...'

'Salma will stay in the room. You may carry on.'

Shaukat looked at her for a couple of seconds, then said, 'As you wish. Don't take offence at my words. I am no longer connected to you but I still get distressed if I hear a word against your honour.'

Umrao's voice brimmed with sarcasm. 'I can't thank you enough for your concern, but I'll be obliged if you could come straight away to the point.'

'The fact is that a lot of trash is circulating about you and Narendra Kumar. It will be in your interest to be a bit more judicious.'

Umrao arched her eyebrows, that were like the wings of a hawk, further. 'I thought you are aware that you and I are no longer connected in any way...'

'Ji!'

'Then, Mian, it would be advisable for you to mind your own business. There will always be a bunch of dogs who'll bark on the streets. When you are not one of them, why trust them and try to caution me?'

Shaukat had no words to say in reply. His fair-complexioned

face went pallid, his thin lips quivered in an effort to speak, then stayed still.

Umrao continued. 'Perhaps you don't remember how much a day's shoot costs. But then why should you, when you don't have to bear it?'

Shaukat was startled. He looked at Umrao and replied slowly, 'I understand what you are hinting at. You're right. I'm a fool. I apologize for having disturbed you with my loose talk. We're ready, we'll shoot as soon as you step on the floor.' He immediately left the room, head lowered.

Umrao gritted her teeth and spat out, 'Shameless brute!'

'Ji...' Salma made as if to say something.

'He has the cheek to counsel me! '

'Bibiji!'

'Shut up, Salma! I'll show the faithless weasel his place!'

'Ji, Bibiji.'

'Scoundrel! Bastard! Swine!'

It took Salma quite a while to calm her down. Umrao fell silent but kept panting, outrage refusing to let go of her.

The beggar has such gumption! A crook, and with so much gall! I am a free woman, I can go where I will, meet whom I want to, love whomsoever I wish to... Who cares what the world banks, I am not afraid of anyone. I will not kowtow to any soul. Just because I was once tied to him, Shaukat presumes he can play guardian to me even after the divorce. Umrao will teach him a lesson!

Shamsuddin, ever polite, arrived to request her presence on the sets.

Umrao sent word that she was suffering from a migraine attack.

She went to the set an hour later and gave one shot. She then left because she just *had* to make a call.

Shaukat interjected, 'It would be nice if you could complete this shot.'

'That would be really nice, Shamsuddin-sahib, but it is really urgent that I make this call.'

She left the floor and spent an hour speaking with Narendra Kumar, who was shooting in another studio.

'Hello, Roopa... Umrao!'

'Tell me.'

'What good fortune!'

'Really?'

'Truly. Now I feel life is beautiful.'

'Truly?'

'Yes. And then I feel like weeping.'

'Weeping? What are you saying, Hero-ji?'

'It's the truth, Roop Kumari. I could not sleep last night.

'*Raat ro ro ke guzaari humne*

Aasuon pe yeh rang tab aaya...'

(I spent the night shedding tears

That's how my teardrops acquired their hue)

'Bahut khoob, huzoor! Lovely sher, Sir!'

'Roopa...'

'Tell me...'

'I'm thirsty...'

'Ask for a Coca-Cola. Or a Mangola!'

'Roopa!'

Umrao broke into full-throated laughter.

'Roopa-ji!'

Umrao turned around. Shamsuddin was at the door.

'What do you want?'

'We're ready.' Shamsuddin joined his hands.

Umrao thought for a while before responding, 'I'm coming.'

She wound up her chat and returned to the floor. Shamsuddin's behaviour had softened her but the moment she spotted Shaukat, her mercury shot up. This happened every time she was in the presence of this creature. Her whole body was aflame. She ought to shoot him, mow him down. *What does he think of himself? A poet laureate? A director? A legend? Fake! Some people are born on this earth with a sharp instinct for serving their self-interest even at the cost of other people's well-being. And to do that they'll laugh or cry, speak homely truths or recite poems, perhaps even kill people! Shaukat is one such offspring of Satan.*

'Monitor please!' an assistant called out.

'All lights!' the cameraman yelled. The lights came on.

'Start rehearsal!'

It's a night scene. The hero and the heroine are locked in an altercation. The hero is fond of a poor girl; he thinks of her as a sister. The heroine doesn't approve, she misunderstands him and bans him from meeting her. She wishes him well but she's too headstrong and power-hungry. She loves and therefore wants to command the people around her. But the hero cannot accept this and fall in line. He says, 'I'm not your slave.'

The heroine turns ashen. 'What was that again?'

'Yes, I said exactly what I mean. You are a heartless woman. You pretend to be in love but in reality you don't know what it means to love somebody. You want to own people and rule over their lives in the name of love.'

'What was that again?'

'You are a selfish woman. As of today I have nothing to do with you anymore.'

The hero speaks his lines and leaves the room. The heroine stares in his direction for a moment. She then takes out her exasperation and frustration on the cup of tea placed on the table, and throws a paperweight at the large mirror on the wall. Her siblings scamper into the room at the sound of the mirror crashing. They stand still on seeing the heroine flop into the bed and break into bouts of tears. The very next minute she sits up, gnashes her teeth, and mutters, 'No, I shall not cry. Tears are not for me.'

Umrao rehearsed the scene. All eyes were upon her. From the light-man to the setting coolie, her co-actors, the boys on the set; every single person present was watching Umrao and Shaukat, who had been husband and wife until the only other day, but were now divorced. They could see hatred surfacing in Umrao's eyes, and a helpless loneliness in Shaukat's.

The rehearsal was repeated.

'Roopa-ji,' Shaukat told her, 'your evocation is not quite right.'

Umrao turned her neck and glanced at him through the corner of her eyes, 'What's that?'

'Please, put more feelings into your words. It seems like your mind is elsewhere. Your action feels lifeless and mechanical.'

'Really?' One enemy looked at another. 'Well, then why don't you act out the scene for me?'

'I'll do so.'

Shaukat enacted the scene. He suggested a couple of changes in Umrao's movement. Umrao watched his movements and became livid. Was it this same person who had been avowing love to her for the last two years? So much adulation, so many idylls, such serenades! The same man who read the marriage vows to her, insulted her love day after day by pretending to be in love with her! *Liar! Cheat!*

'All lights!'

'Ready please.'

Umrao rehearsed again. Shaukat creased his brows and said, 'All right.' It was pretty clear to all that he meant: 'It's not quite right.'

'Take, please!' Shaukat urged.

'Make-up,' Shamsuddin yelled.

'Lights!'

'Ready for take!'

'Ready sound?'

'Sound ready-y,' the recordist's voice boomed out over the set.

'Ready camera?'

'READY!'

'Clap!'

'Scene 60/3! Take 1!' The clapperboard was sounded.

Umrao started counting her steps. The camera began whirring when Shaukat's voice rang out: 'Cut!'

The scene had ended before it could start. Umrao had given a wrong action.

'Sorry!' Umrao said in a sing-song voice. She was laughing away to herself. She knew she was going wrong, and she would continue to go wrong. *I will bring Shaukat to tears.*

'Take two!'

This time the action was right but Umrao messed up her dialogue. Thus it went on until eight takes were labelled 'NG'. Each shot being 250 to 300 feet long, the crew was tiring.

'Sorry!' was all Umrao would say after every take.

Ten takes were declared 'No good'.

'Sorry, the next one will be fine!'

'Lights please!' The lights came on.

Shaukat came forward all at once. 'Would you like to rest for a while?'

'Why?'

'A little rest might help you to not go wrong.'

'No, I'm ready. Take, please.'

'No madam, please rehearse the scene once.'

'I'm tired. I can't rehearse again.'

'Then why don't you rest a little and then rehearse?'

'No, please take the shot right away.'

Shaukat's face reddened with anger, 'Don't you consider me the director of this film?'

'That I do but you seem to forget something...'

'Which is...?'

'That you are being paid by me to make this film. You have no right to waste time and money with rehearsals.'

Everyone on the set was stupefied. Salma was fear-struck. Would the reel-story of the two protagonists repeat itself in real life? Standing in the circle of light, these now-separated souls were unspooling a dark tale of confrontation.

Shaukat knitted his brows. He looked at Umrao for a while and asked, 'Won't you take back your words?'

'NO!'

'I urge you to.'

'You don't have the right, you perjurer!'

A pin, had one fallen on the set, could be heard.

Salma put her hand on her own mouth as a cry escaped her: 'Bibiji!'

Shaukat turned around and said to his team, 'Pack up please.' As soon as these words were said, he walked off the floor.

'Pack up!' Shamsuddin ordered the crew. Umrao bit her lips, looked at Salma and stepped forward. One by one the lights started to switch off.

Shaukat took ill that same night.

The set had to be scrapped. The studio had to be compensated for a loss amounting to five days.

Hamidul expressed regret. 'The loss is ours, Beta. Complete the film any which way.'

'Don't you worry, Abbajaan. If I've caused this loss, I'll make good the loss through my earnings.'

Hamidul slunk away. He must put up with the whims of this person who ended his itinerant life in a nautanki company and the hardships of Mumbai slums. Besides, he was very taken with a young widow from Hyderabad and would enter into a nikah with her in the next couple of months. There was no point losing his cool at this juncture. And, then, he was the owner of *Roshni*.

Salma also wanted to speak her mind.

Umrao shut her up. 'Quiet! I'm not a child.'
Salma had to seek a quick exit from the scene.

Umrao had derived much satisfaction from the insult to Shaukat. It
was still spreading a lot of sweetness in her heart and mind. *Aah!*

The news spread faster than lightning. And it added to the
adulation and the demand for Umrao. That made her reckless.
Shooting for films, watching movies, attending parties, and
Narendra Kumar—nothing else mattered.

Now Narendra Kumar had risen above the touch of her
fingers and tasted the nectar of her lips. But Umrao shied away
from permitting him greater intimacy. Every night, lying in her
dimly lit bedroom, she found her bloodstream matching the
ceaseless waves of the ocean and she lay tossing and turning.
But never could she spot the Prince Charming of her dreams.

A few days later her driver Abbas had news for her.

'Shaukat-sahib is down with typhoid, Madam!'

'Let him die! Why do I need to hear about him?'

'No, Madam,' Abbas stuttered, 'just so...'

'Just? What do you mean?'

'No Madam, nothing...'

'Nothing? Don't you hide anything from me, tell me why
you brought him up.'

'Ji... Shaukat-sahib's wife is here to look after him.'

'Well done!'

Abbas lost no time in making himself scarce.

About ten days later.

A two-day break in the schedule—a shooting stint has been
altered because the hero, Shyamsundar, has taken ill. Umrao
spends her time roaming the garden of Happy Nook, watches
colourful butterflies flit about, returns to her room and plays a
record, switches on the tape recorder and orders Salma to recite

poems, she plays them back to her, then banishes her from her room as she dials Narendra Kumar.

'Hello!'

'Roopa!'

'No, Shanta here!'

Shanta is Narendra Kumar's wife.

'Impossible! Do you think I don't recognize Roop Kumari's voice?'

'Do you?'

'I do! I do! I do! I recognize even your shadow. If I don't see even your shadow, I feel your presence when you're around.'

'And Shanta?'

'Don't even mention Shanta; she's making life miserable for me.'

'Why?'

'Because of you. What luck! She doesn't know that you are still beyond my reach—she never will know.'

'Don't lose hope, Narendra!'

'So you think I have hope?'

'But what will become of Shanta?'

'I don't know, nor do I care what happens to her. She will live as she pleases.'

'What will she do?'

'Perhaps what she's been threatening to do. Go to her parents and seek a divorce. '

'How dramatic!'

'Isn't life a collection of little dramas?'

'Yes Narendra, that is life.'

'Roopa!'

'Tell me...'

'Come over today.'

'I will.'

After she hung up the phone, Umrao sat still for some time.

She was ruffled by an unknown emotion she could not put a finger upon. She was setting ablaze the happiness of a family.

Let it burn. She was scorched too. She glanced at the Arabian Sea outside her window. The fishermen's boats out there on the horizon. The breakers crashing against the boulders lining the shore spray upwards, reaching for the sky, shining like zillions of diamonds in sunshine. A chiaroscuro on the heart of the ocean...

All of a sudden Umrao was rocked by a gust of wind. She ran out of her room. Feet covered in brocade slippers, she walked over the marbled floor of the veranda and the stairway to reach the garden below. She found Abbas sitting under a tree on a chair next to the garage, reading a book and puffing on a Charminar. She walked through the garden shaded by jhow trees, and across the soft carpet of a green lawn, lightly caressing the roses and jasmine, to come and stand before the garage.

'Abbas.'

Abbas was startled. Turning around to find Umrao, he quickly dropped the lit cigarette from his hand and stood up, all attention.

'What's that book you're reading?'

'It's the story of Heer and Ranjha, Madam.'

'Enjoying it?'

'Very much, Madam!'

'Why, Abbas?'

'Ji? It's a love story, Madam! How much they suffer because they love each other! They even die but do not stop loving each other...'

'Hmm. Okay, go on reading.'

She walked a couple of steps away, then stopped.

'Abbas?'

'Ji Memsaab!'

'Has your Shaukat-mian pulled the plug?'

'Ji? I just learnt that he had remission from fever a couple of days ago and has gone to Mahabaleshwar to recover.'

'Really? With his wife and children?'

'No Madam, his wife and her parents are all here in Bombay. They'll all return to Ghazipur, I believe. That's where they come from.'

'Why? Why will they go back?' Umrao's arched brows arched further.

'Ji? I can't really say...'

'Hmm.' Umrao walked over to a swing hanging from a mango tree in the backyard. She was angry with herself. Where was the need to enquire after Shaukat? Chhi! It was because she was so infantile that Shaukat could deceive her into a marriage. Stupid!

She jumped off the swing, returned to her bedroom, lay herself down on her bed and looked out of her window at the ocean and the sky above it. She watched the daylight roll on from midday to afternoon and evening. How the bright rays of the sun slowly turned fickle. How the sun looked wan and spent by the time it touches the ocean. How the bright orange of sunset turned purple and grey and slate-coloured. She was overcome by a dark ache: What was heart longing for? What did she miss in her life?

She suddenly yelled out, 'Salma!'

'Ji!' Salma hurried into the room. 'Should I get you another tea?'

'No.'

'Coffee?'

'No! No! No!'

'Ji.'

'Ask Abbas to bring the car around. I'll go out. You also get ready to come along.'

'Ji, where to?'

'To DIE!'

Half an hour later Hamidul Haq saw his daughter leave with Salma in her Impala. His brows creased as he guessed her destination. Then he unlocked his drawer, took out a passbook, and made sure of the amount he had saved up in the bank. Thirty thousand two hundred and forty rupees and eighty paise. He had spirited away this amount in an account that Umrao was unaware of. He had kept it a secret from her because he was fully aware of the whimsicality of actresses, heady with success in their youth. Be it an actress in a small-town nautanki company or a film actress with national fame and international recognition, the difference lay only in the digits of the price they quoted and the number of people who prized their photos. Hamidul was well aware of this and so he was lining his own nest.

That night, in an undisclosed hotel room, Narendra Kumar embraced the mirage he had been chasing for months.

Something was the matter with Umrao.

Salma had been noticing this from that night.

She paced about her room restlessly; when she sat still, her mind wandered. A moment later, she might ask Salma to play an LP on the gramophone. And then she might just want a relaxing massage.

'Memsaab, what's bothering you?'

'Uh?' Umrao looked at Salma. 'Why? What's the matter? What do you want to know?'

'No ma'am, just.'

'Just?' Umrao mimicked Salma. She retreated.

That's when the phone rang. Umrao looked up, startled.

Salma picked up the receiver and chuckled. 'Narendra Kumar-ji!'

Umrao sprawled out on her bed. 'Tell him I'm sleeping!'

Even as she repeated the message, it dawned on Salma that Umrao had not met Narendra Kumar since that night. What was going on?

A manservant arrived to convey that the renowned and

much-respected scriptwriter Satyendra Sharma had come to see Umrao. She rose from the bed and went downstairs. Everyone looked up to Sharma-ji; Umrao Mahal was no exception. The minute she walked in, Sharma-ji declared that he had come to plead on behalf of Shaukat. Since Umrao was an artiste beyond compare, he told her, she ought to complete the film *Roshni*, and follow the instructions of the director on the floor as a seasoned professional would. No personal issue should be allowed to come in between them.

'Dear girl, if you can't do this, then you fail as an artiste. An artiste *must* rise above personal happiness and sorrow to serve the arts.'

Satyendra Sharma's words touched Umrao. Being skilled with words, he convinced her and got her consent to shoot for *Roshni* again after a month.

Umrao learnt from Sharma-ji that Shaukat was still in Mahabaleshwar. He had recuperated and would return to Bombay as soon as his wife and children went back to Ghazipur.

Umrao couldn't quite comprehend this. Why wouldn't he come to Bombay while his family was still there?

She couldn't catch a wink that night. As she listened to the lullaby of the waves, under the dreamy blue of the night lamp, she missed someone on the softness of her bed.

Early in the morning Umrao showed up at her garage. Abbas was busy washing the car.

'Abbas…'

'Ji?'

'Isn't your chacha's house is right next to Shaukat-mian's?'

'Yes Ma'am.'

'Doesn't your aunt frequent their house?'

'She does, Ma'am.'

'Take me to your aunt's.'

'Madam!' Abbas wasn't quite sure he'd heard her correctly.

'Yes, do as I'm saying. Get a cab. You'll take me along with Salma to your aunt's house.'

Just imagine! Salma was surprised, Abbas was taken aback. But her bidding had to be done. Umrao pulled on a burqa before getting into the cab. Then, straight to his aunt, who heard everything and was alarmed as much as she was amazed. What was Umrao saying?

But if the entire country was charmed by Umrao's whims, how could Abbas's chachi ignore her? She took the burqa-clad Umrao to Shaukat's mother-in-law. She introduced her as her own niece from Allahabad who was visiting Bombay for a couple of days and would leave the very same day.

Umrao and the other ladies were offered seats by Shaukat's mother-in-law. There was chit-chat, and gossip. But where was Shaukat's wife?

'Where's your daughter, Ammi?' Abbas's chachi asked her.

'Allah is upset with us, child! My daughter's insanity has taken a turn for the worse. She's under lock and key since yesterday. She's tearing up the pillows and throwing the cotton wool in the air and breaking into songs.'

'Insane?' Umrao wasn't ready for this. 'Since when?'

'Almost eight years now, child,' Ammi replied. 'She wasn't completely there but we could pull along. She has been uncontrollable these last two years. I heard about jamai raja's illness and brought her along, hoping that the sight of her husband would bring her around. That's not to be. It started after the birth of the first child. She lost it completely after the second delivery. Dulha-mian pays for their upkeep but refuses to live with them. We can't blame him. He is so talented, so educated, so respected. And my daughter? A village bumpkin who keeps raving and ranting...' The old lady's voice choked with emotion.

A faint strain floated into the room:

'*Naina milani kari le re saiyyan, naina milani kari le*
Abki baar hum naihar raibo, Jo dil chahe kari le'
(Look into my eyes, O beloved,
Look deep into my eyes
This time I'll stay back with my parents
Just fulfil the longings of your heart!)
'Didn't you get her any treatment?' Umrao wanted to know.

Ammi sighed. 'We've left no stone unturned. She was kept in the asylum in Ranchi for almost a year. It didn't help at all.'

Umrao caught a glimpse of Shaukat's wife through a window in the room.

Just a rustic village girl, but she was too sickly and her eyes had an unnatural gleam. The room was filled with scattered cotton-wool. And she was sitting in the middle of it, swaying and singing away.

As they prepared to leave, the old lady said, 'God alone knows what lies ahead for my girl. But no matter what, I pray for Shaukat's happiness. Poor man, he married again, but that too was not fated to last!'

Umrao had gone to Shaukat's house in a trance. The same house that had soaked in so many unaccounted-for days and nights of her life. She left the house in a trance, too. Shaukat's mad wife was still singing away to herself.

Umrao felt a stinging in her eyes. She recalled her dead mother after a long period of forgetting.

Salma noticed it all. Umrao was returning to her normal self. She was eating at her usual hour, going out for shoots, getting massages, conversing with Miss Sheridan in English... She was listening to the radio, playing records and, once in a while, chatting with Narendra Kumar over the phone.

'Roopa!'

'Tell me.'

'What's the matter with you?'

'Too busy.'

'I'm busy too, Roopa, but what do we work for?'

'For the sake of that work.'

'But I'm going out of my mind!'

'Please don't, Narendra; it won't benefit you. You will lose in every possible way.'

'Roopa, listen!'

'What news of Shanta?'

'She's gone off to her parents' in Delhi—yesterday.'

'Did you fight?'

'Viciously. I'll divorce her.'

'Make sure you have the best lawyer, Narendra.'

'Roopa, don't make fun of me. Please come over today, there's a lot to talk over.'

'I don't have time. I must memorize dialogues for tomorrow.'

'Roopa!'

'We'll chat again tomorrow. Please dear, let me disconnect.'

Salma noticed everything. She could read between the lines, but she couldn't fully comprehend the developments. Umrao seemed to have returned to normalcy, but was she herself yet?

The Arabian Sea turned and changed colour with day and night. The waves crashed. Days passed and, then, the dates for *Roshni*'s shoot came around.

'All lights!'

The lights sprang to life one by one. It was the garden of the heroine's house. Two songs were to be picturized, and five or six scenes with full dialogue.

Umrao gritted her teeth and rehearsed. No, she had given her word to Sharma-ji. She would keep it.

But she couldn't help the stab of pain she felt every time her eyes alighted on Shaukat. He had become pulled down. He had taken to wearing his hair close-cropped after the bout of typhoid. The man looked spent; he would flop into a chair every few minutes. Was he trying to curry sympathy on the pretext of this illness? Umrao's lips could not suppress the curve of a bitter smile.

'Monitor please!'

The film's climax was being canned. A complex shot. The camera was on a trolley and there were to be four different movements. It was a 300-feet shot at least. Subsequently, a number of close shots were to be canned too.

After a lot of misunderstanding, the lead couple meet dramatically in a different city. By then they've realized that a small lapse in their own understanding has led to the gulf in their relationship. But when they rediscover their love for each other they are separated—one doesn't even know where the other is. The lady's family has just moved into a new city. One evening, she's sitting under a tree in the garden, lost in the memories of that evening when her paramour had proposed his love to her. And today? Suddenly, overcome by the burden of memories, she suffers a blackout. Her younger sister is close by. She screams for help. Somebody runs for a doctor. When the lady returns to her senses and opens her eyes, she finds her love, her dearest, right before her.

'A filter on that 5 kilo...' The cinematographer's assistant was issuing instructions.

Shaukat goes for a look through the camera, then tells the cameraman, 'Mr Iyer, I need the soft glow of the sunset hour.'

'Yes Sir, that's what I'm working towards.'

'No. 5 to the left; a bit more...'

The cameraman called out in a while: 'Rehearsal please!'

'Ready for monitor.'

The rehearsal started, and ended too.

Shaukat called out, 'Not good! Once more.'

Rehearsal, again.

Shaukat shook his head and walked over to Umrao. 'It's not happening.'

'Not happening?' Umrao mimicked him. 'Then why don't you enact how it should happen?'

'If you would permit me to...'

'Go on!'

Shaukat enacted the scene.

'All lights!'

Another rehearsal.

Shaukat shook his head again. 'No, it's still not happening!'

Three more rehearsals were conducted, but Shaukat was not satisfied. He came up to Umrao and stood next to her. His eyes were gleaming with excitement.

'Please don't mind my saying this, Roopa-ji; I'm only a paid servant of your production company. Even so, if you accept me as the director, I'd like to say something.'

Umrao looked at him, daggers drawn. 'Go on.'

'Imagine that you are in love...'

Umrao looked sharply at Shaukat. 'I've never fallen in love.'

'I thought so.' Shaukat smiled weakly. 'But even if you have not fallen in love, you must've read, in story books, about people doing so. Or heard of others falling in love?'

'I am not a scholar like you, Mr Shaukat. Instead of referring to books, why don't you explain the experience to me? What is love all about?'

Shaukat said humbly, 'Love is all about dedication to a single person.'

Umrao's lips curved into a cruel smile. 'To a single person? Why not to two?'

Shaukat realized what she was hinting at. He took a second to digest it, then shook his head. 'No, that's not possible.'

'Why Mian, don't people have two wives?'

'Yes, some do. Some have three, some more than that. But

love is not about marriage, Roopa-ji. And you love only one. Anything more is lust.'

'Really? But you are unable to convey to me what love is!' Umrao ridiculed Shaukat.

He smiled sadly. 'That is precisely what this slave is attempting to do. Love is a sudden sweetness. Someone delights you out of the blue. You long to belong, to become his. It's a fire...

> *Shaayad isi ka naam mohabbat hai Shefta*
> *Ik aag si hai seene ke andar lagi hui...*

(This perhaps is what's known as Love, Shefta
Something like fire burns within my breast ...)

There's a fire constantly burning inside the heart of a lover. There's a constant thirst. A desire to see the man you love. The thought of the person turns your soul into a desert; and the thought of the same person ushers spring into your being. Love is a light that glows within you and, at the same time, fills you with light. Then you fall silent. Like a filled pitcher, you do not create noise. Yet, love cannot be hidden from the world.

> *Dard-e-dil kuchh kaha nahin jaata*
> *Aah! Chup bhi raha nahin jaata...*

(The pain in my heart, I cannot speak about it
Aah! Nor can I keep my lips sealed!)

'Love is a sublime light. Just as the twilight at dusk makes everything appear beautiful, so too with love; all of a sudden the light shines on one person, and what we discover is love.'

Shaukat fell silent.

'And then?' Umrao looked at him with keen eyes.

Fatigue spoke in his voice now. 'Nothing else after that, Roop Kumari-ji. Do try to capture that sublime light of love in your eyes; that's all I beg of you.'

Umrao smiled archly as she said, 'You have skillfully woven the words into a captivating tapestry, Mr Shaukat! Now let me try to digest them...'

'Yes, sure.'

Umrao withdrew to a lonely corner of the set. Salma uncapped a flask and offered her a glass of orange juice. 'No.' Umrao waved her away.

Shaukat was sitting in a chair at another end of the set. He looked exhausted, and immersed in thought.

Umrao sat silently for a while, then returned to the set. Addressing Shamsuddin, she said, 'A final monitor now.'

'Monitor please!' Shaukat rose from the chair.

'All lights!'

The lights came on one by one.

One more rehearsal.

'Take please!' Shaukat called out excitedly. 'Right now!'

He seemed rather pleased. His eyes gleamed with excitement.

The shooting ended.

Umrao finished in the make-up room and headed for her car. Salma followed.

'Memsaab,' she called out.

'What's it, Salma?'

'Narendra Kumar-ji called when you were in the last shot.'

'Why didn't you tell me?'

'I...just... I thought I'd tell you once you had taken off your make-up.'

'What's new?'

'He's waiting in the hotel room.'

'Poor guy! Let's go and have a chat.'

Umrao abruptly came to a halt. There, in the distance, seated in a chair under a mango tree, right outside Floor No. 3 was Shaukat Hossain. His head hung low. He look tired, spent and broken. The setting sun was not visible from where Umrao stood but the twilight—strange and sublime—filtered down to his chair.

'Salma, you proceed to the car,' Umrao instructed. 'I'll join you.'

Before Salma could speak, she moved towards Shaukat.

Shaukat was startled as if an apparition stood before him. He rose from his chair and attempted a smile. 'You haven't left?'

Umrao shook her head. 'No. How are you keeping now?'

'I'm fine, Ma'am,' Shaukat said, but it sounded like he meant the opposite.

Umrao asked, 'Shouldn't you be going home?'

'In a little while...'

'No,' Umrao said, 'now.'

'Ji, I will. You proceed...'

Umrao shook her head once more. 'No, I'll go with you.'

Shaukat was taken aback. 'With me? You don't have your car today?'

'I do, but I want to go with you.'

'With me?'

Shaukat had lost his capacity to think. He stared and stared at Umrao. And as he did so, his eyes started glistening. And the setting sun chose precisely this moment to drop into the ocean. To paint the coral red all through the night. To breathe life into the pearls in the womb of shells.

Umrao looked at Shaukat with unblinking eyes.

'Yes, I want to go home—with my husband.'

Translated by Ratnottama Sengupta

Happiness

Standing on Park Street, if you look towards Chowringhee, you will see a narrow lane to your right. Walk on it for about fifty yards and you will come to a two-storeyed building situated inside a large compound. Inscribed on the marble plaque at the gate is the name of the building: 'Happiness'.

Within the compound is a garden laden with mango, palm, eucalyptus, parvati and bakul trees. In keeping with the mood of the winds, they sometimes sing happily and sometimes they sigh heavily at the thought of happiness; at other times, realizing that happiness is a mirage, they shake their heads wildly.

The garden has seasonal flowers too, which change with every rotation of the sun. Butterflies fly in to flirt with these flowers. In spring you can hear the cuckoo singing away, regardless of whether the inhabitants of 'Happiness' are happy or not.

The ground floor of the house is occupied by Mr Malhotra, a wealthy businessman from Punjab. The gentleman, his wife, their two sons and daughters-in-law and a five-year-old grandson, Makkan—alias Makhan—and their servants. On the upper floor lives the owner of the house, Arati Basu. The thirty-four-year-maiden lives by herself; aided by her maid Anila, who joined the household when she was nineteen and has grown up to be forty-five. Anila is also a spinster, but she has no time to even think about marriage, engrossed as she is in thinking about her paan and her zarda tobacco. There is Haran, aged forty; the short-statured cook Jagannath, aged fifty; driver Bipin Das, aged forty-eight, and the gardener Adhar Mahapatra, aged sixty. The remarkable thing about them is that, like their mistress, they are all unmarried.

The people upstairs and those downstairs don't visit each other often, but not because they lack in civility. When they do meet, they are most cordial, but there's no intimacy. Arati doesn't want it. She likes to keep her distance. She has no one in the world; no brother or sister, let alone a parent. Even those who might be termed a friend seldom visit. She prefers to live with her loneliness, alone.

Arati observes herself in the mirror every single day, so she knows the value of time. That is why she is punctual. In this matter she's very strict with the servants. She has gifted each one of them a wristwatch which they have to wear. Besides, the giant clock in the hall rings in every hour with a chime.

You can hear Arati calling out, 'Anila. '

'Ji, Didi?'

'What's the time?'

Anila looks at her wristwatch before replying, 'It's 12, Didi.'

'Hasn't Jagannath finished cooking yet?'

Jagannath, who has just arrived on the scene, replies with a smile, 'Ji, Didi.'

One morning you might hear, 'Adhar?'

'Ji, Didi?'

'What's the time now?'

'Ji, it's 7 o'clock.'

'Then why have you not finished watering the plants?'

'I finished Didi, just now.'

Then again, 'Haran?'

'Ji, Didi.'

'Why haven't you finished sweeping the floors yet? It's past 8...'

'I'm only fifteen minutes behind time!'

'Has your watch stopped working?'

'It's in first-class condition, Didi! I'll never be late again...'

'Mind that.'

And every evening, before the clock strikes 4, Bipin parks the old, well-maintained Austin in the portico and lights up. Minutes later, the grandfather clock in the hall faintly strikes 4, and Bipin throws away the bidi he has been smoking. He knows that Didi will be down before he can count to ten and ask him, 'Have you washed the car, Bipin?'

That is what Arati said this evening too. 'Ji haan, Didi,' Bipin replied, smiling.

Makhan's mother was in the lawn, drinking her evening tea. She waved to Arati, who waved back from the moving car.

The Austin was wending its way through the regulated Park Street traffic like it did every day. Arati took the compact out from her vanity bag and looked in the tiny mirror to check her lipstick. This scarlet was her favourite. Arati suddenly thought of Rekha. The friend, now a mother of three, had once remarked, 'You're looking like Goddess Kali. Charming, but with blood on her lips!'

'Thanks for the flattery,' Arati had replied. 'Yes, I do cover my lips with blue blood! And I'll keep doing so as long as he doesn't...'

'He!' Rekha couldn't resist the bait. 'Who's this He?'

Arati had replied, 'If I knew, you would've met him too by now.'

Arati looked at her reflection in the mirror. It didn't look like that of a thirty-four-year old's... She was what, twenty-five years old? 'Thanks, Max Factor.' Arati smiled to herself. Was she conceited? How would she be rated? Would she be considered beautiful? Was she pretty? Her features were not perfect, yet she was alluring. For, as Rekha put it, beauty can't be defined by a Roman nose, doe eyes, and a pearly complexion; it was an extra something that made even a dark-complexioned woman riveting. No, Arati couldn't be termed beautiful but she was quite good-looking; and she had a lovely body. Even the previous night, changing into her nightwear, Arati had carefully examined herself in the wardrobe mirror. Yes, she still had it: the fullness of youth.

Arati shut her vanity bag and looked out. Bipin parked at his usual spot on Red Road.

Arati slipped off her stilettos and started walking barefoot on the carpet of grass. She walked for a while. In the meantime Bipin finished smoking another bidi, drew out a photo of Hema Malini from his wallet and adored it. Arati returned just as he was placing it back in his wallet. She sat down on the grass and gazed up at the clouds. After a while she looked at her wristwatch. Bipin sat upright in his seat, his hands on the steering wheel, as Arati got into the car. The vehicle moved at 70 kmph. Bipin dare not go slower, for if he did so, he would invite a chiding. After a while the car stopped again. As on other days, outside the two-storeyed restaurant on the Strand. Arati climbed up to the first floor.

'Salaam Memsaab!' Ganesh, the forty-year-old waiter flashed her a warm smile and pointed to a table right next to the window, with a small wooden board on it that read 'Reserved'.

Exactly as it does every evening until 6.30 p.m. Exactly as it has done for the last five years.

Arati sat on the table and said, 'Get me a plate of samosas, and then a steaming cup of coffee.'

'Ji.'

The Ganga flowed by the restaurant, gurgling, splashing.

The evening sky stretched out over it, softened by the twilight. Looking out of the window, one could see its expanse with ships and boats floating upon it, heaving with the waves. It was almost as if Arati were sitting on the deck of a ship.

Arati looked around her. There were so many faces of happiness, in so many forms. Everyone seems to be thirsting, she thought, no one is satisfied with what they have. Everyone seeks more, some more, even more.

The samosas arrived.

But the food is merely an excuse to sit at the table. Every day she must sit at this table at dusk and look out of the window to witness darkness descend on the Ganga. Or perhaps watch the moonlight transform the landscape into a Japanese watercolour; or, for that matter, the flames of desire in the eyes of the men and women around her. All of these are but a pretext. In reality, she just wants to let go of herself in the flow of time. The truth is that she comes here only to while away the hours. She is eagerly waiting for her ship to sound its siren. Perhaps it will set sail for an unknown destination. Will the destination be happiness or sadness? Pain or pleasure? The finality of death or a new life?

Yes, Arati merely whiles away the hours. Evening and morning. She is up between 8 and 8.30, presses the bell on the table twice in a row, and glances at the wall clock. Then she goes to the washroom. Ten minutes later, Anila carries in a tray with tea, biscuits and the morning daily. Arati scans the headlines as she sips her tea while Anila chews her paan and combs her mistress's hair. Then she goes on a tour of her garden. When she returns, she finds breakfast waiting. She finishes it with a second cup of tea. She then discusses the day's menu with Jagannath and proceeds to the drawing room where magazines await her. Once in a while, she focuses on the listings section of the newspaper to decide if any movie or play merits her attention. If she fancies a title, she leaves home an hour earlier, finishes her routine walk on the Maidan and tea in Floatel, then heads for the theatre playing the movie or the play of her choice.

After the newspapers and magazines, it is time for her bath. A time-consuming, long-drawn-out process. Then she stands before a life-sized photograph of her mother. It was a tiny photograph when her mashi lived. Once she died, Arati got it enlarged. This is the only icon she bows to. No Ram-Sita, Shiv-Shakti for her, nor Jesus, Chaitanya, Ramakrishna, Vivekananda. She is not bothered about any of them nor the philosophies they represent. She doesn't believe in a past life because she retains no memory of it; nor does she believe in an afterlife because rebirth is yet to be proven. But Maa and her love are so real, so deeply experienced, that she reveres her mother, loves her, worships her, bows to her. The only form of greatness she has known was in her mother.

And Mashi, her aunt?

Arati picks up a novel after bowing to her mother. A Bengali novel. She continues to turn its pages till she feels the pangs of hunger. A glance at her wristwatch confirms it is 1 o'clock. Time for Jagannath to announce lunch. No, he is never late. She cheerfully sits down to eat. She won't carry on any conversation. She had to, when Mashi was around. She had to converse and also listen to her aunt.

A little rest after lunch. In other words, get immersed in a detective novel—English or Bengali, that depends on her mood—until the mystery is overpowered by sleep. A light siesta. But just as the clock hand touches 3, she is up on her feet. She picks up a couple of toffees from a jar on the shelf and, followed by Anila, goes down to the garden. There she keeps talking to Adhar as he walkss around the flowerbeds. And the moment he sees her, Makkan Malhotra comes running. 'Aun-tty!' His smile widens as he stretches out his hand. Arati places a toffee on his palm and grabs his hand. Holding him, and followed by Anila, she takes stock of every single plant in the garden. Makkan keeps sucking on the candy while recounting tales of his bravery: 'Aun-tty, I demolished the savage Babbar Sher Khan today with just one karate kick.' Once she's done with the garden, she gives the second candy to Makkan, hands him over to Mrs Malhotra, exchanges a few pleasantries with her, and goes up the stairs.

Anita fetches her a pot of tea. She casts a glance at the clock and gets busy for her outing at 4 p.m. Dressed up, she gets into the car and leaves for Maidan and the floating restaurant, Floatel. At 7 p.m. she returns to her nook, shuts the door, puts on some music and starts swaying to it. She is a good dancer with a good sense of rhythm. While in college, she'd even received a medal for dancing. But once her aunt made a nasty comment about it, she stopped; not just in public but even her daily practice. Then she switches off the music and brings out her sketch book. When she loses interest in that, she brings out the novel. Dinner at 9.30 p.m. From 10 to 11, she surrenders to the detective again. Then she takes her sleeping pills and goes to bed.

Precisely, this is her daily routine. Day in, day out. She doesn't do anything else, because she has no monetary need. And to think that her father died in sheer poverty!

Her mother had married him out of love. Neither Arati's grandfather nor Mashi, her aunt, had approved of her choice. Her grandfather had passed away shortly after their marriage. Arati was born after that and, when she was barely three, her father died a sudden death. In all the years, her mother had never gone to her wealthy sister for any help. Mashi suddenly took note of them when she heard that her sister was terminally ill. Arati had just turned seven. By then, she had witnessed how bravely her mother had had to fight off attempts to violate her modesty and how she had to struggle to keep the kitchen fire aglow. After Mashi arrived with doctor and medicine, Maa could breathe her last with the assurance that her didi would take care of her Arati.

Meshomoshai, her uncle, had been alive then. He owned a factory where he manufactured nuts and bolts. In addition, he had inherited shares in various companies. But he was not on good terms with Mashi. Mesho used to drink regularly and, under the influence of alcohol, he would abuse Mashi for being childless. Mashi would break into tears, and that would scare Arati. Mashi used to think of her as her own child but Mesho never bothered. When Arati was about twelve, Mesho died of cirrhosis. Mashi found a meaning for living. She sold off the factory and put the money into a fixed-deposit account. Of the two houses they owned, one had already been rented out to three tenants. Now she rented out the ground floor of the Park Street house where they themselves lived.

Apart from the shares, Mesho had inherited ancestral land of about 30 bigha and a mango garden. So Mashi was never in want. Arati grew up in prosperity, along with the various whims and idiosyncrasies of her mashi. She learned to dance and paint and gradually completed her studies and became a Bachelor of Arts. After that, Mashi didn't want her to study any more. Secretly, Arati was relieved. Mashi started to find a match for her. And why not? She was twenty. After unsuccessfully trying to attract a handful of 'suitable boys', Mashi started dubbing her 'unlucky' and 'ill-fated'. She was all of twenty-four.

Turning a deaf ear to these words, Arati concentrated on improving her skills with the pencil sketches. Mashi would see the sketches and, some morning or late at night, when about to retire, she would tell Arati, 'Beautiful! You have got magic in your fingers, Arati!' Those precious moments found Mashi affectionately caressing her hand.

Arati cautiously sips her coffee. The scarlet-tinted lips should not lose the 'Goddess Tara' look. Suddenly the word Maa makes her think of Makkan. What fantastic stories he would concoct! 'You know Aun-tty, I was passing through a forest when a lion came out of nowhere! A lion! Bigger, more ferocious than a tiger... Both its eyes were blazing like fire... You follow me Aun-tty? The moment I saw him, I fired the gun... Brooom! The lion screamed ... believe me Aun-tty. I fired again, Brooom!'

Arati decides that, on her way back, she will buy a new toy for him and invite him to the Toys Room, a room which Makkan visits at least once every twenty-four hours. The toys are all for Makkan but he is only to play with them, not take them home with him. Watching him play and cackle in delight, Arati folds him into her arms, draws him to her bosom and kisses him on his cheeks and forehead. Makkan is used to this and now, while playing with the toys, he sometimes walks up to her and says, 'Aun-tty gimme a kissy!'

The very thought makes Arati want to break into laughter. But that can't be. Surely she can't laugh here, so her eyes start twinkling. Has anyone caught her smiling to herself? She looks around her, to her right and her left. All at once, her eyes are arrested and they come to rest upon a gentleman. Tall, well-built, bearded, wearing thick glasses, with a touch of silver in his hair. Dressed in expensive trousers and shirt, he is turning the pages of a magazine while nibbling at a sandwich and sipping coffee. She can observe only his profile—and, all of a sudden, she remembers Captain Aditya Roy. That unleashes a storm of memories.

Arati can almost see them unfold before her eyes.

The Past Unfolds

Mashi had Obsessive Compulsive Disorder. She would wash her hands every five minutes. This had increased after Mesho's death; she would take longer to wash her hands. Go on and on, she would.

Mashi glared at me with her hands still under the tap. 'So

many girls are getting married in this city and you can't hook a groom, eh? You are no beauty queen, but you're not an ugly duckling either! You're a B.A.-pass girl who can dance and sketch beautifully...'

A gulmohar in full bloom was swaying right outside the dining-room window. The fiery orange set off by the high-rise beyond our boundary wall had prompted me to bring out my sketchbook. I intended to finish the painting in watercolour.

'I've forgotten the dance steps since you derided me, Mashi.' I spoke in a soft and serious tone.

'What was that?' Mashi shot back, her brows knitted in anger. 'You're finding fault with me!'

'Why would I do that, Mashi? I just pointed out a plain fact. The fact of the matter is that it matters little whether one is highly qualified or not. It is all a matter of destiny. You're right, Mashi, when you say I am ill-fated.'

As I spoke, tears welled up and washed out the passionate colours of the gulmohar. That stalled Mashi. The next moment her voice boomed higher: 'What the hell! She has started lecturing me!' She stomped out of the room.

That very moment someone pressed the calling-bell. Haran walked in a moment later to ask, 'Where is Maa, Didi? The new tenant is here with his wife.'

'She's in her room...' I replied.

The previous day, an array of vehicles had brought the furniture which belonged to the new tenants. Three or four men in khaki had washed, cleaned and set up the rooms, then locked them and left. The tenants had arrived today: Captain Aditya Roy and his wife.

Mashi came out of her room. 'Ask Jagannath to put on the kettle, Arati,' she said. 'Bring out the tea and sweets for the new tenants. I'll seat them in the hall downstairs.'

Mashi went down the stairs. I followed about fifteen minutes later with Anila carrying the platter of tea and savouries.

'My daughter... I mean, my niece Arati. And here's Captain Aditya Roy and his wife Seema.'

I folded my hands in a bashful namaste.

Aditya Roy must've been about thirty-two and his wife was younger to him by five or six years. They greeted us in reply.

The robustly built and fair-complexioned captain spoke with a smile, 'A little more than one sugar for me, Arati Devi.'

'And you?' I looked at Seema Roy.

She replied with arched eyebrows and a miserly smile, 'Even one is too much for me.'

Mashi told them to let her know if they needed anything at all. They had been married only two years, it turned out.

'You know, Mrs Majumdar, he got a promotion right after our marriage!'

Mrs Majumdar, Mashi, replied: 'This is worth remembering at all times, Captain Roy!'

Captain Roy kept a serious face and said, 'How can I forget it? The number of people to remind me seems to be growing!'

A collective burst of laughter filled the room. Mine was among them, but the one that stood out loudest was Captain Roy's. And the softest was Seema Roy's. She seemed to be raised in Western ways. Not only did she speak accented Bengali, she could not be faulted for lack of etiquette.

In the course of conversation, Mashi told them that although the hall was our drawing room, they too could entertain their guests there.

'Thanks, Mrs Majumdar!' Captain Roy was quick to respond. 'And in that case, I will make use of this screened-off portion. It will provide some privacy when we receive guests and, at other times, I can use it as my writing corner. I will ensure that you face no discomfort.'

It has been ten years since all this happened. I was twenty-four then.

Aditya Roy's laughter floated up. I was standing next to the window.

Aditya and Seema were out for a walk in the garden. It was just about 6.30 in the morning. I had not yet turned robotic. I was yet to become the owner of 'Happiness'.

Aditya was laughing over some humorous exchange with his wife. The burst of laughter seemed to deepen the flame-orange of the gulmohar. The joi de vivre in his laughter was so infectious that I caught myself smiling.

Seema walked a few paces ahead, humming a tune to herself. Aditya lit up a cigarette. Seema stopped before a flower and called out, 'Darling!'

'Chhi!' Mashi's voice startled me. I had not noticed her entering the room.

Mashi creased her eyebrows as she said, 'Shameless hussy! With a Hindu Bengali's blood coursing through her veins, she keeps parroting, "Dal-ling! Dal-ling!" Fie!'

I laughed at that. My laughter added fuel to fire. 'And why are you laughing? Am I joking with you!'

'No Mashi, I'm laughing at the term of endearment.'

Mashi smiled at that. 'Right you are. What awful times we live in!' The next moment her smile was gone. 'But why on earth are you standing at the window and prying on the peccadilloes of a married couple? I have been seeing your eyes popping out of their sockets since they arrived!'

I shut the window with a bang. Aditya Roy's laughter still penetrated the room. As did Seema Roy's voice, calling out to him, 'Darling!'

Mashi was livid. 'It's been two years since they got married, but they still behave as if they are honeymooning. The guy is in the army and the girl has been Anglicized. What did she say? Her father is a Major, now retired. After her mother passed away about five years ago, he married a fifty-year-old Madrasi slut. Disgusting!'

'Why did you take them in as tenants, Mashi?'

'How bright you are! If I were to be so choosy, would I get any tenant? A good tenant is one who pays a decent rent dot on time. These guys have given me a hefty amount as advance payment; plus, with military in the house, we won't have to worry about thieves and robbers. Right?'

I kept my counsel to myself.

Mashi did not worry about my response, or the lack of it. 'And if they cross the limits of decency,' she kept up her soliloquy, 'I will issue a notice and throw them out!'

A tenant, Mashi said, must live like a tenant. 'They will live downstairs and we upstairs. There's no need to mingle, understand? Let them live by themselves. Let them dance, sing and shout themselves hoarse with their "dal-ling" "dal-ling". You don't need to listen to them or keep a watch, okay?'

Once again I did not respond.

'What's the matter?' Mashi demanded, 'Cat got your tongue?'

I lowered my voice to say, 'It will be just as you say, Mashi.'

That's how it might have been if Anila had not disposed otherwise. The following morning, as she was combing my hair, she gulped down her paan and asked, 'May I say something, Didi?'

'What is it, Anila?'

'Promise you won't get angry?'

'How can I promise anything without knowing whether I will be fuming or shedding tears?'

'These two, the sir and madam downstairs...' Anila sniggered as she spoke into my ears.

'What about them?' I was all ears, although I pretended to be unperturbed.

'They are much in love, Didi!'

'A married couple ought to be...'

'You are right, Didi.' Anila was much excited. 'But marriage does not necessarily spell love. Take for instance Dutta-sahib, the owner of the three-storeyed red building; you tell me what hell their marriage is? Love is not easy to come by, Didi, much like God!'

I got irritated. 'Don't go on and on about their love! How do you know about their love?'

'You know Jenny, the Christian ayah they have?' Anila lowered her voice. 'She was saying that Sahib is besotted with Madam!'

'And what about Madam? You didn't care to know if she loves him as much.'

Anila widened her paan-painted smile and said, 'I'll ask her tomorrow.'

I felt like needling her. 'Anila, how do you know that love is like God and not very easy to find?'

Anila started laughing.

'What's so funny?'

Anila could not stop laughing. She then checked it with this observation delivered in a mournful tone: 'Everyone in this world seeks love, Didi! I have seen this all my life. And I have realized it through my own life...'

'What have you realized?'

'That it is not easy to come by. Love is a matter of luck. Fate. Destiny. It is as difficult to get love as it is to reach God.'

'Anila, do you seek love?' I asked in a soft voice.

'Yes, Didi.' Anita's voice quivered with emotion. 'I am a Hindu widow; my best years are behind me. I have lost my husband, so I won't know the love of my children. But siblings? Brother, sister, mother father, friend; you need somebody to share your life with, don't you, Didi? Am I right, Didi?'

'Yes, you're right, Anila,' I said forcefully. 'And I have learnt something from you today.'

'What are you saying, Didi!' Anila was beside herself.

Ten years ago I used to fall asleep at 10 p.m. I had no need for sleeping pills then, like I do today. But after Anila's dissertation on love, I was up till 1 in the morning, tossing and turning in my bed.

Love. Yes, we are all in search of love. I received love from my mother, but I lost her. Mashi scolds me, but she loves me too. However, a spoonful of rice won't fill your stomach. Two spoonfuls of water will not quench your thirst. And then, there are so many shades to love. Life goes on even without the love of siblings, but what is life without that special one? The one that binds Aditya Roy and Seema? The one between man and woman?

I felt a dryness in my throat. I poured a bottle of water down my gullet, then fell asleep but, until then, I felt parched. I didn't realize it then, but now I know what I was thirsting for. All the water of Ganga flowing towards the ocean could not have quenched my thirst.

The next day, curiosity got the better of me, a hidden desire perhaps. How does a husband, a man, express his love for the woman of his life, his wife?

I was hooked, as if I was watching a movie. Avoiding Mashi, I would watch the Roys' live out their conjugal life. When they would spend time in the garden. When they would entertain their friends or relatives in the hall downstairs. When Aditya Roy left for work in the military jeep and when he returned at 6.30 p.m. I would closely monitor their glances, their smiles, their waving of hands, their paces, their steps… There would be a deep look in Aditya's eyes, Seema's eyes would have a misty softness, and a rhythm to her walk when he was beside her.

'Darling, where would you like to go today?'

'To Sheela's at 3 p.m. I will call you from there, okay?'

'Yes, darling.'

'When will you be back?'

'The usual time. Bye darling.'

'Bye dear.'

This was the pattern when he left for work. In the evening, when he came back, the exchange would be different.

'Hello darling.'

'Just hello! What's the matter, Mimi?'

'I'm angry.'

'Angry? That's the other side of love.'

'Clever, aren't you, Captain?'

'Meaning?'

'You are a wordsmith.'

'Wonderful. A little more love and I will be a poet. For now I can only quote the World Poet: "I fail to fathom the mystery that is you... Here I am, all these long years; and still I know not where you are..."'

Aditya came up to the door and stood there. There was an enchantment in his eyes. He walked softly up to Seema. She looked at him while continuing to play. Aditya sang out, in tune with the notes. 'I'm dying of thirst, darling. Do quench my thirst, darling!'

Seema didn't even pause to reply, 'Please go to the fridge, darling!'

Aditya continued in the same vein, 'No darling, no fridge can quench this thirst! I am on fire and only two moist lips can put out the fire!'

'Get lost!' Seema burst into laughter and turned away. But Aditya turned her around to face him and lowered his mouth. The piano stopped playing. I scooted from the spot, red-faced. I went directly up to my room, switched off the light, and flung myself on the bed. I was shivering for quite a while after that.

'Didi, are you there?' Anila was at the door.

'Yes, switch on the light.'

'Goodness, why are you in the dark, Didi? What thoughts are you lost in?'

'Thinking of the elusive love you talked about the other night. Stop laughing, Anila, and keep chewing your paan.'

Anila giggled even more at this. I picked up the dictionary and started leafing through it.

'What are you seeking there, Didi?' Anila was curious.

'The meaning of the word love.'

'What a thought!' Anila was in the grip of another bout of laughter. I opened a page of the dictionary and started reading aloud: 'Love means affection, attraction, romance, passion, attachment... Understand, Anila?'

She couldn't stop giggling. 'What's the matter with you, Didi?' she managed.

I said, 'I will complain to Mashi about you, Anila.'

'Why?' She was scared.

'You're brainwashing me with all your discourses on love. Now, day in, day out, I can think of nothing else.'

Anila was older than me by almost ten years, yet she fell at my feet and cried out, 'Please Didi, don't get me turned out! Please don't.'

'Okay, let me think over it.'

'No Didi, please don't...'

I pulled on a grave face and said, 'Okay, you are excused this once but on one condition. You will update me on any other discovery regarding love and keep me informed. Agreed?'

'Sure and certain, Didi. Without fail.'

That night, I dreamt that I was a schoolgirl sitting in a classroom with thirty other boys and girls. Standing in front of the blackboard was Anila, wearing thick glasses and chewing a paan. She was writing away on the board: 'Love, affection, endearment, attachment = God = affection, romance, passion = paan and tabac.' I started laughing at this. As a result, I woke up very early to see sunlight breaking out in the east, to the accompaniment of the chirping of birds.

I created a record of sorts that day by waking early. I saw a light in the puja room and realized that Mashi was in there. I stealthily opened the door and started walking down the stairs. But what was this? The main door was open. Which meant Munshiram, the butler downstairs, was up too. I walked out to the garden.

The grass felt good under my feet. The flowers had created a carnival of colours.

I came to a sudden halt as I was about to walk past a mango tree. I then crept behind the tree to watch Aditya Roy under a bakul tree, holding Seema in a tight embrace and thirstily kissing her. The balmy morning suddenly lost its cool touch and began to scorch me like a summer noon. The mango tree was like a pillar of fire. I was drenched in sweat. I stealthily fled the scene.

Back in my room, I flung myself on the bed and tightly shut my eyes. Still, the image of the couple in a tight embrace would not go out of my sight. I felt a kind of rage coursing through me. I was not angry with any individual but with the entire universe. My body was on fire and my lips were burning.

Seema would ask me to join her when she went shopping or to the movies. But, despite the friendliness, I felt I couldn't confide in her. And I felt Seema, too, couldn't do so in me. There was an intangible stiffness in the companionship which lacked in warmth. It was a mere formality, or 'time pass'.

After lunch one noon, I went down to Seema's and found her playing a record. She had a good collection of Indian and world music. I started listening to Ravi Shankar on the sitar.

'One can dance to this, no?' Seema looked at me.

'Yes.' I nodded.

'So get started.'

'Me? I don't dance.'

'Don't lie. Your aunt told me the other day. We are aware of your talents and we are trying to find a good match for you.'

'Dhut!' I waved my hand.

'You may make light of it but it's a fact that you are good at it. So please dance Arati, please...'

I had to succumb to her pleas. I chose to enact a Radha-Krishna episode in the Kathak style. With a preliminary introduction to the situation, I went on to enact Krishna trying to appease Radha who is sulking. It felt good to dance after ages. Deep inside, I was delighted that I had not fallen out of practice. The movements were peppered by Seema's laudatory 'wah-wahs'. I got back in form. The minute I stopped, I heard non-stop clapping. It wasn't Seema. I turned around to see Aditya Roy clapping from the bedroom. 'Well done, Arati! Excellent.'

'Sorry, Arati.' Seema giggled. 'We'd conspired to make you dance today because it's his holiday.'

'Why aren't you smiling, Arati?' Aditya asked. 'Are you angry?'

'Why would she be angry?' Seema exclaimed. 'She's a darling. I'll treat her to Bhim Nag's sandesh.'

'Just you try!' I faked anger.

Aditya laughed so loud it seemed as if the roof would come down. When I went upstairs a little while later, Anila came to me. 'Mashima's calling you. What's the matter, Didi?'

I was taken aback. 'Nothing!'

I entered Mashi's room. Her face predicted a thunderstorm. 'You wanted to see me, Mashi?'

She was knitting. She lifted her eyes, measured me with her gaze, and turned to her knitting again as she asked, 'How old are you now?'

'Why?'

'There can be only one straight answer to my question, Arati.'

'Twenty-four...'

'Are you married?'

'You know only too well that I'm not, Mashi!' I could not keep irritation out of my voice.

'Really?' Mashi put down the ball of wool and said, 'See, you've become combative after your growing friendship with military folks. You have to counter every sentence I speak. Who can imagine that this is the niece I picked up like a kitten from the street and raised!'

I was like one possessed. The words flew out of my mouth. 'If you think of me as a kitten off the street, you should put me back on the streets, Mashi!'

Mashi's eyes were spitting fire. 'Utter one more word and I'll slap…' She left the words hanging in the air and went on to say, 'You are at a marriageable age. Why must you entertain them and join them in their shameless ha-ha-hee-hee? Why are you rubbing shoulders with a married couple? They're a young couple; what draws you to be the third angle in their life?'

'Mashi!' My voice was mournful.

'Enough! I have lived long enough to read meaning in even the sneezing of a lizard. I have been watching you; you even look different.'

'What are you implying?'

'The cut of your blouse has changed. You've asked the tailor to stitch three sleeveless blouses. Showing off your skin! Why? Do you want to be a memsahib like Seema?'

I was stunned. Mashi kept at it: 'What are you gaping at? Why have you gone dumb? Should I speak on? You have even bought the same soap and scent that Seema uses. You have ordered the very same curtains as theirs. Why?'

Tears welled up in my eyes but I didn't want to let the floodgates open in front of her, so I fled to the sanctuary of my room. I once again flung myself on the bed, this time to cry my heart out.

Then I sat up to think. Mashi was right. I was indeed aping Seema.

That very day I stopped going to their apartment.

Two days passed.

On the third day I was up at daybreak. It struck me that I was going to another extreme. Why should I not interact or mingle with people? That was normal. I was not sinning.

Daylight had not yet touched the trees in our garden. Like a butterfly I went from flower to flower, walking barefoot on the dew-drenched carpet of grass. I even plucked two blood-red roses in full bloom.

'Hey, what are you up to?' Aditya Roy's voice was still sleep-laden.

I froze. I surmised that I was in close proximity of Aditya Roy and Seema. I didn't have to make an effort to eavesdrop.

'What's the matter, darling?' Aditya Roy's voice had clarity now. 'Why aren't you looking at me? If I'm enraged, I'll punish you. A sweet punishment!'

My heart was pounding. If I turned around now I might be privy to a sight like the other morning, when two thirsty persons sought relief in each other's lips, both bathing under the same waterfall of lust. And the bakul blessing them with a shower of fragrant flowers...

'Darling...'

It struck me that the voice was right behind me. I turned around, startled. Aditya Roy was indeed there.

He stood there unblinking for a few seconds, as if ossified. Then, with an awkward smile, he said, 'You! Arati! What a blunder... Did you and Seema buy the saris together? They are of the same print!'

Instead of speaking, I simply smiled. I was blushing.

'Please don't mind,' Aditya said, 'I mistook you for Seema. I see you are up much earlier today. Why were you missing these past two days?'

'Just…'

Aditya was yet to regain his composure. He kept talking with some levity in his voice in order to do so: 'I thought you were upset with us.'

'No no,' I cut in, 'why would I be upset?' For some reason I felt embarrassed. I turned my face away.

'These roses are exquisite! What will you do with them?'

'Nothing in particular.' I looked down at the flowers in my hand.

'Will you give them to me?' Aditya Roy smiled.

'Take them…' I offered. As he stretched out his hand, our fingers touched. 'I want more,' Aditya lowered his voice, almost to a whisper.

'What?' I was also whispering.

'A portrait of you, by you. A small one…'

'Why mine?' I was smiling.

'Just a fancy.'

'No…'

'What's going on?' Seema was standing close by. Both Aditya and I turned around. Really, Seema and I were indeed wearing the same print!

Seema blinked. 'Am I wearing your sari or are you wearing mine?'

'Both are from Mafatlal's,' Aditya Roy joked. I simply smiled.

Seema too smiled as she approached. 'What's the matter, Arati Devi? Didn't you sleep well last night?'

Aditya Roy looked at his wife and said, 'I was telling Arati Madam that tomorrow being Saturday, we will attend the new play at Biswaroopa.'

'Yes, why don't you join us, Arati?'

'No.'

'Why not? You need Mashima's permission, right? I'll get it.'

I did not wish to prolong the discussion.

'Yes, Arati will also g—'

Mashima was at a window on the first floor. I hastened to take leave. 'Mashi must need me for something.'

I almost fled the scene. A cuckoo somewhere in the garden chose that very moment to call out.

That day, when Mashi retired for her post-lunch siesta, I peeped out of the window and saw Seema leave for New Market with two of her friends. I was relieved. I was in no mood to chitchat. I was still recovering from the aftermath of the morning's incident.

Anila came in, a paan stuffed in her mouth. 'What're you doing, Didi?'

'Nothing. Just thinking.'

'Thinking? What about?'

'Nothing special. About a painting that appears to be forming in my head.'

Anila smiled. 'It's different with you artists.'

I smiled back at her. 'Right you are, Anila! Now go and give yourself an hour's rest.'

'Yes Didi, I'll do just that.'

Anila left me to myself. I looked at the mirror. My reflection appeared to be lost in thought. Somewhat withered, she looked. A light shone on her unkempt hair. A river deep within her seemed to have flooded its shore...

I stood up with a jolt. I brought out my sketchbook and started on my portrait. It was ready in ninety minutes. By then daylight was taking its leave. I signed off the portrait with the word 'Me'.

Dusk turned into darkness.

Aditya Roy's guffaw floated up from downstairs. Perhaps they had some visitors. I climbed up to the terrace to escape the soundscape. I spent some time in solitude. I was chased by a restlessness, as if there was a storm brewing in the distance that would soon overpower me.

Quite a while had passed when Anila showed up at the door frame. 'My God, you're standing here? I was searching for you downstairs.'

'Why? Why did you need to search for me?'

'Maa's asking for you.'

'Carry on, I'm coming.'

But Anila didn't leave. She looked at me, then at the sky, and said, almost to herself, 'It's so nice to watch the stars in the open sky, no Didi? It reminds you of so many things...'

I looked at Anila. She was admiring the star-studded sky, a paan stuffed in her mouth. There was no difference between the two of us at that moment. I climbed down the stairs without rupturing the magic of the moment.

'Where were you all this while?' Mashi asked as soon as her eyes alighted on me. 'You seem to be rather flighty today. Have you written down the expenses? Go get the diary.'

I sat down with the diary. Then I attended to the chores one after another. The lights were switched off one by one. My room, too, succumbed to darkness.

But sleep evaded me. Two questions would not let me be. One: Aditya Roy had asked me for my portrait, sketched by me, but why did he not reveal that to Seema? Two: Why didn't he tell her that, because we were both wearing saris of the same print, he had mistaken me for his wife? Why?

The search for answers revealed a chemistry I had not tasted before.

The clock struck 1.

Then the clock struck 2.

I sat up and switched on the table lamp. I took out my portrait, switched off the lamp and stealthily came out of my room. At the end of the passage I opened the door and climbed downstairs. With every step I took I experienced the thrill of a detective novel.

In the hall, across the partition, was Aditya Roy's table. His diary was my target. I would fulfil a small request of his by placing my portrait within it.

By the time I reached the other side of the screen I had sampled how the visually challenged make their way around. Now the table was to my left. I felt around until the diary was in my grip. I placed the portrait in it and was about to put it back on the table when the accident occurred.

The bone china vase on the table fell to the floor with a resounding crash. Startled, I tried to quickly move away and dislodged a few other things. As I tried to back off, I bumped into a chair which protested loudly. In a chain reaction, Aditya Roy bellowed from his bedroom at the other end of the hall: 'Who's there?'

I was petrified.

I heard a door open.

I leaned against the wall and contemplated breaking into a run. But my legs let me down. Someone was striding forward— Aditya Roy. I moved forward as soon as I could reclaim my feet but Aditya Roy's hand stopped me. The hand seemed startled by what it felt and withdrew. It had worked out the fact that the figure wrapped in darkness was a woman.

'Who're you?' a surprised Aditya Roy roared.

'It's me, Arati...' I was compelled to whisper.

'You! But...'

Before Aditya Roy could express his amazement Mashi's voice floated in, 'Who's there?'

I immediately entreated him, 'Please go!'

Aditya Roy was about to retreat and I was making to move forward when the light in the stairway came on. Mashi witnessed the unexpected drama of two dumbfounded adults exchanging startled looks in a neon-washed hall in the dead of the night.

'You two!' Mashi could barely believe her eyes. Spots in her eyeballs rained fire. She put us in the dock and demanded like a public prosecutor, 'What's going on there? Why are you two standing in the darkness?'

Aditya Roy was shaken out of his amazement. He said, 'I came out on hearing the shattering of a vase. And before I could gather my wits, you came down...'

Mashi walked down and stood before him. Narrowing her eyes, she spit out, 'What do you take me to be, Aditya? Have I not lived long enough to sift the truth from lies?'

Aditya Roy's face turned pallid. 'What are you saying? Ask Arati if you don't believe me!'

She demanded of me with a stern look, 'Out with it; what were you up to here, at this hour?'

What should I say? I debated with myself. The truth would smear my intentions; even daylight loses its shine to tinted glasses.

'So? Why are you speechless?'

'I heard a sound... and...' I stammered.

'What noise? What kind of sound?' Mashi interrogated me like a seasoned lawyer. 'You were sleeping upstairs in your locked room. And the passage door too was closed. What was the terrible sound that pierced through all these doors and woke you up? Hussy, do you think I am an imbecile?'

The very next moment she addressed Aditya Roy. 'I don't believe you either. You heard a noise and came out to see what's going on without switching on the light? Only predators can see in the dark, not humans.'

Aditya Roy furrowed his brows. 'What are you implying, Mashima?'

'I'm speaking the truth, Aditya. You're an educated, married man, and this is what you are up to? Taking advantage of a simple, foolish girl...'

'Don't utter crap, Mashima!' Aditya Roy cut her short.

'Crap?' Mashi snarled. 'Just because you're caught red-handed?'

'Yes, crap!' Seema's voice cut in.

Mashi turned around to see a sleepy Seema at the door. 'What balderdash are you uttering, Mashima? What a shame! It was I who heard the noise and sent him to check what was going on.'

'If you had sent him, where was the need to be so intimate?' Mashi snorted viciously.

'I'm certain the need was not on his part.' Seema's voice was pure poison. 'You should ask your daughter: what was the need that drove her downstairs at this hour. And you're talking about switching on the light; did you give Mr Roy the chance?'

Mashi took a step towards me. 'Harlot, why did you come downstairs? What was your intention?'

I made no attempt to break my silence. What was the point? No one would believe anything I said. Nor could I speak the truth.

'Why are you reprimanding me in this manner, Mashima? It benefits no one...'

'What do you understand about benefits and losses?' Mashi raised her pitch. 'You Anglicised people raised with Western mores, at the drop of a hat you go "dal-ling dal-ling"...'

I could have sunk into the ground.

Seema too raised her voice. 'Right you are, madam. Because of my Western education, I don't go "harlot" and "hussy" at the drop of a hat. But please, Mashima, let's not go on in this unpleasant manner. The servants are lapping up the scene and, next, the neighbours might show up too.' She turned towards her husband and said, 'Darling let's go inside.'

'Yes, let's go,' Aditya Roy said, adding, 'Sorry...'

He left the scene with rapid strides. Seema bolted the door from the inside. Did Aditya Roy apologize to me? I wondered.

Mashi looked around her. Anila stood at the head of the stairs, Jenny at the far end of the hall, Jagannath at the other end. Mashi grabbed my left arm. 'Come upstairs...'

I set foot on the stairs but could hardly keep pace with Mashi's hurricane strides; she virtually dragged me up all the way. Anila made herself scarce, Jenny and Jagannath too disappeared. Mashi switched off the light on the landing. Darkness descended upon the stage where the drama had been unfolding all this while.

Mashi pushed me into my room and shut the door. Then she asked me in a glacial voice, 'Tell me why you went downstairs.'

'Just like that...'

'Tell me the truth: were you getting intimate with that military guy?'

'You have a dirty mind, Mashi.' My voice was frosty.

Mashi landed a stinging slap on my face. 'Come out with the truth,' she demanded, 'were you on a rendezvous with Aditya Roy?'

'No.' I said. That earned me a second slap. 'Speak the truth, you tart! Is Aditya Roy avowing love to you?'

'No.' A third slap landed on my cheek.

'Liar! You are in love with him.'

'No.'

'No again! Slut! Whore! Tramp!' Each word was accompanied by an indiscriminate blow.

I gritted my teeth so that no sound would escape me. With each blow I was swaying this way and that. And then, everything blacked out and every sound ceased to be. I fainted.

But I did not die.

I regained consciousness after a while. I was lying on the floor, my head in Mashi's lap, water sprinkled upon my face. Mashi was gazing at me. I sat up.

'How are you feeling now?' Mashi asked in a soft voice.

'All right,' I replied, eyes fixed on the floor.

Mashi stood up. 'Go to sleep,' she said as she left the room, closing the door behind her.

I sat still. I can't recall what I was thinking to myself. I could hear an occasional car shattering the midnight silence with its raucous horn. 'How shameful! Chhi! Chhi!' the cricket seemed to repeat in my ears. It crossed my mind that it might be better to die.

The clock on the wall struck four. I rose from the bed, switched off the lamp and came out on the passage. The door was locked from the inside. So was the door leading to the stairs. That was Mashi's doing!

'Arati!' Mashi called out softly. I turned around to face her. She came out of her room, stood next to me and said, 'Go to sleep, child!'

'Let me go, Mashi,' I pleaded in a soft voice. 'There's no point in my living now.'

Mashi drew me to her chest and said, 'Nonsense! Don't utter or even think such nonsense. Don't worry. Every flesh-and-blood creature is a bundle of urges. In trying to balance them, things go off the edge once in a while. Tell me dear, who do I have in my life other than you?'

Mashi tightened her embrace and I could feel her crying. Her frame was rocking, quivering, her tears falling on my shoulder. They somehow acted as a balm and soothed my anger, pain, desire, excitement, apathy...

I spent the following day looking at the sky out of my window. Sky, the epitome of empty space.

I did not peep down from my window. Nor did I ask anybody, and yet I realized that the apartment downstairs was vacated by 4 in the evening. I felt an unbearable lightness.

And then the days passed by.

I got used to keeping quiet.

Mashi tried to find a suitable match for me—in vain. She became morose after that. After the Roys left, she never once called me a hussy or a harlot.

One morning, about six months later, Anila rushed into my room and shook me out of my slumber. Fear was writ all over her face. I rushed to Mashi's room. She was lying on her side; her stiff body cold to the touch, her eyes wide open. Mashi was no more.

I felt I had lost the very ground underneath my feet.

Where should I go now? What should I do? What would happen to me? Should I try to look for a job? What if I didn't get one? A million doubts beset my mind.

Three days later, the solicitor, Mr Chatterjee, came over to announce that, in her will, Mashi had left me her entire property, all her assets, the shares and liquid cash.

Mashi had taken care of me. I would live. She had ensured that I would not starve to death—even if I wished to!

Ten years passed by after that.

Today, Once More...

The past fades away.

The coffee's finished too.

Arati looks at her watch. It is time to leave.

She glances sideways at the gentleman who triggered her journey into the past. What is this? He is also peering at her! Her head starts to spin. Who is that? Why is he watching her so closely?

He leaves his table and walks across to Arati.

'Namaskar!'

Arati looks at him. Is the restaurant swaying? It is supposed to resemble a ship on the ocean... Is it really floating?

He speaks in a soft voice. 'Please don't mind my asking you... Do you live on Park Street? Or lived there in the past? Are you Arati Devi—Arati Basu?'

'Yes...' Arati gazes back at him.

The gentleman smiles a clipped smile. 'I am Aditya Roy.'

A siren sounds off a ship in the distance.

Noticing her fixed gaze, Aditya Roy asks, 'I...I hope I am not an unpleasant presence for you. You are not upset to see me, are you?'

'No.'

'May I take a seat? I have to say a couple of things to you.'

'Here?' Arati speaks as if reciting a rehearsed line.

'Who knows if we will meet again. Life has no dearth of high drama!'

'Please seat yourself.' Arati stirs to life.

Aditya gestures to a boy who appears with a chair from somewhere. He sits down.

'Coffee?' Arati enquires of Aditya.

He shakes his head.

'Something to munch on?'

'No.'

They look at each other, then look away. A few minutes pass in silence as they keep their heads lowered. They are oblivious of the noise in the restaurant or even the lap-lap-lapping of Ganga flowing down to the ocean—like Time.

'How are you, Arati Devi?'

'Good. And you?'

'Fine, thanks.'

'How's Mrs Roy doing?'

'Haven't heard from her for days now.'

'Meaning?' Arati looks at him with the question in her eyes.

'She's been Mrs Mukherjee for the last seven years. We got divorced eight years ago.'

'What? This... I am so sorry to hear this!' There are questions galore crowding Arati's eyes.

Aditya Roy smiles but there is neither joy nor grief in it. 'Nothing is wasted in life, Arati Devi. Destruction contains within it the seeds of a new creation. When this shore crumbles, a new chunk of land shows on the other shore. I'd heard this statement earlier but have come to realize the truth of it only now.'

'But why did this happen?' Arati mutters, more to herself.

'Drama. Or destiny.'

'True…'

'Mashima—your aunt—how's she?'

'She passed away six months after you left.'

'So where do you live now?'

'In the same house!' Arati smiles wanly. 'Mashi left me her entire property.'

'But you…' Aditya Roy tries to guess. 'Are you…'

'No, I'm not yet married!' Arati layers her reply with levity. 'I am not one to kowtow to anybody. I don't have the desire to arrange my own match nor do I have the smartness to seek one through matrimonial columns…'

Aditya continues to watch her.

'Where are you posted now, Mr Roy?'

'I live in Poona. I retired six months ago, as a Major.'

'Retired? So early?'

'Yes. I didn't feel like continuing with the job.'

'So you are all by yourself?'

'Yes. All alone. And lonely.'

'But why did this happen?'

'You mean the divorce?'

'Yes…'

'As a consequence of the dramatic developments of that night…'

'Oh my God!'

Aditya fishes out a packet of cigarettes from his pocket and lights one. He slowly lets out a mouthful of smoke. He then speaks. 'You may remember, that night Seema had said that she had sent me on hearing the sound of the vase shattering …'

'Yes.'

'But that wasn't true.'

'Really?'

'She saved me from Mashima's furious attack with that lie and rescued me from an uncomfortable situation. Then, after you returned to your floor and darkness returned to the hall room, she faced me in our well-lit bedroom and said in a calm voice, "Go to sleep." I was in complete agreement as I felt like a fallen tree. My mind refused to work. I couldn't gather my wits about me. I preferred the darkness to the light. I crumpled on the bed like an inanimate lump, unable to sleep.

'I don't know if Seema could sleep that night. I moved to our Mess the very next day and sent Seema to her uncle's house in Baghbazar. We had to scatter the furniture in three lots—some with me, some with her, and some with a friend. It was a month before we could move into a flat in Ballygunge. When we got together, I realized that there was a gulf between us. She had gone quiet, she giggled no more, there were no more "darlings" at the drop of a hat. I realized even I could not burst into laughter the way I used to. Gradually I felt she was constantly scrutinizing me, analyzing every word I spoke, every action I took, every movement I made... I realized she was suspecting me of infidelity. What she did suspect, I knew not, but the lack of trust in her eyes bothered me. I got worried.

'One day, I asked her point blank: "Is something weighing on your soul, Seema?"

'"Yes." Seema looked at me and nodded. "That night I lied to save you from an unpleasant situation, remember?"

'"Yes, I remember."

'"But what is the truth then?"

'"I had gone out on hearing the sound of the vase crashing to the floor..."

'"But it's possible that Arati had sent word for you to meet her." Seema smiled.

'"No Seema, it's not possible because Arati really did not do any such thing."

"'Then why did she come there so late at night?" Seema's eyes lost their glow.

"'I really am unaware of why she did that. Only Arati will have the answer to that question."

'Seema cut in before I could finish, "Why were you standing so close to her in the darkness?"

'I calmly explained to her that everything had transpired in a flash. Within seconds. I was searching for the switchboard, I suddenly touched Arati; before I could understand who was standing there, Mashima switched on the light.

'Suddenly there was an ugly shadow in Seema's eyes. "What did you feel when your groping fingers felt Arati's curvaceous body, Aditya?"

'I was numbed into silence. "Go on..." Seema prodded me.

"'What's wrong with you, Seema?" I was shocked. "Are you insinuating..."

"'I'm not quite convinced of the truth."

"'Why?"

"'You..." Seema cast an arch look at me. "You had fallen in love with Arati."

'I sat up and looked her in the eye. "Can you prove what you are charging me with?"

"'I can't speak about what I've not seen but one can taste the ocean in a drop. I'll tell you what I saw. That morning, you were standing so close to Arati; it was just like you two were that night in the dark."

"'Seema, listen to me..."

"'Let me finish. Arati gave you some roses. A woman can read the terms of surrender in another woman's eyes. And your eyes were speaking the same vocabulary. It was a repeat of the warmth I had noticed when Arati finished dancing..."

'I helplessly tried to explain to Seema that an unexpected turn of events had led to the precipitate situation that night, and

I really was unaware. Seema chortled at that. Raising her hand, she stopped me mid-sentence. "Hold on, wait a minute..." She extracted a sketch from a corner of the bedroom and placed it in front of me. It was your portrait, which you had sketched. An excellent portrait, signed off with the word 'Me'.

'In a flash I recalled that I had asked you for one such painting in the garden that morning.

"'I found this in your diary the next morning," Seema quietly finished.

"'Why didn't you tell me all these days?"

"'All these days I was trying to figure out why you never showed this to me." Seema chuckled, as if she was thrilled to remembering something.

"'Don't think I'm a cretin, Roy. The word 'Me' hides within it an unarticulated other: 'You'. A stricken smile played on Seema's lips as she held me in a cold gaze.

'I looked at the portrait that was signed off with a "Me". It meant you. Which meant...

'Suddenly everything went topsy-turvy. The very earth received a jolt. Lightning flashed, piercing the blue sky of my home. I had a revelation.

"'Go on, Roy, confess." Seema was positively savage. "Were you not in love? Come on, be a man; a military officer at that. Have the courage to own up..."

'I nodded. "Yes Seema. I now realize that you are right. But all of it was only in my heart."

'Seema lowered her head. "The heart is all, Roy. If you give your heart away, what remains?" she finished with a plaintive smile.

'I had no answer to that.

'Slowly Seema retired to her room. An insurmountable peak stood between us now. I felt stifled.

'The phone rang after an hour. Seema was at the other end. "I have come back to Dad's, Roy."

'"What do you mean, Seema?"

'"I will no longer live with you. Bye..."

'Four or five days later I received the lawyer's notice. Six months later, we were divorced.'

Aditya Roy falls silent. He lights up another cigarette to avoid looking at Arati.

She sits with her head down for a few seconds, then she looks at him. There is a touch of silver in his sideburns.

'Where will you go now?' she asks him.

Aditya Roy looks up. 'The Park Hotel.'

'No.'

'Why?'

'You'll go to Park Street.'

'Your house?'

'Yes,' Arati replies with a steady gaze.

Aditya Roy can read all her unstated feelings in that gaze. A rueful smile plays on his lips. 'Ten years later...when my hair is rich with silver!'

'But the heart never ages,' Arati replies firmly. 'Seema was right; the heart is all that matters.'

She stands up even as she speaks.

Aditya Roy stands up too. 'Let's go.'

They walk out side by side.

The clock shows 7.40 p.m. Half an hour later they will enter the house where the simple English word on a 1X2 marble plaque at the entrance reads: 'Happiness'.

Translated by Ratnottama Sengupta

That Bird Called Happiness

Rao came to a sudden halt. 'No, I simply cannot walk any further.'

We stopped too. We, meaning Nimbalkar, Choubey and I, along with the two Garhwali coolies, Sunderlal and Rooplal, who had joined us at Hrishikesh.

We had completed the pilgrimage to Kedarnath and were on our way to Badrinath. We had left Joshimath before daybreak, at 5 a.m. Rao had been complaining about a severe headache from the previous night. He was feverish by the time we were setting out. We suggested postponing our travel plans, but Rao would not hear of it. He was the most enthusiastic traveller in the group. So we did not stay back. The first two miles out of Joshimath were descents, so we did not feel any pressure. However, by the time we reached Vishnu Prayag, the sky was overcast with rain clouds. The distant peaks were lost in the mist. The downpour was compounded by icy winds. The narrow winding lanes became slippery and dangerous as we were now on an ascent. But Rao said it was better to keep forging ahead. We ploughed on for a mile, then stopped to rest at Baldeo Chatti. It was drizzling when we resumed our journey but we ignored the rain, as we did the mounting clouds that engulfed us. The chir pines were swaying madly to keep up with the wind's velocity. It seemed the mountains were suddenly sighing deeply. Rao was clearly in need of rest but there was no way that we could stop in the middle of nowhere.

When we had covered three miles on level ground we arrived at Ghat Chatti on the banks of the Alakananda. Rao's temperature had shot up to 101 degrees. We had packed in some brandy from Delhi for medicinal use; a dose of that with warm water revived him. But he refused again to halt for the night. We decided to take a call at the next chatti, Pandukeshwar, about two miles away. So move on, move on. But after about a mile on the road, we could no longer face the onslaught of sleet. Underneath our raincoats we were equipped with overcoats, woollen sweaters, flannel shirts, cotswool banyans, tights, gloves, boots, terry wool trousers and monkey caps. And yet we were freezing to our bones.

This was when Rao came to a sudden halt and declared, 'I simply cannot walk any further.'

'Have another brandy,' Nimbalkar advised. Rao did that. He ignored the drizzle and the wind and stood still to gather his breath.

Rooplal, the elder of the two coolies, spoke at this point. 'Saab, let's trudge another half-mile.'

'We will carry you, if need be,' I assured Rao.

'No need for that yet.' Rao smiled. 'The brandy seems to be working its trick again.'

Rao walked on. 'Jai Badri Vishaala-a-a...' Rooplal called out the call of every pilgrim on the way. Praise be Lord Badrinath! We echoed his call as we joined Rao. To keep his mind off his pain, Nimbalkar engaged him in amusing tales. Choubey and I lent support on either side. Inch by inch, we braved the chill and the downpour until we reached Pandukeshwar. The clock showed 1 p.m.

We were carrying an introductory letter from the lodges at Joshimath. That made it easy for us to get a room on the first floor there. We spread out a makeshift bed and got Rao to lie down. By now, his temperature had touched 102 degrees. We were carrying some basic medicines with us. Nimbalkar was fastidious in these matters. After administering a dose to Rao we decided to stay put in Pandukeshwar until he recovered. We were barely 11 miles from Badrikashram, but what could we do? All willed by Badri Vishala! May His will be done. He will give us an audience as soon as Rao is better, we consoled ourselves.

It was too late to cook a proper meal. We were carrying chapatis, so we bought some potato curry, moong ka laddoo, and tea from a nearby food stall. 'Lunch' over, Choubey and I wrapped ourselves tight in a blanket and sat down with our smokes. Neither Rao nor Nimbalkar cared for our vice.

We four are from four different states of India. I'm a Bengali originally from Dhaka. Nimbalkar is a Maharashtrian from Sholapur. Rao hails from the southern city of Kanchipuram while Choubey comes from Ghazipur in Madhya Pradesh. But though we come from different corners of India, we have many things in common. All four of us are disenchanted souls from not-so-flamboyant backgrounds. We all live in Sholapur. All four are teachers at Kelkar's English High School; we are all approaching fifty and, together, responding to the call of the Himalayas.

Nimbalkar, the eldest in the group, doesn't get along with his wife. He lives in his rundown ancestral house with his widowed elder sister. His wife has made her home with her two earning sons in Nagpur. Nimbalkar teaches Marathi at Kelkar's. Sadashiv Rao teaches geography. He leads a solitary existence since his wife passed away, childless, about five years ago. Ramanath Choubey never married. He loved and lost once upon a time and went adrift in life. He arrived at Kelkar's some twenty-five years earlier to teach Maths and now teaches Hindi too. And Amiya Banerjee—that's me—has taught English for twenty years now, since I left Nagpur after cremating my parents. No, I had no time to marry nor any urge to seek out relatives who might want to take care of me.

One fine morning this quartet set out of their homes in Sholapur on a pilgrimage to Kedarnath and Badrinath, in that order.

The peaks were standing yonder, heads raised, defying the dense clouds and the incessant downpour. The raging wind combined with the raindrops to give rise to a kind of melancholy. I can't vouch for what the others were thinking; I can speak only for myself. Some 1,500 miles from Sholapur, I suddenly came alive to the duality of this world and my life. Day and night, light and darkness, multitudes and solitudes, love and hatred, bondage and freedom—these contradictory streams are constantly flowing by each other. The friction between these forces keeps the world pulsating, throbbing, rotating on its axis.

This is when the song floated in. The song, rather than the singer, is the protagonist of this story, in which we are peripheral characters, providing merely the preface.

The song went thus:

Chal hansa wah des jai, piya basey chitchor,
Surat suhagin hai panharin, bharei thaad bin dore...
Wahi deswan baadar na umre, rimjhim barsei meha,
Chouware mein vaidh raho naa, javijhoon nirdeha...

(Let's go, O Swan, to that land, where dwells the Beloved Stealer of Hearts. There, the beautiful damsel needs no rope to draw water from the well. There, the clouds don't thunder, they softly pour in droplets. Do not stay bound to your courtyard, let's go beyond the confines of the body.)

I sat up and took note. I can't say that the voice was very mellifluous; in fact, it had a scratchy timbre that lent the song a texture, a catchy sharpness, an alluring passion, a meditative resonance. It was the madness of a crazed soul.

Rao opened his eyes to comment, 'Good singer, this guy!'

Nimbalkar joined in: 'There's passion in his song, that of renunciation.'

Choubey listened intently for a while, then responded, 'He's singing Kabir.'

We all listened in silence for a while. There was no let-up in the downpour outside, the clouds and the mountains had become indistinguishable. Which land was the invisible singer referring to in his song? Was that land hiding somewhere in the unsurmountable Himalayas? The melody transformed the wailing of the winds into the sigh of renunciation. Pointless, it seemed, was our existence in the chatti, the halt. Move on, move on ceaselessly... Beyond Kedar-Badri or even the Kailash mountains and Manasarovar, beyond the skies too, chanting, 'Not here, not here either... Elsewhere, to some other place.' We have to go beyond all this, and arrive at...

The song came to an abrupt halt. We were engulfed once more in a drizzle and howling winds some 9,000 feet above sea level. Wrapped in blankets, we kept watching as daylight surrendered itself to the emphatic clouds. But a while later, the voice floated into the silence again:

'Baalam aao hamri geh re, tum bin dukhiya deh re,
Sab koi kahae tumari naari, moko yeh sandeh re...'

(Dear one, come into my embrace. My body aches for you. Everyone says I am yours, but I have my doubts...)

The song cast a spell once again with its harmonious articulation as much as the heartrending emotion in its lyrics. Who *was* singing? Every single note of the song was heightening our curiosity about the singer.

That song too came to an end. We administered another round of medicines to Rao, prepared more tea, and tried to get the better of the freezing cold. Then we settled down once more with our minds and the meandering moves they made.

Half an hour must have elapsed when the voice announced itself again.

'Rehna nahi des virana hai.
Yeh sansar kagad ki puria,
Boond padey, dhool jaana hai...'

(Not for us to live in this land. It is a paper bag, this world: unto dust it will go with mere drops of water...)

'Every single song is a Kabir composition,' Choubey kept repeating. Rao sat up with his 102-degree fever. The disenchanted dusk was steeped in the pathos of the lover's lament. Who? Who *was* singing?

We summoned Rooplal for an answer. 'Some madman in the basti directly beneath ours,' he informed us. In other words, he could hardly enlighten us.

Gradually, the sunset surrendered to the growing darkness. The Himalaya plunged into a profound meditative silence. The dim light of our hurricane lamp bravely soldiered on as we geared up to cook dinner even as we shivered away. At this point, once more, the voice joined us.

'Dulhin tohi piya ke ghar jaana...
Kaahe robo kaahe gaabo, kaahe karata bahana?'

(Oh bride of mine, you know you must leave to make your home with your darling. So why the tears and the whining, why dilly-dally with pretences?)

At this precise moment the manager of the lodges, Kapil Prasad, walked in to inquire after us. If needed, he would supply us with more firewood or blankets. A well-mannered, middle-aged Brahmin, he stayed back to chat with us for a while. I could not help but ask him, 'Someone was singing away in the chatti somewhere that way, Kapil Prasad-ji...?'

'Yes, the man has been there for the last three or four days.' Kapil Prasad smiled. 'He is a pilgrim on his way to Badrinath but is held up here as he took ill. No attachments, near stoic. He seems to be quite an educated person but, going by his clothes, he seems to have fallen on bad times. He is attired in saffron dhoti-kurta, and is carrying two blankets with him—one he sleeps on, the other he covers himself with. His only other belongings are a few books and a reading glass, contained in a saffron-coloured thaili. He rings in the hours with a song, and every few hours he takes a pinch of grass. He sings only Kabir. Maybe he is a Kabir Panthi, or he could be a Sahajiya, I don't really know nor, frankly, am I bothered. There is so much diversity in God's creation, who is seeking Him, in what particular way, who cares? It is enough for me that he is a seeker, scaling mountains to rest his head at His feet inside a temple. I have noticed another thing about the man. He hardly suffers the pangs of hunger or thirst. Two days had gone by before a god-fearing elderly lady gave him two chapatis; he returned one and ate just one.'

My curiosity was already whetted. I decided to have a look at the person from a distance the next day. Kapil Prasad returned to his quarters.

Pandukeshwar is a largish village; quite a few families make their homes here. Folklore has it that this is where King Pandu, the progenitor of the Pandavas—the heroes of the *Mahabharat*—meditated. The village has two temples that come alive with the sounds of temple bells and conch shells being blown to announce nightfall. Darkness rapidly sets in soon after. All of Pandukeshwar falls silent and every inhabitant goes to sleep wrapped in the warmth of blankets. We were no exception. But I could not float into slumber. I was kept awake by nagging thoughts: What is the purpose of my life? Is it only to teach English in that far-off school in Sholapur?

'Sukhwa pinjra chhodi bhaaga...
Is pinjare mein dus darwaje, dus kiwarwa lagaa!'

(The bird has flown away! The cage has ten exits, and all ten are locked. Still...)

The song wafted into my thoughts. But I could trace exhaustion in the singer's voice. Now and then his voice would trail off in the gale which defied the darkness itself. It was as if a wounded bird was crying out and then falling silent. I could not contain the tears in my eyes. Everything seemed meaningless, life itself appeared to be a pointless exercise, the body a birdcage made of multi-hued desires, and liberation from this body was what would spell happiness!

I was up before the sun, to the chant of Nimbalkar's 'Shiva Stotra'. I sat up even though I was shivering violently. I felt Rao's forehead and realized that he had had a remission. 'No fever,' Choubey was up too. 'His temperature reads 98 degrees and he is sweating.' No more worries, we agreed.

Rao smiled. 'I think we will be able to make it to Badrikashram today.'

'Are you mad?' Choubey responded. 'It is an eleven-and-half mile climb. And who knows what the weather gods have in store for us?'

However, in a little while, the chirping of birds put our doubts at rest. We cracked opened a window and were greeted by a clear sky. But the squall was still icy, piercing us right through to our bones. We promptly shut the window.

Pandukeshwar stirred back to life much later. We downed two cups of tea each, doubled under the weight of the woollens we had covered ourselves with from head to toe in, and stepped out into the open. It was freezing! The rain-washed range had pulled a veil of mist over itself. We took a call: We would stay back another day in Pandukeshwar and set out for Badrinath by sunrise the following morning.

We ran into Sundarlal just outside the lodgings. With a wide grin he informed us that the other side of Hanuman Chatti had had snowfall through the night.

Choubey was furious. 'What is so funny about it?'

Sundarlal grinned some more, then added: 'One more news, sirs! The man in the basti down there died last night. Finished!'

'Which man?'

'That sadhu who was singing.'

What! Was the song that had brought tears to my eyes the swan song of the singer's imprisoned soul?

'The guy just left us in the lurch.' Nimbalkar sounded resentful. 'Let's go and see him.'

Sundarlal reported: 'Many persons have come to one end of the row there, Sir, the police have also been informed.'

The man had breathed his last around midnight directly fifty feet below our dharamshala, walking to the right, at one end of the row of huts in the habitation close to the road. Some ten to twelve people had assembled there by the time we reached. Our innkeeper Kapil Prasad was amongst them.

'He seems to have suffered heart failure,' Kapil Prasad informed us. 'The old woman who had been feeding him roti noticed that, despite the weather, this door was ajar. She discovered the body. The police have been informed just a while ago.'

We peeped through the open door. The man was lying on his left side on a torn blanket spread out on the floor. The second blanket was pulled down to his hips. His left arm was pressed against the left side of his chest, the right arm sprawled on the floor. His eyes were turned upwards as though he had been intently watching something before death came. He had turned stiff—it had been hours since the bird had fled the cage.

The old woman who had fed him joined us. She said in a tear-filled voice: 'Hopeless chap! He came all the way and still could not fulfil his pilgrimage.'

'Who is the man? What is his name?'

'No one seems to know,' Kapil Prasad said. 'The police might have an answer once they have gone through his thaili.'

The cloth bag placed right next to the corpse had some books and a few tin cans. Next to the bag was a matchbox and a chillum to smoke ganja from. One corner of the room had the remains of ashes.

The man was dark-complexioned, lanky and sickly. A rudraksha mala hung around his neck. He had a salt-and-pepper beard, like was his matted hair. A scar just above his left eyebrow lent a touch of the sinister. Near his feet lay a pair of rubber chappals crafted out of worn tyres.

Who *was* he?

'Astounding!' I heard Rao blurt out at the back of the crowd. We turned around and realized that he must have joined us at some point.

'Why have you ventured out with your fever?' Nimbalkar was not one bit pleased.

'To see him,' Rao said, his gaze fixed on the dead man's face. 'Yesterday his songs had me mesmerized too.'

Rao kept watching intently. Then he uttered a 'Hmm...' and paced off to the other end of the verandah. We followed him there.

'You should be resting, Rao,' Choubey advised him.

'I am fine.' Rao smiled at us. 'Please don't treat me like a patient now. Let's start off for Badrinath without wasting any more time.'

Nimbalkar would not relent right away. 'Let's return to our lodgings now. We can decide over a cup of tea.'

'Rao,' I quizzed him across the steaming cup, 'why did you utter the word "Astounding!" and say "Hmm" when we were near the corpse?'

'Really? How come?' Choubey wasn't pleased to have missed any detail at the scene.

'So, Rao?' I prodded him again.

'Okay then, hear me out. I was feeling miserable lying here all by myself when you three were gone. So I summoned Sundarlal. In the course of our conversation he mentioned that the singer was dead. I wanted to check out the person whose impassioned singing had become a part of us since the time we arrived here the previous day. I had sketched an image of the man through his songs and was tempted to ascertain how close to reality I was. I set out all by myself, and when I saw the body I was astounded. This man had an amazing likeness to a person I once knew. That accounts for my first reaction. On closer inspection, I was certain that the saffron-clad body was none other than the man I knew in the past. So I responded with a "Hmm". Any more queries?'

'This is just the beginning, dear friend,' I replied. 'You will have to satisfy all our curiosity about him: Who is the man? What did he do? How do you know him? How long ago? What happened then?'

'Yes Rao,' Nimbalkar chimed in, 'tell us.'

Choubey was all ears too, he said.

Rao had a wan smile on his face. 'It is not a happy story, friends. I don't think it will cheer you up.'

'Don't forget Rao, we belong to a culture where sadness too is considered a rasa. So speak on,' I urged.

'You are right, Banerjee, about karun too being an emotion worth dwelling upon,' Rao said. Then he cleared his throat to go on.

Raso vai sah ... the name of God, just like God, is filled with rasa, our shastras maintain. But to be able to view it as such we need a certain objectivity; and most of us don't have that. Which is why tragic incidents spell only sadness in our lives, they seldom transcend to the level of a tragic observation. If we had a heightened sense of objectivity, the entire world would appear to be a vast stage where countless dramas are being incessantly played out. These dramas are not enacted as per the rules of Bharata's *Natya Shastra*. The thunderbolts here do strike from the heavens...'

'Why don't you cut short your preface?' Nimbalkar cut in.

'I will do that.' Rao nodded with a smile. 'But allow me to add one more observation before I start. What was the reason for me to fall sick and stop in Pandukeshwar for a rest? Was there a purpose in my coming across the dead body of Shiv Shankar Pillai after twenty years?'

'So this man was called Shiv Shankar Pillai?'

'Right.' Rao smiled.

'Where were you twenty years ago?'

'In my own city, Kanchipuram. That is where I got to know Shiv Shankar Pillai,' Rao was on his way into the past.

Actually we have to start twenty-two years ago. The country was still under foreign rule. Like millions of others, I too was smarting under the enforced subservience. But being from a humble middle-class family, and not wanting to compromise on my idealism, I followed up my graduation with a job as a teacher in a private school. I truly believed that teaching was a noble profession through which I could raise a generation of compatriots to follow in the ideals of nationalism. A year later, when the founder of the school, Shree Raghavan Iyer, died, his eldest son, the middle-aged Shree Madhavan Iyer took charge. An erstwhile Congress worker, he followed the principles of his late father but differed in their execution. Shree Raghavan wanted to educate the students, Shree Madhavan wished to enlighten them. He wanted to mould them into such citizens who would never forget their responsibilities to society and to the nation. Quite naturally, he effected a lot of alteration in the mode of education. He would suggest revolutionary changes in the way teachers treated their students. And the way he went about it, we came to firmly believe that we were dealing with a crazed mind. This belief emanated from a question Shree Madhavan Iyer put to every single teacher: 'Are you happy?'

What an absurd question!

Most of the teachers said they were far from happy. And I gathered from reports that the reply did not please Shree Madhavan.

One day I was summoned by Shree Madhavan. He was all by himself in the principal's room. A short-statured, healthy person with a shiny pate, he had firmness written all over his face. And the yellow-tinted white of his eyes shone with an ethereal light; you couldn't look into them for any length of time.

After the initial pleasantries, Shree Madhavan put the same question to me: 'Mr Rao, are you happy with your life?'

I was prepared for this. 'Yes Sir,' I instantly replied, 'I am a happy man.'

Shree Madhavan leaned forward.

'What makes you happy, may I ask?'

'Sir?'

'Why do you think you are a happy man?'

Another absurd question!

I was breaking into beads of perspiration but I had to think of a convincing answer. 'Well Sir, I do not want much. My parents are alive, and they are decently off...'

Those yellow-tinted white of his eyes could perhaps see through my effort. 'Hmm...' he said, 'okay, you may leave now. Namaskar.'

I virtually ran out of the room. I was smarting under the pinprick of 'fabricating a truth'. For the truth was that I was unhappy with the social construct around me. I was unhappy that there was so much want in society.

The following day onwards, Shree Madhavan's madness climbed a pitch higher. The teachers who had confessed to being unhappy were reassigned to different jobs in his other businesses—at the same salary. Needless to say, I retained my job as a teacher, as did the others who had not disclosed the truth about their 'happiness'. In all, just four of us were left in the school, but ninety-eight percent of us had admitted to being unhappy with our circumstances. Hence, the search for more teachers was begun.

Consequently, six months elapsed before we could muster up the minimum number of teachers required to run a school. Shiv Shankar Pillai was the last one to join this new lot.

Pillai was from Kerala but had been around the country with his father. His infancy had been spent in Quilon; when he was eight they'd moved to Uttar Pradesh and then to Bihar; once he finished school, he completed college from Madras. He was equally conversant in Malayalam, Hindi, Tamil and English. He was to teach English. If the similarities between Shiv Shankar Pillai of Kanchipuram and the man lying dead in Pandukeshwar are many, the differences are no less. Twenty-two years ago Pillai was aged about twenty-seven or twenty-eight. His dark-complexioned features would shone with good health and his eyes glowed with intellectual brightness. His visage reflected the calmness of a lamp that is never swayed by stormy thoughts.

Like love, friendship too can be kindled at first sight. Or perhaps the birth charts ordained it! However you look at it, it took only some hours for us to become friends. I grew very fond of him. Soft-spoken and reticent, Pallai seldom spoke out of turn but, whenever he spoke, he would arrest your attention.

One day I asked him, 'What did you think of Shree Madhavan's interview?'

Pillai promptly replied, 'Striking in both, his personality and his thinking.'

'What? You didn't think he has lost it?'

Pillai was taken aback. 'What made you think so?'

'Didn't he ask you whether you are happy?'

'Yes, he did.'

'So what was your reply?'

'I said I was happy!'

'Is that the truth, Mr Pillai? Are you really happy?'

'Of course I am happy. I do not lie, Mr Rao!'

'What makes you think that you are happy?'

'Shree Madhavan posed the same question to me,' Pillai replied. And with that an endearing smile spread across his face. He paused briefly before speaking, 'I told him that I have loved and I have been loved, that is why I am happy.'

'Please don't mind my asking, this person whom you love, is she...?'

An enchanting smile played on his lips as he replied, 'I am proud of my love and so I have no shame or hesitation in disclosing that my love is my wife. I love her, and have her love, so I love everything surrounding her. I don't hanker for others' love, I am not consumed by anger, my life has become meaningful. I have something to live for.'

'How did Shree Madhavan respond to your reply?'

'He smiled, as if he were pleased by it. Then he said, "Go on loving, Mr Pillai, because love purifies us. Your love will lead you to the almighty."'

I laughed at this. 'Do you know that he has put the same question to every single teacher?'

'No.' Pillai shook his head. 'I didn't know that. I was somewhat taken aback and wondered why he wanted to know this. Now from what you are saying, I feel there is a deep-seated reason for this.'

'There has to be. Else why would he sack or reassign those who confessed to being unhappy?'

'Are you aware of the reason, Mr Rao?'

'No, I'm not.'

'But I must know why he quizzes everyone about happiness. I will ask him at some convenient point.'

It did not take long for Pillai and me to strike up an easy friendship. Neither was there any lack of camaraderie with the other teachers. Rao was a good teacher. Everybody was impressed by his ability to make the students learn. However, I could not help notice that he did not become friends with anyone nor did he uninhibitedly chat with anyone. Well, he did not seem keen to seek out people's company. If he did talk to anyone, there always seemed to be an unseen wall between them. Perhaps he was self-content, complete in his own world.

Of course, all the other teachers read this as arrogance. And why not? He spoke so many tongues, he was a good teacher and, above all, the proprietor of the school, Shree Madhavan had a soft corner for him. Consequently he kept a distance from everybody else, as though he belonged to a different class! Oh, the spice of gossip! We came to the conclusion all by ourselves and decided to accept him, warts and all. Yet, if truth be told, he had a special bond with me. I was perhaps the only one he would open his heart to once in a while. I doubt he did it of his own free will; he had to succumb to my goading!

For nearly four months Pillai stayed in a boarding-house for single men. He wasn't very buoyant in these months. His wife was with her parents in Madras. I was also married, so I could understand his despondency. I tried to help him find a suitable house. Eventually I fixed up the ground floor of a double-storeyed building in my own neighbourhood. Two rooms, kitchen, bathroom—sufficient for a childless couple.

Pillai took four days' leave right away to fetch his wife from Madras. I was at the railway station to receive them; and that's when I first met Pillai's wife. In indirect proportion she was as Westernised as he was Indian. Europe made its presence felt in every action and move of Mrs Pillai. And I could not take my eyes off her. She seemed to me a pond of a hundred lotuses. She was tall for an average Indian. And her neck! It made me think of the golden champak flower. And her dreamy eyes? They would suddenly be transformed as she was charged with a laughter that echoed the flight of a herd of deer.

Pillai too was a transformed man. The unseen wall that existed between him and those he spoke with seemed to grow taller. I visited the Pillais along with my wife a couple of times. Nothing was lacking in the welcome they offered us. Yet we got the feeling that we were not really welcome. There seemed a hollowness in our conversations. And Shanta—yes, Pillai's wife—had a highly superficial manner of articulating her words. The third time I proposed to stop by the Pillais, my wife yelled at me. 'Go if you must! I have no need, nor any desire to step into their house again. I too have self-respect; can't they visit us at least once?' Needless to add, the Pillais never bothered to visit us although I did visit them at least twice after that, all by myself. After all, he's a colleague and a neighbour, I reasoned with myself. And, all said and done, Pillai is knowledgeable, and talented.

But one day even I ran out of patience. No, I told myself, no more visits. Pillai, to quote Kabir, was in a rapturous state all through the day and night—*aat hu pahar matwaal laagi rahe*. If I dropped in, he would chat with me but his gaze would be riveted

on Shanta. It was as if Shakespeare's Romeo could not draw his
eyes away from the sun of his life, Juliet. As a geography teacher
I am conversant with the movement of Norwesters and gentle
breezes. I have it in me to describe a barren desert, elucidate a
coral reef, evoke a mountain peak, but I cannot analyse or expound
the recesses of human psyche. To sum it up, I could see Pillai
flushed with love and felt like an intruder in their intimate life.
Gradually, my visits tapered off.

The other teachers would tittle tattle about the Pillais.
Ramamurthy would lead this pack. He had an insatiable appetite
for gossip. His caricature of the Pillai couple entertained us for
some months. The 'fun' rose to a higher pitch when Pillai was
heard singing. Since his return from Madras Pillai would sing to
the accompaniment of a tanpura. It won't be a lie to say he had
a charming voice. In fact, I would stop in my tracks to hear him
sing. Every single song was a love ballad. I loved them and yet
joined Ramamurthy and Co. when they joked about Pillai's dazed
demeanour. You heard Pillai sing yesterday, all day and late into
the night; so you can imagine how he must have sounded twenty
years ago. A man who never smoked in the past had taken to
smoking ganja; you have sampled what that can do to a voice.
Raucous, scratchy and yet with compelling power to cast a spell,
right? From that you can gauge what enchantment young Pillai's
voice cast. He would start singing when the neighbourhood
was retiring for the night. Listening to him I could visualize
sunflowers transform into peacocks and the peacocks would start
dancing in my mind's eye, as if to woo peahens.

Aat hu pahar matwaal laagi rahe—that was Pillai. He taught
the class as if in a trance. The students would listen to him
spellbound. It is a fact that he cared for his students. He would
selectively invite the bright ones home, offer them treats, play
carrom with them, narrate stories. Morning or evening a handful
of boys would go over for special guidance. This, to Ramamurthy,

was a calculated move. 'He invites them home and treats them to dosa so that they take tuitions from him!'

Pillai did not care to socialize. Once in a while husband and wife would go out in the evening. They would either go to the movies or enjoy the solitude of suburban parks. Those who set their eyes on Shanta even once could not stop murmuring words of praise. Ramamurthy and Co. would snidely remark, 'Did you ever notice the expression on Pillai's visage when he is on an outing with his wife? Any day he will burst with pride! Ai aiyyo! Is he the only one on this earth to claim a beauty queen for a wife?'

A few months had elapsed when I noticed that Pillai had taken to gardening. He had fenced off the patch of green outside his apartment and started in right earnest to hoe the soil, plant seeds and saplings, water them with care. Within days his garden was smiling with roses, zinnia and passion flower. When the rains came the garden was bursting with blossoms of every possible hue. One morning I was compelled to stop short as I walked past his garden. Three astonishingly rejuvenating sunflowers were in full bloom. The plants stood about four or five feet from the ground, and each of them was adorned with a sunflower the size of a dinner plate. What a brilliant shade of yellow the petals wore! I could not stop myself from entering the garden.

Pillai came out in person in answer to my call. He was pleased to hear such high praise for his garden. He asked me in for a cup of coffee. Shanta served us steaming coffee, enquired after my health in the manner of a European, then excused herself to supervise work in the kitchen.

Pillai was back to the topic after his heart. 'You really like my garden, Rao?'

'Yes, I love it.'

'I was never into gardening. I was inspired when I saw Shree Madhavan's garden.'

'So you are in regular touch with Shree Madhavan.'

'Not often, Rao. I do visit him every month or two. We ordinary people have a lot of time to while away but important people like him have much to attend to. By the way Rao, I have the answer to your question.'

'Which question?'

'Arre you wanted to know na, why Shree Madhavan asks everybody, whether he is happy or not?'

I sat up sharply. 'What did Madhavan say?'

'Yes, I'll tell you. Actually I should have shared it with you three or four months ago but I somehow never got around to it. One day I had gone over to Shree Madhavan's house. I have never gone there to gain favours, Rao. I hope you agree that I pass any test as far as teaching is concerned; so I really don't care to ingratiate myself. That saps one's self-confidence. I am drawn by Shree Madhavan's personality. No matter what others say, the man is a learned, affable patriot.

'That day I found Shree Madhavan next to a bed of sunflowers in his patch of green. Every single plant was crowned by a sunflower in full bloom, just like you have seen outside my house. The entire garden had come alive in the golden light. The minute he spotted me, Shree Madhavan gesticulated for me to walk cautiously up to him. I noticed that he was intently watching something. When I reached him he directed my gaze to an enchanting sight. A bright green parrot had perched itself on the curved stalk of a golden sunflower and its red beak was immersed in drinking the pollen and pecking at the brown seeds. I was transfixed by this gorgeous sight. Just picture it: A flamboyant splash of yellow, a vibrant dash of green, a vivid touch of red…

'The bird was lost in the joy of tasting the nectar. Then all at once, satiated, it flapped its wings and whooshed off into space.'

'Did you see that?' Shree Madhavan turned towards me, his eyes sparkling with a keen light.

'Yes.' I nodded. 'A rare sight.'

'No no, not rare.' Shree Madhavan's voice was full of conviction. 'Parrots frequent the gardens of happy people.' This bird, he said, is an externalization of contentment. 'There is a sunflower in the heart of every man in love. And it feeds the parakeet of happiness with the nectar and pollen in its heart. If you grow sunflowers in your garden, you will have parrots in your garden too!'

'Madhavan Sir, I've been wanting to know something from you.'

'Go on.'

'What difference does it make to me as a teacher whether I am happy or not?'

Shree Madhavan smiled at me. 'So you too have wondered whether I had lost it.'

'I have deep respect for you, Sir,' I hastened to reply.

He was touched by the sincerity in my voice. He walked up to a bench and waved for me to sit down. 'I am aware of that. This could be a form of madness, Shiv Shankar, but I will not give up on this quest for happiness. Shall I tell you why? I believe that he and he alone is fit to be a teacher whose heart is overflowing with contentment. Frustrated, forlorn, unhappy, sad people nurture many complexities in their soul. They have not loved or have been loved. So they do not find liberation from their negative emotions. Consequently, they envy others, are jealous of people's happiness, want to hurt them with their words, strike at their harmony, all to retain their own balance. This only spreads violence and discontent. If such a man becomes a teacher, how can he ensure the well-being of a student? The quest for knowledge then becomes a dry routine, education a burden on the young souls and not a life-giving fountain of wisdom.'

'Rao, I was left speechless. The logic in Shree Madhavan's words was inspirational. Mine is a miniature effort to imitate him. Now the sunflower of love is spreading joy in my garden too!'

Honestly, it seemed like he too was infected by Shree Madhavan's madness. And yet I could not laugh at his sincerity and satisfaction. I found myself responding respectfully with these words: 'Now the parrots will grace your garden too, Pillai.'

At this, a charming smile spread across Pillai's face. Almost at the same time a burst of laughter from behind us rent the air. It was Shanta. 'Do you believe these words, Mr Rao?'

Shanta's eyes were restless, like sprinting deer.

'I do, Mrs Pillai,' I humbly replied, 'because they couch such an alluring thought!'

About a week elapsed after that. Shree Madhavan's conversation with Pillai would not leave me alone although I saw no reason to be overwhelmed by it. That evening, after school hours, Pillai drew me aside and reported excitedly, 'Guess what, Rao? Yesterday a bright green parrot visited my garden, and perched on the sunflowers!'

Pillai's eyes were aglow with an unknown excitement. I smiled to myself after I managed to extricate myself from the conversation. Perhaps this madness was required to be in Shree Madhavan's good books!

Days went by. Gradually Pillai's craze became a mundane part of our everyday routine. Night followed day as Monday follows Sunday and, then, the other days of the week. By this time we had marked two years since Shanta Pillai had made her home amongst us.

That morning Ramamurthy lowered his voice to ask me, 'Rao, is something the matter with your Pillai?'

'Why?'

'I cannot say what but something surely is cooking. Why don't you find out? He is quite friendly with you.'

That same day I caught hold of Pillai after school break. He was hurrying down the road towards his house. 'Pillai... Here...'

Pillai did not hear me. I raised my pitch to draw his attention. Startled, Pillai looked back and noticed me. 'Oh, Rao.'

'You didn't hear me when I called you! What thoughts are you lost in?'

'Sorry... I... just...'

'Why do you look so spent, Pillai? You are keeping well I hope?'

'Yes yes, all is well... Please don't mind Rao, I am in a bit of rush...' Almost rudely Pillai turned his face away and darted into a lane in the opposite direction of our house. Clever Ramamurthy had correctly surmised...

Before the week was over, Ramamurthy lowered his voice again. 'Your Pillai is surely breaking down.'

'Breaking down?' I could not quite figure out what had gone wrong.

'He is breaking Shree Madhavan's rule; he is beating the students.'

'Really?'

'Absolutely.'

It was easy to verify the truth in Ramamurthy's words. It was hot news in the Teachers' Room that Pillai was resorting to corporal punishment. He couldn't even hold the attention of his class. He was punishing the students in peculiar ways. Sometimes he would place a pencil between a boy's fingers to crush them. Sometimes he would tug at their sideburns. At times he forced a student to stay back at tiffin break and write out ten pages. At other times he asked one boy to box the ears of another. A slap here, a kneel-down there, these were not to be counted among the punishments.

I decided to speak to Pillai. But the chance did not present itself as he was studiously evading me. So, before I could, the headmaster summoned him and told him off about the way he was treating the students.

Pillai did not raise his voice, but replied, 'Whatever I am doing, I'm doing as part of my duty.'

'What do you mean? You believe in beating children?'

'I didn't earlier; now I do.'

'But I don't, Mr Pillai; neither does Shree Madhavan. You would do well to bear that in mind.'

'Okay Sir.'

I tried to speak to Pillai that evening. He held me in a hard gaze as he chewed out the words: 'Mind your own business, Rao.' I gave up hope. That was probably the day Pillai hit the bottle. His immediate neighbours were, of course, the first to know, but it did not take long for the news to reach the school. I was worried for him. What was wrong with Pillai?

About a month later, I ran into Pillai on my way home after visiting an ailing relative. He was swaying.

'Pillai!' I was dismayed.

'Stop it,' Pillai raised a finger as he muttered incoherently, 'I don't drink on your money, Rao; don't you dare say anything to me.'

I didn't. I was too angry to utter a word. Pillai staggered on and dived into a narrow lane.

But the next day the drama reached its climax. Around 3 in the afternoon the entire school was in a turmoil. A peon rushed in to inform us that Srinivasan of Class X had fallen unconscious in the class following a beating by Pillai. The headmaster rushed there and we followed him. We sprinkled water on Srinivasan and brought him around. His face was swollen from the beating. From the other boys in the class we gathered that Pillai had struck him because he could not answer some question. When Srinivasan protested, Pillai lost his temper and started beating him right left and centre. Srinivasan had collapsed within minutes.

Srinivasan was sent home in a car accompanied by a teacher. Pillai had turned to stone. When the headmaster tried to admonish him, he realized that Pillai had come to school dead drunk.

We slunk away from there, shamefaced. I did not care to know Pillai's fate.

That very evening, at about 11 in the night, just as I was preparing to retire, someone started banging on the front door. I opened the door to find a sozzled Pillai at my doorstep.

'I would like to have a few words with you, Rao.'

'Come back in the morning, Pillai.'

'No Rao no, tonight. Let me say it tonight. Why, are you worried that I will be incoherent?'

'Fine, spit it out.'

'I lost my job today. Shree Madhavan had sent for me. I saw him in the evening. He held me with his gaze and asked, "Tell me the truth Pillai, are you happy?" I had to say, "No." Shree Madhavan merely said, "Then stop coming to school from tomorrow." I said, "All right." That's it. I headed straight for Venkatesh's booze shop and downed four pegs. Right then, goodnight good man...' He turned around to leave.

'Pillai,' I called out. 'Tell me, what is making you so unhappy?'

'Don't ask me. It is not something I can talk about. Don't leave me bereft of even the fig leaf, Rao! Let me go. Out, out brief candle...' He left with Othello on his lips.

I spent the night tossing and turning in bed. I gave tuitions to two boys in the morning and coached a third in the evening. The school accounted for the better part of the day. But, for the first time in two and a half years, I felt lonely. There was no Pillai. I had no patience for the crocodile tears of Ramamurthy & Co., so I left early. But though I had the urge to, I could not see Pillai.

The following morning I hastened to his residence. Shanta was in the living room, having coffee in the company of an elderly gentleman. This person was completely and unmistakably European in his ways. When Shanta introduced us I realized this was Pillai's father-in-law. It was clear from his words that the gentleman was both well-placed and well-off. I asked for Pillai only to be told that he had been missing from home since daybreak. They did not discuss his loss of job with me, nor did I have the courage to raise the topic. I set out from the house but stopped short in the garden. The patch of green was set on fire by a handful of golden sunflowers crowning the plants standing about six feet high.

The stillness in the morning air was suddenly ruptured by cackles of laughter. It was Shanta. She had silently followed me to the courtyard. 'Admiring the sunflowers, Mr Rao? Go on, I'll send words as soon as the parrots arrive!' And then, once more, the 'Hee hee hee…'

'Shanta!' Her father sharply rebuked her. Still Shanta kept laughing uncontrollably, her eyes dancing like a wild herd of fleeting deer!

I came away without another word. But throughout the day I was chased by a sense of unease. At dusk I set out again in search of Pillai.

He answered my knock forthwith. 'Come right in Rao…'

Pillai was sitting with a glass of whisky, the bottle resting on the table right next to him. 'Say nothing yet, Rao.' Pillai disarmed me with his smile. 'I have the means to go on drinking for some more days. Oh, by the way, Shanta left for Madras with her father this afternoon. Busy man he is, and still he came down the minute he received the telegram from his daughter. He is not one to let her life go waste, so he has taken her back with him.'

I could not think of anything to say in reply.

'Rao…'

'Tell me.'

'Have you noticed? This year, too, the garden is smiling with sunflowers!'

'Yes, I have noticed that.'

Suddenly Pillai burst into peals of laughter. Pardon me, as a Geography teacher I do not have a vocabulary fit to describe that laughter. 'Pillai,' I said, as I rose to leave, 'goodbye.'

'Yes Rao, it is time to bid goodbye. You know that I am too refined to digest your sympathy or your counsel; it is better for both of us if you keep those to yourself. Every man has to bear his own cross. So… goodnight, Rao.'

I dashed blindly out of his house and on to the streets. I had no desire to rest my eyes on the sunflowers.

That was the last time I met Pillai. By this time I knew him well enough to realize that he was a man of indomitable spine. I did not want to weigh down my soul with wasted efforts to set things right. Some days later I heard that a bearded sadhu from the northern belt had made his appearance under a banyan tree near the bazaar. He, I was told, had two constant 'companions', ganja and Kabir. I also learnt that Pillai, flush with country liquor, had taken to idling by his side.

And then, one morning, the sadhu was gone. And Pillai too had disappeared along with him, leaving the doors of his house ajar.

I went across to check things for myself. I found the windows, too, wide open. All his belongings, his clothing, books and papers, kitchen utensils and cutlery, everything was lying intact.

In the courtyard some new plants were crested by the golden petals with a heart of brown. The sunflowers were swaying in the gentle breeze.

Rao fell silent. You could hear a pin drop in that room in the dharamshala.

Nimbalkar broke the silence. 'Sorry, I am totally lost.' He wanted further explanation.

'Really,' Chaubey joined him, 'what was the reason for Pillai's transformation?'

'Hold on,' Rao spoke again. 'Before I say anything more, I must clarify that whatever you heard so far, I personally witnessed. When Pillai went missing I too wondered what happened. Where did things go wrong? And why? For three months I had no clue what the truth was. Around this time we employed a new maid, Kupai Amma. She used to work for the Pillais. Soon after she joined us, my wife took me aside and said, 'Listen to what Kupai has to say about your friend and his wife.'

I asked, 'What tale does she have?' I then told Kupai not to withhold anything that could throw light on Pillai's tragic life. What you will hear now was all gathered third person, from her.'

Kupai would report to the Pillai household every morning at 9 and stay till 1, when she would go home for lunch. She would return to work at 4 and retire for the day at 7 or 8 p.m. Initially, she was enchanted by the love the Pillai couple had for each other. A pair of love birds they are!' she would say to herself. In particular, she was fond of Pillai. Such a decent person!

The wife was a little too Westernised for her own good, but never mind, so long as she loves her husband just the way he does—this is what Kupai thought. But she could not take kindly to the fact that Shanta spent her days idling in bed or just sitting around while Pillai did the household chores including, at times, the cooking. She even protested that on one occasion. At that Pillai requested her to take on the responsibility of the kitchen and gave her a raise of 5 rupees. Of course she agreed, happily so.

Days went on to become weeks, months, years. It was almost two years when she was first startled by a quarrel between the husband and wife. But she could only hear a word or two from the kitchen. Pillai was saying something to the effect of: 'I don't like such things at all.' And Shanta had roared back, 'Don't you dare to interfere in my freedom! It will do you no good.'

Kupai couldn't quite fathom what it was all about, but this much she could see: instead of blowing away, the storm kept brewing. She couldn't read anything on Shanta's face. And then, why should she bother much about their private lives? She was, after all, only a paid servant! Besides, which husband and wife doesn't quarrel once in a while?

But another unpleasant episode occurred a few days later in her presence. She was cooking dinner in the kitchen and Shanta had stepped in for a drink of water. Pillai walked up to the kitchen door and, in a forbidding voice, called out, 'Shanta, come this way for a minute. I want to discuss something.'

Shanta looked at him from the corner of her eyes, turned her head away, and said, 'Hold on.'

Kupai Amma's curiosity was roused. She stealthily followed Shanta towards the bedroom and tried to hear their conversation. 'Who had come here after I left for school today?' Pillai had asked his wife.

'No one,' Shanta had replied in a steady voice.

'Didn't Ganesan come here?'

'No.'

'Then where did this cigarette come from?'

'What nonsense are you speaking? Go wash your face.'

'Shanta, tell me the truth.'

'Don't drive me out of my mind Shiv! I have wasted my life by throwing in my lot with you. Don't spoil my happiness any further.'

'Aren't you happy, Shanta?'

Suddenly Kupai Amma heard Pillai gnash his teeth. 'Why? Why don't you love me anymore?' his impatient voice demanded of Shanta.

'Let go of me or I'll scream! Leave me alone!'

Kupai could hear no more as she returned to her post in the kitchen. But the little she had picked up whetted her appetite. There is a natural tendency in humans to find loopholes in people. If needed, they will fabricate faults in others. Kupai was not beyond this human failing. As long as she was working in the Pillai household she would keep her eyes wide open. She would scan even the boys who came to Pallai for tuition. Gradually their number dwindled. Pillai hit the bottle. Kupai Amma could see a happy household crumble before her eyes.

Amma would go to her own house in the afternoons. But she was not one to give up so easily. She started posting one of her grandchildren on a watch near the Pillai residence. Sooner or later it would yield some result!

One evening, her granddaughter reported that a handsome man dressed in a smart suit had alighted from a taxi around 3 in the afternoon. He let off the cab a little distance away from Pillai's residence, scanned the houses to his left and right, threw away the cigarette he was smoking and hurried up to their house. He walked up the garden and had barely knocked on the door when Shanta opened it. The visitor had left hours later.

'Pillai had got wind of the affair,' Rao continued his narration. 'He had even guessed who Shanta's paramour was. I was depressed by what I heard from Kupai Amma. I did not wish to hear anymore. I don't enjoy dissecting people's illegitimate affairs; I believe it weakens one's own character. I had got my answer. I realized that life goes awry when it is bereft of love. I also realized that love is, simultaneously, a life-giving nectar and a poison that destroys lives. It rejuvenates those lucky in love, it destroys those who love and lose.'

Rao ceased to speak. The room was thick with silence once again. None of us dared open our mouths.

Footsteps. We looked up. Kapil Prasad came in, accompanied by a middle-aged sub-inspector. 'May I come in?' he asked.

'Certainly,' I replied, 'take a seat.' Both Kapil Prasad and the SI sat on our beds.

'Someone is dead in the basti,' the SI opened the conversation.

'Yes Sir,' Nimbalkar responded, 'we had gone there to see the body.'

'I got these books and some letters from his thaili,' the SI said.

'What are the titles?' Rao wanted to know.

'One *Complete Works of Shakespeare.* The others are all religious literature. The letters are all penned by the deceased. They are in Malayalam. I thought perhaps one of you could help me read them.'

'I will be happy to be of some help,' Rao responded. 'Let me see them, I can read Malayalam.'

Rao ran his eyes over the letters. There were five of them, all discoloured, written at various stops in his journey, on different dates. All of them were to the same effect. Pillai could not forget Shanta, he just could not get over her. Addressing her, he wrote that he had sent several letters to her but they had all returned to him, unopened, unanswered. He wanted nothing from her, if only he could meet her once and exchange pleasantries. He had taken to sanyas, become an ascetic, yet there was no peace in his mind. He had become a sadhu in vain. At every step, his very breath reminded him that he had lost his love.

Rao read the last letter aloud. It went thus: 'I write to you but cannot bring myself to post them. I don't have your address! And still I write because you have a permanent residence in my heart. When I lost you, I had decided I would offer all my love to God. The flower of happiness would again blossom in my heart. The green parrots would again descend to savour the nectar of love with their crooked red beaks. But that did not happen. I kept parroting Kabir's devotionals. I went around the country to savour the ceaseless variety of His creation. And still He could not command all the love in my heart. You are the veil of Illusion still standing between us. But yesterday I had a new realization. I have failed to give you true love. That is because I did not stop at loving you, I wanted you to return that love in equal measure. All my pain and suffering is because I desire your love. So, from this day on, I will not pray for your love. All I will do is go on loving you, Ratnamala...'

Rao suddenly stopped reading and looked at the SI. 'What's the name of the deceased?'

'The books show the name as Shri C.D. Ramachandran,' the SI replied. Rao quietly returned the letters to the SI.

'Did you know the person?' the SI asked.

'No,' Rao shook his head.

The SI thanked him and left with Kapil Prasad. The body had to be sent off to Joshimath, as early as possible, for a post mortem.

'So this man isn't Shiv Shankar Pillai, Rao?' Nimbalkar mumbled once we were by ourselves.

'I was wrong.' Rao smiled wanly. 'I had not focussed on the dissimilarities.' After a pause Rao added, 'But this man too is a Shiv Shankar Pillai, isn't he, Nimbalkar?'

Nimbalkar nodded in silence. We did too. All four of us, middle-aged singletons with no love in our lives, looked at one another. The distant peaks visible outside the windows were silent too. The rainclouds at the foot of the mountains appeared to me like the sacred smoke of camphor aarti offered to Lord Badri Vishal.

Suddenly I felt frightened by the lovelessness I had discovered within me. Had I ever recited the mantra of true love in my heart? Had any of us? How, then, could we be worthy of offering our loves to Badrinath?

Perhaps in an echo of my thoughts, Nimbalkar spoke out: 'Friends, we will all go back... Today.'

Translated by Ratnottama Sengupta

Papui Island

I live on Papui Island. Having travelled all over the world, I know there is no peace and no love anywhere. And when I tired of looking, I came here. Here I can breathe. There is love here, and peace. That is why I call this home.

Papui is a tiny country, just twelve miles across. It lies to the east of Japan, tucked away deep upon the Pacific. Beyond it stretches a hundred miles of ocean. Imagine a land far, far away from every sign or vestige of human civilization. There are no railroads, steamers or aeroplanes here. Possibly, that is why it is so calm. Papui floats like a lotus in the middle of a vast expanse of water. The dormant volcano Kijima rises on one side, two thousand feet into the air, to touch the sky. At the foot of the mountain is a dense, silent forest. Here and there gush a few waterfalls. Wild and unknown birds have made this forest their home and their twittering and calls are the only sounds one hears. Tall coconut palms cast their shadow on the parts of Kijima that bears human habitation. Bamboo groves abound, as do gardens of banana and papaya trees. Countless colourful flowers twinkle through the undergrowth like stars come to earth. And one glimpses from afar the glittering blue and yellow plumage of hundreds of tiny honey-sucking birds that come here to draw nectar from those exquisite flowers. There are no wild animals in this forest. Only some harmless foxes and herds of deer roam the jungles.

Completing this idyllic picture is a natural lake called Haisanu, created by rain water and by waterfalls, ringed by coconut groves. The inhabitants of the island live upon the shores of the lake. Their complexion is like bright almonds, and their features bear a slight likeness with the Japanese. It is believed that Hanaka—one of the thousand sons of the Sun Goddess—built his kingdom in Papui. So the natives are known as the Hanakans or the Hanakai. The men and women dress identically, wrapping a piece of colourful garment around their waist and leaving the rest of their bodies bare. Unlike the rest of the civilized world, they are totally unselfconscious about their nudity. They truly are children of Nature. These peace-loving yet brave Hanakai are a small tribe. Their numbers are, in fact, declining. This is a grave problem for them. The old priest in the temple at the foothills of Kijima sends up an occasional prayer to the Goddess to not hold the innocent Hanakans responsible for the terrible sins being committed by the rest of the world.

From the mountain, the island slopes gently towards the sea. The sandy beach, like a vast shawl, is dotted here and there with black bead-like stones.

Half a mile from the shore is a mile-long coral reef. The water there is so clear that one can see the ocean-bed right at the bottom, where countless exotic fish dart about, shimmering like rainbows. On full-moon nights, when the golden disc rises from the depths of the Pacific Ocean and sits like a crown atop Kijima, the winds sigh and the palm groves rustle. The intoxicating waters of Lake Haisanu slip under a spell. And, two by two, the young lovers of Papui make their way to the reef holding aloft baskets made of coconut fibre. On that ridge they give themselves up to the romance of the night. They raise their languid voices in songs of love that swell the tides of the mighty ocean. In a playful mood, it sends wave after wave to wash the reef, much to the delight of the young lovers.

There is love in Papui. And peace. That is why I am here too. Over there, where the coconut palms start thinning, if you start climbing past the sanjini flowers that shine like dewdrops in the sunlight, you might come to a huge fort-like structure made out of rock. Nobody remembers when it was built or who used to live in it. People say it is Hanaka's palace. It is difficult to say how old this tumbledown ruin is—perhaps over a thousand years! I believe it was the home of Mongolian pirates. Here and there are narrow channels where the sea has made inroads and through these the waters of the great ocean wash the stone constantly, as though to wipe out the memory of a blood-filled history.

I wander about all day on the island. I breathe in the air on Kijima's peak. On moonlit nights I sit atop a massive dam, and when I am sleepy I fall asleep somewhere on that ancient island that is my home.

But I am not human. I am not flesh and blood, I am nameless, I am a ghost and I wander about unfulfilled. I am a ghost but I am not evil. I am a part of nature and nature's endowments to earth. Nature has no substance; I and my companions are nature's agents. We spread the fragrance of flowers in the wind. We help the sunlight reach the farthest corners. We help seeds to perpetuate, and turn flowers into fruit. We help snow to fall, and melt.

We are busy souls. Yet my life is very lonely. There can be no relationships in this world of ours; there are friendships but no attachments. I feel lonely and miserable. When I am done with my day's work and I sit by the ocean, my past rises like a mist in front of my eyes. I was once very rich. I loved a girl very much. How beautiful her thick-lashed eyes were, how intoxicating and sweet her ruby-red lips. But this same girl who came home to me as my bride poisoned me one day...

The memory of that dark deed haunts me and tears me apart although I lack the physical body to feel it. This happened fifty years ago, and much time has flown by. I have crossed all the spirit worlds, through light and darkness, and now I seem to hear a message from I know not where and it is telling me that the time has come for me to walk the earth again... It is a command to take birth once more.

But I do not want to be born. I know that everything in the cosmos, even planets and satellites, desire to come into being in some form or the other; humans are an embodiment of God, and there is a strong desire for rebirth inside each soul. But I am afraid. Because I know my own past, and I know that the Devil rules over darkness and even Devil's denizens look for an opportunity to take refuge in a human body. Why else would my wife have fallen in love with another and poisoned me? Besides, even as a spirit I have been noticing that Man's greed and violence is increasing day by day. Selfishness is on the rise. Be born again? Fall in love again? Never. Get involved or fall into the clutches of a lesser mortal with evil intentions? The very thought terrifies me.

I traversed many lands in search of peace and love. I did not find it in forty-eight years. Everywhere I saw the forces of darkness defeat light. It's a universal fact that human beings want to live but cannot survive, they want love, and lose out. Wherever I went I found war, riots, and clashes... I felt choked by the clouds of greed, deception, selfishness and violence. I ran away from there. In the end I came to Papui Island, and found the peace and the love I was seeking.

I spend my days and nights on this island. On some nights friends come by to visit me. We exchange stories, and we sigh deeply. The world is being torn into fragments by the fight between good and evil. We talk about other lands, shake our heads and say, 'No, unless humans turn over a new leaf, we shall not take birth ever again.'

Sometimes the wind turns hot. It howls eerily across the land until I feel suffocated. Mere mortals will not sense these winds. For these are the collective sins of the world roaming the earth. They suck water from the clouds, they derange the sun's orbit, they cast an unholy shadow over planets and satellites, they cause diseases. This never ceases, nor will it end until the Devil ceases to dominate Earth.

And sometimes, either in the day or at night, an icy wind sweeps the land like a tornado and benumbs all. If spirits like me get caught in it, it renders us unconscious and, in the form of light, scatters us in the floating clouds. Then we fall to the ground as rain, we lie hidden in grains and fruits. That is how we enter a mother's womb and are reborn as a life form.

At such times I tremble in fear. I clutch one of those ancient stone pillars with all my might and never let go. No no, I will not take birth just yet. I know it is unavoidable, a part of the natural order of things, yet I run from the much-coveted human birth. Let love and peace be established in this world, I will be born then. Until then I will live in Papui because the men and women here have love and peace.

The Hanakai are a loving race. Parents love their children, friends love friends, there is deep love between brothers and brothers, brothers and sisters. The love that binds lovers is like the sublime rays of the sun. And the most passionate is the love of two young people I perpetually follow like an invisible bodyguard. Their names are Nagasi and Lusan.

Twenty-two-year Nagasi loves eighteen-year-old Lusan. Their love makes the air of Papui more salubrious, the pohutukawa blossoms more fragrant, the birdsongs more mellifluous. Nagasi is the epitome of manhood, and Lusan is grace incarnate.

They have known each other since childhood. There are no strangers in Papui. Nagasi knows Lusan is a good singer and can dance gracefully. Lusan knows that Nagasi is matchless at throwing harpoons and expert at hunting whales. Nagasi and Lusan have met frequently in the rice fields next to Haisanu Lake when men and women sow the seeds, plant the saplings, reap the grain. They have also met at the temple of their god Akamaru. Each meeting has intensified their devotion to each other. And then, one day...

That day I had fallen asleep. When I woke up it was dusk. The blue of the sky and the sea had been dyed red by a bleeding sun. The top of Kijima was clouding over and a flimsy mist had drifted in from the Pacific Ocean upon the wings of a restless wind. I looked towards the shore and saw Lusan bathing in the sea, all alone.

Nagasi appeared at that very moment. He stood still on sighting Lusan. Seeing him, she came out of the water. Her long hair clung to her wet body, droplets dripping off the ends of her dark tresses. Freshly bathed, the almond-skinned beauty seemed even more dreamlike in that mystical evening light.

Lusan was walking away. Nagasi blocked her way.

'I must go home...'

Nagasi did not reply, he just stared at the sea-drenched beauty. Lusan looked at Nagasi in surprise but sensed the churning within him. She instantly blushed, crossed her arms over her breast, looked down and made to leave.

Forthwith Nagasi rested a hand on her shoulder and said, 'Stay, Lusan.'

'What is it?' Lusan asked with her head bowed.

'Look at me...'

'No.'

'You must answer me.'

'Ask.'

'Will you be mine?'

Lusan quivered like a creeper. Nagasi saw that. She slowly raised her head, gave him a fleeting look, and smiled shyly.

'Please Lusan, answer me…'

'No,' Lusan said with a grave face.

'No?' Nagasi's male ego was hurt. 'No!'

'No.'

He took his hand off her shoulder.

Lusan moved forward but stopped after a few steps, looked back at Nagasi, and burst into a musical laughter.

Pretending, was she? His humiliation evaporated and he regained confidence. He moved swiftly towards Lusan. Laughing, she started to run but how could she outstrip Nagasi? He caught up with her in the middle of a field of bright sanjini flowers that shone like dewdrops. Lifting her face with his hands, he said, 'Now tell me.'

'No,' Lusan was laughing.

'No!'

'Yes!' All at once she threw her arms around him in wild abandon.

That night the stars twinkled more brightly over Papui Island. The ocean roared to create an orchestra with the trade winds that wafted through the coconut palms. And, at midnight, as a sleepy slice of half-moon rose from the ocean, a group of fairies came riding on moonbeams and danced in the pohutukawa garden.

The following day news of their romance spread through Papui.

The Hanakai people are farmers, they grow rice, and they fish. These are their staple foods. The island is rich with banana, papaya, the tisang fruit—and fowl. Once a week a market springs up to the east of Haisanu Lake. There they barter their produce for what they need for themselves. Once a year, in the winter months, people from Taihan Island a hundred miles away bring clothes and woolens and, in return, carry back pearls and coral. This is all their contact with the outside world.

Limited are the needs of the Hanakai people. So they have no greed, nor conflict. After a hard day's work, they have all the time in the world to relax in the evenings. Then, they sing and dance by the Haisanu Lake, or dream dreams on the coral reef...

That day the sea was very calm. The young men of the island went off in boats and rafts to catch fish with spears made of bone and stone. As the day wore on, a wall of clouds rose in the east. In the late afternoon the islanders stood anxiously on the beach. Lusan, too, because Nagasi was among the men who had gone out to sea.

But where was Nagasi? There was not a speck on the horizon. Only, the bank of dark clouds grew more ominous. Lusan's eyes turned increasingly sad and stormy.

The boats finally came back in the nick of time. Nagasi's face lit up on seeing Lusan. He leaped out of the boat to show her the prized catch of the day—a baby whale. But, to his surprise, his beloved was furiously walking away from him! 'Lusan...' he called out but she was so angry that she did not stop.

And why would she not be angry! Had Nagasi been caught in the storm, there was little chance of his return, for just a while later a huge gale struck the ocean. Kijima's peak vanished behind a mass of inky clouds. The palms moaned and howled as giant waves lashed the ancient walls of the citadel. And that toxic mist made up of mankind's sins wafted over the island. I felt stifled. To ease myself out of that miserable state, I sought the company of Nagasi. He was dashing through the storm to Lusan's home.

Her parents greeted Nagasi at the door and welcomed him in. They asked their daughter to serve rice wine. Lusan brought it out and quietly stood aside, glancing sideways at Nagasi from time to time. The intoxicating brew reddened Nagasi's eyes. Lusan's father, old Kangchin, was also slurring as he told stories: about a strange boat that had come to the coral reef a good twenty years earlier. It was like a big house, and it was called ship. It carried men from that faraway land, Japan. They were not good people, old Kangchin said; they brought along iron weapons called guns with which they killed four or five islanders. Before leaving they went around Papui for four days, and during those four days none of the women and girls could come out of their homes. When the strangers left, some livestock and young girls also disappeared, never to be seen again.

'No!' the drunk Nagasi shouted in feverish anger. 'Never will a ship from another land come here again! The world is an evil place. If they come, we will kill them.'

Leaning against the door, unseen, I smiled. How little this youth knew the world!

Outside, the storm was abating. The windswept clouds hurried off to the west. The waxing moon, set in the blue canopy of the sky spread over the ocean, lit up the island with its shy glow.

Old man Kangchin was now lying prone on the floor. His wife had gone inside a room. Nagasi raised his drunken eyes to look at Lusan, who was watching him from the doorway. Her eyes were shining and the pearl necklace round her neck and the corals dangling from her ears glowed in the light of the fish-oil lamp.

Nagasi's body rocked. He stepped forward to take Lusan by her hand and dragged her outside.

'Where are you taking me?' Lusan whispered. Without a word Nagasi picked her up in his arms and carried her, as light as a bird, past the pohutukawa garden towards the shore.

'I'll be angry, Nagasi!'

In reply Nagasi hugged her more tightly. Feeling his strong arms about her body, Lusan grew delirious with anticipation. She spoke no more.

Nagasi reached the moon-washed shore and stopped. There

was silence all around. His footfall sent a company of red crabs scurrying to safety. Tiny shells in ruby red and sapphire hues dotted the sands like sequins adorning a velvet sari. He laid Lusan down upon that exquisite bed of sand and sat down next to her.

Lusan smiled.

'Why're you laughing?'

'My wish.'

'Why were you angry with me in the evening?'

'Why were you so late coming back from the ocean?'

'Men can't afford to be afraid.'

'They can!' Lusan laughed out loud.

Nagasi was in the throes of passion. Peace lay over the world. The sea was roaring, the snowy foam cresting the waves were luminous. The trade wind whistling through the coconut palms caressed the sanjini flowers. Sitting on a pile of rocks, I was fascinated by this heavenly play of human love.

Further away stood a few houses on stilts. Nobody lived in them. When the Hanakkai married, the newlyweds would honeymoon in them for seven days.

'Look!' Nagasi turned Lusan's face toward the huts.

'I've seen them.' Lusan hid a smile.

'When shall we go there?'

'You tell me!'

'On the full moon that follows the next full moon.'

'Shall I tell my father?'

'All right.'

'And then?'

'Our numbers are dwindling.' Nagasi's voice was intense. 'I will pray to Akamaru to empower me to gift my people with a hundred children.'

'Dhat!' Lusan buried her face in his chest.

How many unspoken words of love hung in the air of Papui, like the fragrance of jasmine! Late at night Nagasi carried Lusan back home.

I sat alone and dreamt that the world would soon become like Papui—a kingdom of true love.

I have no idea how long I sat like that, lost in thought. Suddenly, I was hit by a blast of hot air. The moon had traversed to the other side of Kijima. Darkness descended and a band of wicked ghouls came dancing to hover over Papui. Some were without legs, some had no hands. Gross, repulsive, terrifying— their appearance churned the ocean and the waves jumped. The moon paled and fog engulfed the island. The ghouls tittered, pointing at me, and chuckled amongst themselves.

I was alarmed. Why were they here? There was no disturbance here, no sin. Is the whole world ruled by the Devil, then? But that's not true. I have seen a number of people all over the world working for the welfare of mankind. So?

Daybreak intensified my fear. The air over the island became very stuffy. Then a strange drone rent the air, as if thousands of bees were buzzing in unison. The sound closed in. Looking up at the sky, I saw four aeroplanes. They circled the island a few times, then flew so low that the terrified Hanakai ran off to hide in the jungles or in their homes. Only Nagasi and some courageous men came out to observe the planes. They sallied down with an infernal noise, as if to study the island's topography and its contours.

A mighty cry of distress rose from Papui.

The planes flew away after half an hour. Climbing atop Mount Kijima, I saw them departing in four directions. Then, two planes started to fly side by side. I perched on the wing of one of the airplanes and peeped inside. Two white men, dressed in soldiers' uniforms, were speaking into a wireless radio. 'Hello, Control,' one of them said. 'Listen, we've found what we were looking for. There's a partially deserted island with nothing for a hundred miles around it. The sortie is on…'

I climbed down. On Mount Kijima, the ghouls of last night were hanging like bats from the haiti trees. They startled me with their laughter. The islanders did not hear them but the unholy glee swept over the bamboos and spread afar like a foul smell in the wind. Wracked by the stench, Umanga and other devout Hanakais huddled inside Akamaru's temple redoubled their prayers. 'Oh God,' they prayed, 'protect us! The machine-birds of the civilized world have trained their sights upon us. Let not those birds bring catastrophe and death upon us…'

An unholy shadow now hung over Papui. The island seemed struck by gloom. The islanders were at their wits' end. They gathered here and there in groups. The heaving ocean and the sighing wind reinforced the suffocating sensation. And that searing heat, that noxious, asphyxiating gas! I was gripped by anxiety. Would I lose this beautiful sanctuary of Papui Island? I flew far from the island and over the ocean but did not see a single friend or familiar face. I was no wiser.

Day ended. Night fell. The full moon rose. But even the moonlit night did not draw a soul to the coral reef. The cooing of love seemed to have been stilled. Lusan and Nagasi did not meet or talk anymore. Nagasi and his friends had started patrolling the island.

Something was about to happen. At nightfall those wicked souls would clamber down the haiti trees and go romping around the island. There was an unmistakable foreboding… Some evil was about to befall the island.

And, sure enough, it did.

Early one morning, five days later, everybody was surprised to see a ship as large as a palace anchored offshore. The Hanakai were unaware of what I knew: It was a naval ship with machine guns and cannons mounted on its deck.

The news spread like wildfire. The islanders gathered on the shore while the soldiers lined up on the forward deck of the ship. They shouted something which the Hanakai could not understand. I could see that they were offering a friendship that was patently false.

'A ship,' old Kangchin whispered, 'like the one that came twenty years ago.'

All the old men knowingly nodded their heads.

Umanga said, 'This one is ten times bigger...'

Two boats were lowered from the ship. The Hanakai watched breathlessly as thirty men scrambled down a rope ladder onto the boats. Twenty of them were carrying machine guns, tommy guns and rifles. Kangchin lowered his voice to say, 'They have iron weapons—guns!' The islanders stepped back a few paces.

The boats closed the distance between us. We could see them clearly now. The soldiers waved. 'Do not be afraid! We come as friends.'

The boats came to rest on the beach. The soldiers jumped down. Four men with rifles slung on their waists led the way. Behind them, in a semi-circle, stood the men carrying machine guns, followed by those with tommy guns. They came up to the islanders and smiled. 'We are friends,' the leader said. 'Don't be afraid, we're here on a short visit...'

The Hanakai understood nothing.

Some soldiers were dragging large chests towards us. Inside were colourful silk cloth, dresses, toys, biscuit tins. 'Take these.' Their leader started distributing the articles. 'These are our offerings, our gifts of friendship to you.'

'No,' Nagasi cautioned, 'don't touch their things!'

A rumble of discontent now rose in Papui. Opinion was divided. One group wanted the gifts, another refused them.

A young soldier approached Lusan with a colourful scarf and draped it over her shoulders, smiling at her bare body. Nagasi angrily rushed over to throw the scarf to the ground. The machine guns and the tommy guns swung upwards at once. Their commander laughed out loud, and clapped a hand on Nagasi's shoulder to make light of the matter. He smiled. 'Don't be angry. We're friends. We have come to get better acquainted.'

Kangchin and one or two of the older men counseled Nagasi not to get overly excited.

Nagasi contained himself with difficulty. Looking at Lusan, he found that she had picked up that scarf from the ground and draped it around her shoulder. Pleased by its softness against her skin, she smiled at the soldier. This almost broke Nagasi's heart.

My heart too grew heavy. 'Beware!' I cried many times. 'Be warned, they're evil! If you submit to them, your souls will grow black like theirs, you will be devoured by greed and lust... Be careful!'

Alas, nobody heard me. My warning floated away like bubbles in the air.

Before dusk fell, the cannons on the ship were pointing towards Papui. The soldiers erected four large tents on the beach, then cut away bamboo to make an enclosure of wire netting covering an area of about 100 yards.

The Hanakai watched, frightened and angry, but could do nothing.

They were divided amongst themselves. One group said, 'Let's see what happens. Don't say anything for the time being.' This was the larger group, led by Kangchin. The dissenters said, 'No, let's tell them to leave.' This was a small group led by Mitsu and Nagasi. Umanga warned both groups, 'Don't make these outsiders the reason to fight amongst yourselves!' Nagasi heard Umanga and fell silent.

Old man Kangchin made friendly overtures to the soldiers. They started communicating with each other in sign language. The soldiers opened a bottle and invited the old man to drink with them. Then they told him to invite the others later in the evening.

Kangchin excitedly conveyed the news to the others. They all came one by one. Nagasi kept a watchful distance. When darkness fell, two young women came down from the ship and joined the soldiers in the tents. How beautiful they were, and how dazzling the clothes they wore!

Some of the girls arrived from the village to stand there. Lusan was with them, and around her shoulders was that offending scarf.

Nagasi's eyes blazed. 'Lusan,' he growled, 'why are you wearing that scarf?'

'It's so pretty!' Lusan smiled primly. 'Why, am I not looking nice?'

'Throw it away!'

'No!'

'Then you don't love me anymore...' Nagasi's eyes burned in their sockets.

'It's you who doesn't love me,' Lusan retorted defiantly.

Their squabble was suddenly drowned by loud music and foreign-sounding songs, with words nobody could understand but were sweet to the ear. The Hanakai noticed that the sound was coming out of a large box. 'How strange,' they thought, 'where are the singers?' Their amazement was now laced with fear. Who were these foreigners? How powerful they were!

'Enemies!' Nagasi muttered. 'These magicians are our foes...'

'Yes, true.' I went up close to him and whispered in his ear, 'They're enemies...'

The music played on. The white soldiers and the young girls poured wine into glasses and began to serve everyone. They hesitated at first, then they drank, then they licked their lips and laughed. Then came biscuits and, then, chocolate.

The moon gradually ascended from the ocean's depths. The crescendo of music pounded the stone walls of the ancient citadel of pirates, almost like the mighty waves. The Hanakai moved their heads to that rhythm. The Hanakai girls laughed from time to time, inebriated by the strong alcohol, and dissolved into shrill giggles. And whenever they giggled, the wicked ghouls giggled along with them. They were perched around the wire fence now, waiting and watching.

All at once the two white girls started to dance intimately with two of the men, arms round their necks. The Hanakai men and women were embarrassed. What kind of behaviour was this? But the dancing was wild, and the drink was spiking their blood. The embarrassment vanished in a little while. They watched the dancing wide-eyed and sat closer to their women.

The young soldier came up to Lusan, a drink in hand. 'You didn't have any wine,' he offered, his voice slurring. 'Drink...' Lusan looked at him with shining eyes, laughed, then shook her head to say 'no.'

'C'mon, you must drink!' The soldier laughed and pulled her by her hand.

Lusan lifted the glass to her lips with a naughty smile and arched brows.

Nagasi could take it no more. He rushed forward and pushed the soldier aside. The soldier blazed fire with his eyes. Uttering an abuse under his breath, he punched Nagasi hard. Nagasi fell to the ground. Mitsu immediately jumped into the fray. But before he could act a white soldier fired a tommy gun into the air. A trail of fire rent the air. The islanders screamed in fear. Mitsu was stalled. Nagasi slowly got back on his feet. Their friends came forward and took them away from the barbed-wire enclosure.

The leader of the white men roared in laughter. He gestured towards his own head to say, 'Hot-headed!' Then he tried to reassure the gathering, 'Fear not! We are peace-loving people. Come, sing and dance... Eat and drink... Enjoy yourselves!'

The soldiers now embraced those two girls from the ship and went back to dancing wildly. The Hanakai resumed nodding their head to the beat. And that soldier came back to Lusan, stood close to her and smiled. She downed the rest of the drink in her glass. Her body was now on fire. How handsome this white soldier was! Lusan smiled back at him.

The ghouls on the barb-wire fence danced in glee. The air was stifling. I fled the scene, trying to stop my tears. Papui Island was in grave danger. The Hanakai had surrendered their good sense. These white intruders were driving away love.

Nagasi and his band were the only hope for the island. But they were a mere handful. What were they planning?

Nagasi was sitting outside Kangchin's hut. He was waiting for Lusan. When she returned with old man Kangchin, the moon was high above Mount Kijima.

Kangchin was humming away and muttering to himself, 'Our brew is just no good... Not a patch on this amazing drink of the white man. This ship is much bigger than the one that came twenty years ago! That one had brought the Japs but these foreigners are so much nicer. Such good-tempered guys!'

Kangchin went indoors, swaying.

Lusan also made to follow him when Nagasi got hold of her and pulled her to his broad chest.

'Who's this? Oh! Nagasi...' She was reeking of foreign liquor and was draped in that offending scarf. She tried to push Nagasi away but couldn't extricate herself from his strong embrace.

'Uff! Let go of me... Leave me alone!'

'No—never!'

'Nagasi!'

'How can you be so heartless, Lusan?'

'Why? What have I done?'

'Don't go to their tent again, Lusan.'

'And why not? They're gentlemen!'

'No! They are our enemy. They surely have some ulterior motive.'

'That's your insecurity speaking.'

Lusan's words were so cold! She had distanced herself from him. Nagasi got tetchy; the primitive man within him was roused. 'Listen Lusan,' he gritted his teeth and said, 'you are mine and nobody else's. You must abide by what I say...'

Lusan glared at him, then forcefully pushed him away. 'I will not be your slave!'

'No?'

'*No!*'

'So now you don't want me...'

'I don't want you as long as you rebuke me.'

'Are these your last words?'

'Yes.'

Nagasi flung himself upon Lusan and grappled with her. He had the urge to strangle her. His sturdy fingers ruthlessly closed in on her neck which was as smooth as a conch. But how luscious her red lips were! How luminous her eyes! Nagasi pushed Lusan away and hastily fled the scene. A painful moan escaped him as he melted into the darkness.

My disembodied self was quaking at the impending doom of Papui Island. What should I do? Where should I go now? I couldn't stay there any longer.

I went over to the coral reef. It was not resounding with the love notes of Hanakai couples. It was dotted with white soldiers serenading girls who had traded their Hanakai code for a luxurious world of drinks, biscuits, colourful pieces of cloth... And the ocean roared, as if enraged by their shamelessness.

I returned to my home in the pile of stones. That miasma of sin was choking my breath. Someone somewhere was weeping. Was it the soul of Papui Island?

At daybreak I noticed something in the foreigners' tent. They had transported at least fifty bags of cement and a multitude of tools in the dead of night. It looked like they intended to erect a wall. But why?

I had guessed rightly. Sunrise found them explaining something to Kangchin. The old man just could not comprehend what they were saying. Someone then demonstrated the way to dig a trench. Kangchin nodded.

An hour later the soldiers were digging a 20X20 feet tank inside the fenced area and a group of Hanakai men were filling up basket after basket with the soil. In another corner four or five men were digging another square area to hold water. Before long, Hanakai girls started fetching water in earthen pitchers from Haisanu Lake to fill up the water tank. The soldiers softened the dug-up soil into clay and cast bricks out of it.

Curious Hanakais came in groups to watch. The soldiers entertained them again. Today they were initiated into the pleasure of smoking cigarettes.

Nagasi arrived with his band but stood at a distance. Lusan came later. Her appearance aroused anger and hatred in Nagasi; he left with his band.

That handsome soldier came forward to offer Lusan a camp-chair. She could not contain her gratefulness.

The mercury was rising. The heat was insufferable. The quantum of sin was peaking by the day. Night followed, day after day.

The soldiers piled up the bricks and fired them. When they cooled down, they bound them with cement.

Another day went by. The walls now enclosed a large room. A concrete room with just one door. An iron rod was placed over the door, it was then laced with all kinds of wires.

Meanwhile, twenty days had elapsed.

In these few days Papui Island had seen transformations. Every house on the island smelt of foreign liquor and foreign cigarettes. The natives were carrying goats and hens, corals and pearls to the white men. In return they received clothes, woolens, watches, biscuits and gilded jewellery. Lusan's neck and earlobes glittered with fake stones set in rolled gold. How glamorous she looked! But Nagasi avoided her like he would a poisonous reptile.

One day that soldier took Lusan for an outing on a boat. She was given a tour of the ship! All the Hanakai men and women stood in a circle around her. Lusan was flushed with exhilaration and wonder. 'It is as big as Papui Island,' she described the ship. 'And inside, there are rooms and rooms and rooms, all full of divine stuff!' Excitement and temptation ruled as the others listened with bated breath.

Every evening after sunset there was music and dancing outside the tents. Those two white women in skimpy clothes regularly took to the floor. The Hanakai also joined in after downing a few drinks. A drunken Lusan tried to dance in step with that young soldier.

And then, one night, very secretively, the soldiers carried something from the colossal ship. They entered the concrete room through the single door. Outside, a number of soldiers stood on guard with machine guns and tommy guns. When some Hanakais came closer, the soldiers drove them away.

On hearing this, Nagasi sat down to confer with his band. What is going on? Why have they built that house? Why are they not leaving the island? What are they housing in there so secretly? A foreign god? One meant to exterminate Akamaru? Some devilish spirit? Will they annihilate Papui Island?

Meanwhile, the soldiers finished their secret agenda. They locked the single door to the room, sealed it with an iron sheet, and then made it impenetrable with brick and cement. Then they opened bottles and spilled champagne. And the dismembered ghouls went on a spree on the terrace of that secured room: leaping, bounding, somersaulting.

Nagasi and Mitsu entered at this juncture, holding boulders and spears made of bones.

'Keep your distance!' yelled the machine-gun-wielding guards.

'Let them in,' commanded the white man's leader.

They came in, twenty of them; the rest of the Hanakai were out of sight.

'What have you kept in that house?' Mitsu demanded.

The white-skinned commander followed what he said. 'Our Akamaru!' he joked.

'You take your god away. Papui Island belongs to us.'

'Have a drink?' The commander tried to make light of the matter.

'No,' Mitsu was firm. 'You leave our island along with your god.'

'Don't be mad!' The commander pushed Mitsu. 'Go home!'

But Mitsu and Nagasi and those others had gone mad. Mitsu suddenly lunged at the commander. A white soldier immediately swung his machine-gun towards him.

Rat-tat-tat-tat-tat!

Mitsu and four others fell to the ground. A cloud of blue smoke rose to the sky. Elated, those ghouls over the concrete room whistled and clapped. The startled cry of the five fallen Hanakai youth evaporated in the evening air. A ruddy spectre with five heads materialized from their blood streaks and started bouncing about. A tornado flew into my face and almost swept me off. I managed to stay put only with severe effort.

The Hanakai were startled by the gunfire but were stopped from coming forward. Nagasi, now afraid, started to back away along with his band.

'What do you say?' The white commander pointed to the concrete room and asked, 'Will our god stay?'

Nagasi, tears rolling down his cheeks, nodded assent.

'You may leave,' the commander gestured.

Nagasi left the place like a cur with its tail between its legs. Some of the soldiers lifted the bodies of the fallen men into

a boat and rowed off towards the muddy waters of the ocean.
The offenders who had challenged the god in the concrete room
deserved no more than a watery burial.

It took no time for the news to spread. Panic seized the
Hanakai. Nagasi was stupefied. Old man Kangchin was frothing
at the mouth with a tirade of abuse at the defiant band.

Evening came. With it came the sound of music and dance
outside the tent. But today no one could muster the courage to
join in. They assembled in small groups along Haisanu Lake.
Suddenly they were taken aback by the sound of military boots
crushing twigs on the ground. The white commander stood before
them along with ten of his soldiers. They had come to invite the
islanders to join in the merriment. They were sorry about the
five dead men. But they had insulted the whites and physically
attacked them, so they had had to open fire in self-defence. An
unnerved lot, led by Kangchin, walked towards the tent with
hesitant steps. Nagasi and a few others moved further away in
the opposite direction.

The foreign liquor was an extraordinary concoction. The Hanakai
forgot everything in no time at all and were dancing in joyous
abandon. Today the white ladies chose to dance with a few among
the Hanakai. Lusan chose this moment to go out, unnoticed,
with that white soldier.

The moon was yet to rise, the island was wrapped in gloom
and reeking with an infernal smell. But they were on a high
wrought by alcohol, the urgency of desire primed by the heady
fragrance of pohutukawa and sanjini blossoms. I followed them.
They headed for my abode: that ancient pile of rocks. They sat
down side by side, then lay on the ground.

'I want to marry you,' the soldier said.

Lusan didn't follow what he was saying but smiled anyway.
She held the soldier's face in her hands and drew it towards her.

I couldn't stand her shameless behavior and fled the place. My life from fifty years earlier, when I had been flesh and blood, came back to me. The time my wife had poisoned me...

Sin, sin will cause the end of the world. Love vanishes overnight. The pious become depraved.

Serving drinks to everyone present, the commander said, 'Hear me. We are concerned about your well-being. Which is why I'm telling you this: Leave this island and go away within four days.'

Nobody understood his words. The soldiers repeatedly used sign language to drive this home to Kangchin. He grasped the meaning of the words and passed it on to the others.

'Why? Why? Why?' The Hanakai were filled with foreboding.

The commander spoke again, 'This island will sink in a few days. Our highly advanced machines have told us this.'

The party broke up. Thoughts of death gripped the Hanakai. They went home without a word, lead within their hearts. The crescent moon emerged from her bath in the ocean waters and started riding the sky. Kijima's peak was clouded by mist.

In the dead of the night, the faithless Lusan and her white soldier came out of the ruin that was my home, hugging each other, holding hands. But that treacherous girl did not go home. The young man pulled her towards the tent. I sat in my home that had been defiled by the vile couple and wondered to myself, 'Where can I go? What should I do?'

I fell asleep, still wondering. I was woken up by a rumble and a roar, and saw in the dying light of the moon that, beyond the coral reef, the foreigners' ship was churning the waters of the ocean.

They were leaving! I jumped up and headed for the tents. But where were they? Not a single tent was standing there. There was not a soul in sight. Only the stench of blood-soaked earth. And a concrete house that looked like a mausoleum.

They had ripped out the barb-wire fence and wrapped it

around the structure. They had made an invincible fortress. Why? What was inside? Which idol? I went over the barb-wire and struck the wall. It was as hard as solid stone. How did one enter? I penetrated the iron and concrete with my formless body and entered the room. Darkness. Airless, thick darkness. Through the darkness, I could discern an iron chest. I entered it. In it lay a small toy-like ball of steel. I carefully examined it and realized it was the devil incarnate. Satan had disguised himself in hydrogen and was sitting there, dreaming of Armageddon. If I had waited I would have dropped down senseless. I bolted.

I figured out that this was the weapon which would be used in the fight that has ensued, for the white man to enjoy the world all by themselves. They had made the bomb to reign supreme, and they had placed it in the home of the Hanakais to test the power of the deadly weapon. Once this experiment succeeded, they would use it to finish off their opponents.

Spotting me there, the wicked ghouls came rushing from every corner and started hitting and biting me. I screamed in pain and ran off.

Papui was in peril. At daybreak I sought out Nagasi and his companions. They were outside his hut; beaten, bewildered, benumbed.

'Beware Nagasi,' I stood close to him and shouted again and again, 'the foreigners have planted seeds of destruction on your island!' But they could not hear me. My words had no impact other than rustle the air. At that moment someone rushed in to inform them that the ship had gone and so had everyone else.

'Gone?' Nagasi ran towards the shore. Everybody gathered near the concrete structure. 'What have the devils left behind? What is in there?' Nagasi asked.

'A bomb,' I replied, unheard.

'They have made a barrier around it,' Nagasi said, 'remove

it.' Someone took a spear and pulled at the wire netting but shrieked in distress and fell aside.

'What happened?' asked the others.

'I don't know! A powerful energy hit me and I feel paralysed!'

I understood. They had placed a powerful battery inside to electrify the barb-wire fence. But the primitive, ignorant Hanakai did not realize what was going on. Seeing the power of the white godman they retreated. 'What will happen?' They began to speculate.

Kangchin came running up at that moment. 'Lusan has vanished!' he said, beating his breast.

Nagasi went up to him. 'What do you mean, vanished?'

'Last night she was dancing with a soldier and didn't come home,' Kangchin said. 'We cannot find three girls: Maitisi, Rangcha and...'

'Where could she disappear?' Nagasi yelled.

'Maybe she went on that ship...' Tears rolled down Kangchin's crumpled cheeks.

But the enraged Nagasi showed not the slightest sympathy. Instead, he went for Kangchin and put his hands round the old man's throat. 'Vile dog! Did you sell your own daughter?' Abruptly he spat upon Kangchin and rushed towards the ocean.

'Nagasi, where are you going?' his friends yelled.

Nagasi pulled hard on a raft as he replied, 'I'm going to catch that ship.'

'Why?' asked his companions, running after him.

'I will bring Lusan back.' He pushed the raft into the ocean.

'Are you mad?' his friends cried out. 'You are out of your mind!'

By now Nagasi was afloat on the ocean.

'Nagasi, do you see the ship? It's gone too far! Come back!! Please!'

'Wherever it goes, I will catch that ship.'

'Nagasi! Nagasi!'

But Nagasi did not turn back. His eyes were set on the horizon. His raft was like a banana leaf upon the breast of the mighty ocean. By and by he and his raft both went completely out of sight.

Papui Island has lost its life and soul. The silence of death has descended upon the islanders. Five young men have died. Four girls have vanished. An alien god has made his home on their island. The Hanakai daily raise their voice in prayer to Akamaru, and the wicked ghosts snigger. They giggle and dance on the tips of the bamboo trees and turn cartwheels in the air.

Days pass. The ocean bellows. The sea water laps at the ancient ruin. The trade winds play with the palms. The aroma of pohutukawa flowers waft about upon the winds just as before. The sanjini flowers bloom and wither away. Ripe tisang fruits fall off the trees to the ground. Haitaru and mangchua birds sing as they have for centuries. And the dormant volcano Kijima dreams of its own fiery youth and hides its face in diaphanous clouds.

One day.

Two days.

Three days.

Each day Papui Island has grown hotter and hotter. I realize it is time for me to leave. Time to seek another sanctuary. But where? I have seen the world!

Night comes. Darkness engulfs Papui. Perhaps the moon will rise halfway through the night. Papui is hushed, and still.

There is no love left in Papui. Lusan has betrayed her lover. Where is Nagasi? Is he still alive?

Out of the blue my phantom friends come riding upon the wings of the winds. 'Quick,' they shouted, 'come away with us... Fly!'

'What's wrong?'

'There's no time... Just come away...'

'Tell me why?'

'The ship has gone 200 nautical miles. On it is a gadget with a tiny button. The minute this button is pressed, a lever will get activated...'

Before they can finish, an apocalyptic sound reverberates through the island and the ocean and the air, as though the world has neared its end. A thousand lightning streaks split the sky. My friends pull me upwards at top speed. Up, up and up.

I look down, terrified. In the blink of an eye, all of Papui Island splinters into pieces and starts to dissolve into the ocean. A vicious explosion turns into a fiery ball that keeps bulging with every second and becomes a vast mushroom cloud of fire that rushes upwards. The stupendous atmospheric pressure it causes unleashes a tempest. Death travels in every direction with the squall. The wind turns into a conflagration. Holocaust prevails for hundreds of miles, exterminating animals, birds, insects and every visible and invisible form of life. It does not spare even space, rising upwards twenty-five miles through the sky. Deadly poison spreads underwater along the sea-bed too. The planet trembled and with it shudder the satellites and stars of the cosmos.

A sphere of death has resulted from that instant of destruction, and no one knows how many aeons it will take for life to blossom once more.

We see all this from the air. When the cyclone subsides, we see that Papui has simply ceased to be. In its place is a massive volcano spouting fire in the belly of the ocean. The ceaseless waves churn like a cauldron.

The storm spends itself. But the ashes of death are carried by the air to every nook and corner. It will rain illness and disfiguration and death into the unborn. It will rob men of manhood, and women of fertility, and encourage animalistic instincts. The reptile of death spreads through space, in slow motion, upon the wings of the wind.

A great cry reverberates through the universe. Spirits come rushing down from the suns, the moons, the stars, the galaxies and the nether world.

'Hear, hear! All of you listen...'

We gather near the Milky Way with only one question upon our lips: What will happen now? If there are more such destructions, the very impulse of life will come to a stop. The human existence that every life form aspires to, now does not respect Life. They want Death. Hatred and violence has turned mankind into votaries of Death. So what now?

'No, that won't do!' the spirits scream in unison. 'Nothing is more important than living. So, human beings, listen to us. Love! Go on loving. Only loving each other can save you from the jaws of death...'

We know that human beings do not hear us. Still we will go on calling out our warning. When the rosy light of dawn falls on their faces, when flowers bloom, birds sing, babies smile and pretty girls look shyly at them, they might realize that we are cautioning them, over and over again. 'Fall in love. Love everyone. Only love has the power to win over death.'

But the world is filled with hatred. Suppose they hear our pleas and still do not accept that love is supreme. What then?

So, in the midst of those cries, I pray to the Lord of Birth. 'Oh Lord, I have avoided being born for full fifty years. But no more. I want to live again. Let me be born now. I have much to do on earth...'

Translated by Aparajita Roy Sinha

Full Circle

'Have mercy on me, my gods, have mercy!' Sreedhar Bhattacharya was praying from the core of his heart. 'Sixty years of my life I have spent meditating upon your name. I have never lied nor have I failed in my duty. All my years have gone into studying and teaching scriptures; why then should I be punished? Why must my equanimity be destroyed? You have restored a part of my fortune, now please help restore all of it. Oh God! Please help... Please keep my self-respect intact. Almighty, please...'

Sreedhar was emotionally charged. His eyes were moist, his voice tearful. The room was filled with smoke from incense and the mild smell of flowers. In the midst of everything was a wooden throne with the idol of a god on it. Sreedhar Bhattacharya's sonorous voice reverberated through the room. His face glowed with emotion and spiritual effulgence. Though he had aged, his complexion was like molten gold. His face was crisscrossed with worry lines. His hair and eyebrows had turned white but he still had the erect body of a youth. The firmness of his body reflected the rigidity of his mind.

Yes, Sreedhar Bhattacharya was a rigid man. He was known to be learned and unbeatable at scriptural debates. He had run a village school for twenty-five years. He had drilled dull students till they had themselves become learned. He lived in poverty but had always kept his word. A man of discipline, he faithfully performed all his duties. Not once had he neglected his home and hearth. He had three sons and two daughters. The daughters were married into good families and the sons were well-established. He had had no disappointments.

His eldest son, Avinash, had a job in Calcutta that earned him the enviable sum of three hundred rupees every month. When Avinash had started working ten years earlier, he had asked his father to quit teaching and stay with him. He wanted his father to rest his tired bones. But Sreedhar did not agree. He had no intention of renouncing his way of life. He enjoyed the discipline and rigour of his existence. However, the younger brothers moved in with the elder one, completed their studies and started working. His elder daughter married and moved to a town in the western part of Bengal. The younger one was married to Tarini Chakravarty's son in the neighbouring village. They owned a garment shop in Dhaka. Sreedhar felt settled in all ways. During their long holidays the boys would return to their parents in the village. The elder daughter came only once in two years because she had moved far away. Only Gouri, the younger daughter, stayed for stretches of three to four months.

There was nothing to worry about. He continued living in the village of Nandapur in Noakhali district with his wife, Dakshayani. Situated by a river, Nandapur had a dream-like picturesqueness about it. And at one end of the village was the tol run by Sreedhar. Quiet and peaceful, the school had a air monastic. Fifteen to twenty students resided on the campus all year round. Day and night they chanted slokas composed by ancient sages and savants. The school, surrounded by trees, had the ambience of a hermitage. Seated ramrod straight in a semi-circle of disciples, Sreedhar, the master of learning and debates, would expound time-honoured scriptures. He would recite immemorial slokas one after another and explain them in detail. Legends, edicts, rules and laws were described to the students. In a full-throated voice, he would confidently proclaim India the best country in the world and Hinduism the foremost of religions. Thus was Sreedhar Bhattacharya's autumn years soaked in bliss and peace.

Contentment, serenity, spirituality—he had everything. Both this world and the other—where he would go when he died—were attractive to him. Life continued in harmony till the day a storm swept through his world and wrecked it. He had never experienced such a terrible disaster in his sixty years of existence. Riots erupted in his district. Not mere rioting, but battles! And...

'Oh Lord, please help me retain my self-respect... Please, God...!' He ended his prayers and glanced at the four-armed statue of Vishnu. The tiny black carving seemed to have come to life; wasn't it smiling at him from the corner of its mouth? This smile inspired courage in the face of every hurdle: sorrow, grief, senility, death. It spurred devotees to action, it drove the faithful to perform great tasks. Almighty, you make the impossible happen.

Sreedhar bowed to the idol with unadulterated devotion for a long time. He then stood up. His eyes reflected peace and his face glowed like that of one who had conquered death.

He strode out of the room, locked the door, stepped into his wooden clogs, and headed for the third storey of his home. *Khat, khat, khat*—the wooden clogs sounded his firm footsteps.

Dakshayani came out of the next room. She was a fit consort for her husband: fair-skinned, and looking every bit a priestess.

'What is the time, Daksha?'

'Ten minutes after ten.'

'Have they all left for office?'

'Yes.'

'I see.' Sreedhar nodded his head. 'Gouri's in-laws will arrive at Howrah by the 11.30 train. It will be another hour before they get to Bhowanipore.'

'Yes,' Dakshayani said. 'Howrah is a fair distance from here.'

'Is everything ready, Daksha? You must complete the arrangements for their bath and lunch before they reach.'

'Rest assured; everything is ready. Our daughters-in-law, Gouri herself, and I have all been busy. Gouri has been working very hard. She alone has performed a hundred tasks.' Dakshayani's voice trailed off into tears. She paused, then went on, 'And why won't she? After all, her fate will be decided today.'

Sreedhar was moved. He felt a shiver rise up his spine. He breathed deeply. Then, in a heavy voice, he uttered, 'Divine Mother!' He started climbing the stairs to the third storey, his khadau making the same, loud *khat khat khat*.

'Should I give you some prasad?' Dakshayani called out after him. 'You did not eat much last night.'

Sreedhar kept climbing. Without turning towards his wife he answered, 'Fine. You can get some upstairs.'

This rented house was in a quiet neighbourhood. A bookbinder occupied the lowest level. Four or five people worked there through the day and went home every night. They were not noisy and, when they left in the evening, the ground floor fell silent. Avinash and his brothers occupied the five rooms on the second and third levels. Sreedhar and Dakshayani occupied the single room at the top. There were three or four children in the house but they were not boisterous as they were not too young. Other than the occasional patter of children running, or their laughter, one could hear at regular hours the loud *khat khat khat* of the learned debater's wooden clogs. Life flowed smoothly like a river.

The room in one corner of the small roof was filled with scriptures and books. The roof was enclosed by a high parapet. The view from the roof stretched far: a forest of tall buildings with the occasional interruption of treetops and, beyond that, the sky. Occasionally crows, sparrows and pigeons called out from their perch on the rainshed. By no means did they sound discordant.

The door to his room was shut. Opening it, Sreedhar Bhattacharya entered the room, sat on the floor-mat, and gazed out of the window.

It was April. The whole town was awash with bright sunlight while a few torn pieces of cloud floated in the sky. Nice, but Calcutta was not Nandapur. You could not see fields of rice or jute stretching out endlessly. You did not see coconut, betel or bamboo trees adding to the lushness of the green. There was no solitude, no silence, no open skies or free-flowing breeze. The days here were not filled with the calls of multifarious birds, or the night with the howls of jackals. Most pertinently, the learned debater did not have his school there. The only thing that Calcutta had in common with Nandapur was the sky. So it was okay, though not quite nice.

Sreedhar stared vacantly. His school no longer existed. His life's work had been destroyed. The hurricane of violence that had stormed in was the worst experience in the six decades of his existence. The assault had shattered the happiness that was his universe. It had annihilated his school.

Riots. He remembered them well.

A small black cloud appeared in the clear sky. It spread slowly and darkness engulfed daylight. Riots. First came the rumours. Next came news of bloodletting in Calcutta. Fear shook the very foundation of every being. Talk of all-consuming violence was heard in their province too. The violence became a reality one morning and spread like wildfire through their village. There was no escaping it. Sreedhar's students were in the village and Gouri was visiting. She had arrived two or three weeks earlier to spend the Pujas with them. She would then go back to her in-laws, to the home she had been happily married into for four years, and where she had everything—except children.

But there was no escape...

The students and the other Hindus in the village decided to take on the mobs. But what could they do against a thousand barbarians? They came in the deep of night with flaming torches. They killed the students and the men. Only those who agreed to convert to Islam escaped death. A few managed to flee. Two of the students somehow covered themselves and escaped with Sreedhar and Dakshayani.

Sreedhar was not willing to run away at all. The sight of his school going up in flames had driven him insane. And tt was at that very hour that the villains had dragged Gouri away.

Screams. Chaos. Blood-curdling shrieks. Scorching heat. Blinding smoke.

The heart-wrenching cries, the spurting blood and the kidnapping of his daughter had pushed him even further over the edge. Sreedhar's students forcibly took him to a safer location. Then they started making cautious enquiries about Gouri's whereabouts. In vain. They could get no information. Sreedhar was struck dumb with grief. Nor could they get any news of Gouri's husband and in-laws in the next village. They had also run away. What was the solution? Sreedhar was given to believe that Gouri had been killed. Broken-hearted, he left for his sons' home in Calcutta. They too were to have come for the Pujas but their cancelling of the trip had proved fortuitous.

Sreedhar became very erratic. Dakshayani wept day and night to lighten her burden. But Sreedhar had not a tear in his eyes. He was dumbfounded. At times he would turn the pages of the scriptures and try to read his books, but they made no sense to him. He did not like anything. Everything had become meaningless. He stopped praying to the gods. He just could not bring himself to seek their blessings. They got news of Tarini

Chakravarty; he had escaped with his family to Bardhaman. On hearing about his daughter-in-law's abduction, he responded with a letter: 'Everything is destiny. Let God's will be done. Other than this, I can say nothing today.'

Mukund, Gouri's husband, visited them once. Dakshayani started crying as soon as she saw him, but Sreedhar locked himself up in his room. The sight of his son-in-law had unleashed endless memories of his lovely daughter. He could still hear her piteous screams emanating from some distant, unknown place. Mukund left soon, with no one to say goodbye or to send a message to. After all, there was nothing to say.

Days went by. Scriptures and God receded into the distant past as grief and sorrow came to rule the heart of Sreedhar Bhattacharya. There was no respite. He mourned Gouri incessantly and recalled her smallest action in all its detail. Her face kept wracking his heart. She was like a beautiful goddess, cheerful and kind.

And every time he remembered her, the terrifying images of that night in Nandapur flashed before his eyes. Those fiery tongues of flames which burnt their homes down and licked their lives! The horror of the fire still raged in his learned heart. Those flames had razed houses, destroyed the village and reduced his world to ashes...

Over time, Sreedhar came to the realization that the call of the heart was stronger than the call of scriptures, rituals, purity and heaven. No, there was nothing greater than the welfare of one's sons, daughters, wife and home. God? He was too abstract, too lofty, too far away. His heart cried for those who were much smaller, finite and closer.

One day, Sreedhar felt suffocated at home. He had no taste for anything. On the spur of a moment he left quietly and roamed around aimlessly for hours. All of a sudden he stopped in his tracks to look at a girl. Who was she? Was it Gouri? The very next moment he realized his mistake and walked on. A fallacious dream! He raised his distressed eyes to the skies. God? No one knew where God resided. Perhaps somewhere high up, beyond the clouds...

While walking around Sreedhar wondered if, some day, he would bump into Gouri. Was that a possibility? He looked around with searching eyes. Maybe someday fate would make the impossible come to pass. Who knew what could happen? He increasingly started leaving home and walking the streets. Calcutta was still wracked by riots. It was not possible to wander about wherever one pleased. Still Sreedhar roamed around. At sixty, he became daring like a careless youth.

One day, by a twist of fate, the impossible became a reality.

Sreedhar was at the Sealdah Railway Station. In the aftermath of the Partition, the place was teeming with Muslim men and women going to and fro. His laser eyes stared at the women amongst them. They were wearing burkhas. It was 10.30 in the morning and the platform was packed with people jostling against each other. Sreedhar stepped aside. The signal was down and coolies bustled around. A train was steaming into the platform. As it came to a halt, the commotion and cacophony increased with the passengers pouring out.

All of a sudden he noticed two women in burqas accompanying three men in lungis. As they neared Sreedhar, one girl came to an abrupt halt. She started swaying on her feet and craned her head towards Sreedhar. Why? What was going on? Sreedhar was trembling and his heart was pounding. Something was afoot here.

'Maa!' he called out on an impulse.

At once the burqa-clad figure broke away from the group and ran towards him.

'Maa!' Sreedhar once again called out the endearment he once used to address Gouri.

But the girl was stopped. Three male companions caught her by her arm and dragged her away.

'Hurry up.'

'Quick.'

'Move quickly...'

Sreedhar lost all sense of propriety and yelled agitatedly, 'Maa! Maago...!'

The girl unexpectedly sat down on the floor and violently shook her head. No sound escaped her lips. Her escorts started beating her and pulling her back up onto her feet. They were fuming but the girl would not budge. Hindus, Muslims, policemen, railway employees... By and by everyone came to stand around them in a circle.

'What happened?'

'What is the matter?'

'Why are you beating the girl?'

'This girl...' Sreedhar screamed like a lunatic, '...she is my daughter...'

Pandemonium swept through the crowd.

'Police! Police!'

The girl continued to shake her head.

One of the three men looked fiercely at Sreedhar and drew out a knife from his waist. The bedlam turned riotous. More people rushed to the scene. More police intervened. The police in-charge at the station scurried to the platform. The three men and the two burqa-clad women were arrested. The policeman in-charge was Hindu. He listened to the whole story, then asked a lady passenger to cross question the girls and examine their faces. The ladies went into a waiting room and took off the burqas. One of them was found to be gagged and had her hands tied at the back. She wanted to come out of the waiting room to the platform. The police permitted her to step out. The crowds waited in eager anticipation and Sreedhar's heart rose to his throat. He had not been afraid of death during the riots. Death ends every suffering but here was a heartrending chance of his hopes being dashed. That is why he stood with eyes wide open.

When she came out of the room, the onlookers murmured, 'Hindu... A Hindu girl...'

Sreedhar ran towards her like one possessed, clutched her to his heart and cried out, 'My daughter! My Gouri! My Gouri Maa...'

'Ogo... Do you hear me...'

Sreedhar was startled. Dakshayani had got him some of the Puja offerings.

'Here, have some of this and drink some water,' she said.

Sreedhar stirred back to life.

Dakshayani was looking closely at her husband. 'Eat!' she repeated.

'Okay,' Sreedhar took the plate of prasad and asked, 'You have almost finished cooking. Right?'

'Yes.'

'You have bathwater ready for both of them?'

'Yes. Don't worry so much!'

'Arrange for them to rest in Avi's room after lunch. Once they have rested, I will address the issue...'

'We are all set. Besides, there is still time.'

'Yes, that is true.' Sreedhar nodded his head. 'What is Gouri doing?'

'Feeding the boys in the kitchen. She is unnaturally silent...' Dakshayani looked at her husband. 'You understand... this is the day of her trial by fire!'

'Maa... Maago!' Sreedhar prayed in a choked voice. He sat still for some moments, then resumed, 'Dress up Gouri very nicely today. She is like a goddess. When they see her, their hearts will surely melt...'

Dakshayani turned her face away from Sreedhar. She was quiet for a while, then stood up abruptly. 'Let me go and see what remains to be done.'

'Do that. And let me know when it is time.'

'I will.'

Dakshayani almost ran out of the room.

Sreedhar was about to put a slice of cucumber into his mouth when he paused midway. Would the hearts of Tarini Chakravarty and Mukund melt when they saw Gouri? For six months, Gouri had been a slave to the hooligans who had captured her on the night of rioting. Those goons took her from village to village. They took her across rivers, streams, canals and marshes and, finally, they were headed for the east. She had been brutalized and tortured. She had become emaciated and had grown darker. There had been no way out of the trial; she had been guarded at all times.

Sreedhar had found her about twenty days earlier. He thought a lot after he rescued her. He calmed down a little, started praying again, and felt hopeful. Gouri had looked after her husband and his family for four years. She had gained the affection of her in-laws and her husband. Everybody acknowledged that she was an excellent homemaker. She would have to be handed over to her husband and father-in-law this very day. In a way, she would be reborn and start a new life.

Sreedhar knew Mukund and Tarini well. He had deep insight into the human character. The son and father were gentle, learned, charitable, broad-minded and large-hearted. They would definitely accept this girl who had been rescued from the barbarians. Scriptures? Yes, this act would have scriptural approval too. Just as the scriptures rejected women exposed to impurity and filth, they had rules for accepting such women too. Which was acceptable? Both. Even if a woman's body had been sullied by beasts, she remained pure if her mind were untouched. Gouri was innocent and unstained because the beasts had attacked her.

'Thakur, please have pity on me...'

These were not Sreedhar's words. It was a prayer that had been offered by a Vaishya girl many years ago.

The words drifted to him from the past and sent a shiver up his spine. Images from a blurry past bubbled up before his eyes. Sreedhar felt shaken.

Punctiliously observant of the canons and rites enjoined by the scriptures, the disciplined Brahmin Sreedhar Bhattacharya was then the head of the village school and an arbiter of social law. He passed judgments on social behaviour and decided what the acceptable code of conduct for the village would be.

This was an evening almost two years ago. Manohar Kundu's beautiful young daughter-in-law was returning from a dip in the river. As she headed home, four beings from hell jumped out of the darkening hedges. She did not return home that evening. The sky turned to night. Her father-in-law grew worried and went out with a few men to look for her. She was not to be found in any other home. They grew agitated and looked in all possible places all through the night. The following day, they located the girl in the jute fields, wounded and senseless. She was lying in a faint.

Everyone in the village was aware of the incident and discussed it among themselves. Manohar Kundu took the girl home and had her treated. Everybody thought this was a humanitarian act. He would obviously not keep her once she was well. She had been violated and her purity had been soiled by the Muslim hoodlums.

But, no, the opposite happened. Manohar Kundu did not show any sign of rejecting or excommunicating his daughter-in-law.

The Hindu pundits found this intolerable. The panchayat

sat in judgment. Its chief was Sreedhar, the learned debater. A lot of issues, a slew of scriptures were discussed, and many debates were held over the fate of the girl and the Kundu family. Manohar Kundu pleaded for the girl to continue in her home. But the gods of society were not to be appeased. Their chief, Sreedhar Bhattacharya, quoted scriptures and judged heartlessly. He declared that dharma was blind and implementing it was extremely tough. One had to be unkind and cruel to keep dharma intact. Manohar Kundu had no option but to abide by the diktats of the gods of society. He had to excommunicate his daughter-in-law, throw her out of his home and family. Else, he and his people would have to leave the village of Nandapur was the verdict of the righteous members of the panchayat.

After this threat, Manohar and his son fell silent. Contradicting society was out of question, as was leaving the village for the sake of the girl. They wept in sorrow. They did not have the strength to protest or to ignore the verdict.

The panchayat session was adjourned.

Sreedhar was sitting down in the verandah that evening. The hedges had grown darker in the dim light of the new moon. He had finished the day's lessons and, sitting alone in the dark, he was basking in the light of his thoughts. Nature seemed to come alive with the star-studded skies and the soft rustle of the wind. For him, this universe and existence itself was honeyed.

A figure suddenly emerged out of the darkness and walked towards him. 'Who is it?' He could not see the face clearly in the absence of light.

The figure did not answer. It stood like a carved statue.

'Who are you? Why are you not answering?'

There was still no answer.

Sreedhar called out to Dakshayani. 'Wife, get me a lantern quickly...'

Dakshayani hurried out with a lantern. In its light they saw that the figure was a veiled woman.

'Who are you?' Sreedhar asked in surprise. 'What do you want?'

The figure removed her veil slowly and wordlessly. Sreedhar and Dakshayani saw a beautiful face full of melancholy, with tears streaming down her eyes. They recognized her in a flash. She was Manohar Kundu's daughter-in-law.

Sreedhar and Dakshayani stared at her, curious and silent. What did the girl want? Why had she come to them alone in the dark? Sreedhar's features hardened. He could guess.

The girl stepped on the stairs to climb up to the verandah.

'Please don't climb up here,' Sreedhar said in a stentorian voice. 'Go back to your home.'

The girl stopped in her tracks. Perhaps she felt dizzy. She stumbled and flopped down on the stairs. Her tearful eyes had the look of a hapless animal out for slaughter. She started banging her head against the verandah and said in a mournful voice, 'Thakur! Have mercy on me. I am not to blame. You know that. I am innocent. Save me, Thakur... Protect me...'

Sreedhar knew that being a god of society was an onerous task. So he nodded his head and uttered a single word, 'No!'

Dakshayani could not hold back her tears but she did not have the courage to speak a word. She stood there speechless as the girl kept beating her forehead. Sreedhar ignored the girl and walked away in stony silence.

After all these days, the cries of that condemned girl seemed to come back from an invisible chamber in the sky.

'Oh Thakur, have mercy on me... Save me.'

Sreedhar was trembling. He trembled because he was not the man he had been two years ago. After losing his daughter and then rescuing her from the clutches of the barbarians, he realized he had been unjust that day. He had wounded her with scriptural canons. He had devastated her life. He had broken a home. He had destroyed a family. He had committed a grave sin. He would pronounce the opposite judgment upon his daughter and, thus, atone for his past sins. The scriptures had given him two options. Bodily impurity and spiritual impurity could be treated in different ways. Never again would he say that bodily impurity and spiritual impurity was the same thing. Yes. After sixty years, he had discovered the real truth. No, there was nothing to worry about. Tarini was a learned, knowledgeable man who acknowledged that Sreedhar knew best and would accept his decision. There would be no hitches. Oh! It would be such joy! After that? Sickness and death? These were a matter of a change of scene. Perhaps he would continue in the same place as long as he lived. He might not be able to return to his village in this life. Never mind. He would open a school here to educate students to become good human beings.

'Ogo, come quickly...'

Sreedhar's heart beat quickly. What had happened? He looked at Dakshayani. Her face was flushed.

Dakshayani said quickly, 'They have come. Both: her father-in-law and husband.'

Sreedhar stood up. His voice was tearful when he tried to speak. 'They have come? May God's will be fulfilled.' He suddenly remembered something and said, 'Is Gouri in the other room? They have not seen her?'

'No.'

'Then let's go.'

There was silence in the room. Sreedhar sat on one side, Tarini and Mukund sat on the other. Dakshayani and her two daughters-in-law waited outside the door, alert. No one spoke in the room, as if they were all mute. Or as if they were aliens from different planets.

All of a sudden Tarini stood up crying. Mukund continued to sit with his head bowed down.

Tarini clasped Sreedhar's hand in his own and said in a tremulous voice, 'Is your daughter not mine? Your grief is deeper as Gouri is your own blood. But she was my family! I am bereaved too...'

Sreedhar's voice shook as he said, 'You are my only consolation in this grief...'

Tarini was a generous man. He kept quiet for some time and then started talking about his daughter-in-law. He recalled many small details: what she said on which day, what new dishes she had made for him with sincerity and love, how much care she bestowed on him... Endless stories of Gouri, at the end of which he started weeping.

'She was like an incarnation of Sati and Lakshmi, pure, sacrificing and devoted. I look around for her whenever I am out walking. If I found her, I would take her home.'

Sreedhar was observing Tarini carefully. He was scanning every line on his face. Were the words sincerely spoken? Was there sorrow underneath the words? Was there a deep affection for Gouri? Sreedhar was relieved after the examination. No, Tarini was not lying. He did have true affection for Gouri.

Sreedhar said in a gentle voice, 'I pray to God all the time that I get my daughter back...'

'How can you get Gouri back?' Tarini breathed deeply and shook his head in negation. 'She must have taken her life in shame and abhorrence...'

Silence!

Sreedhar stood up and said in a faint voice, 'Is there any end to our sorrows? We will eventually talk things over. Now, why don't you bathe and eat lunch? Come, get up, Mukund...'

They finished bathing and sat down to eat. All of Sreedhar's sons were away working. The women of the household were quietly serving food, like automatons. They made small talk over the meal. Tarini had moved to Bardhaman. Mukund had

opened a big shop there. They were also thinking of expanding
their business to Calcutta. But, somehow, there was a hitch in
the flow of conversation. There seemed to be a kind of a wall.
The women of the house said nothing. They were breathless with
anticipation. What would happen? Oh God! What would happen?

'Sreedhar...' Tarini said suddenly.

'Yes?'

'You wrote in your letter that you had something important
to discuss. What is it?'

Sreedhar was caught off guard. But he controlled himself.
'These things never end...' he said. 'We will discuss the issue
after lunch.'

Lunch ended.

Sreedhar's eldest daughter-in-law offered paan and mouth
fresheners.

Sreedhar came outside the room and whispered to Dakshayani,
'Have you finished dressing Gouri up? Hurry...'

'Almost done,' Dakhayani replied in a dry voice. 'We will
not be late...'

'Dress her up well...'

The sight of her husband struck terror into Dakshayani. His
lean, aged body shook with agitation. His bloodshot eyes looked
discomposed. What was going to happen? What was in the girl's
fate! God, let no one be shamed thus! Dakshayani could not
stop the tears from streaming down her cheeks.

Silence. The whole house was steeped in silence, as if it was
waiting to hear a death sentence. Not even the kitchen utensils
clanged to break the eerie silence. Tarini Chakravarty would
announce god's judgment today. The social arbitrator of Nandapur
village would not have the last word. Instead, he would be judged
and, like a beggar, would have to accept whatever was doled out.

Tarini said, 'What is the important thing you want to say?
We must return by the evening train.'

'I will.' Sreedhar's voice shook with emotion. He added softly, 'But before that I will show you something...'

'What do you want to show us?' Tarini was curious.

'Something that will surprise you...' Sreedhar nodded his head. 'And gladden your heart.'

'Really? What could it be? Get it, then, and show it to us...'

Sreedhar left the room with a trembling heart. Dakshayani followed him. They halted in front of the last room which suddenly woke up to activity. The daughters-in-law covered their heads with the loose ends of their sarees and stood up. Gouri sat on the floor with her head bowed. They had finished dressing her up.

Sreedhar called out in a tremulous voice, 'Now, precious, think of God and come with me...'

Gouri got up slowly. She touched her mother's, father's and sisters-in-law's feet in obeisance. Everyone blessed her without uttering a word. Only Sreedhar remained standing stiffly.

He looked at everyone for a few moments with burning eyes, grabbed Gouri's hand, put his foot forward, and said sotto voce, 'Come, my fortune, let us battle with fate this once.'

They moved forward in silence. The mother and sisters-in-law followed behind, as if in a grief-stricken procession.

Gouri came to halt outside the room where Tarini and Mukund were waiting. Sreedhar gently tugged at his daughter's hand. Gouri did not hesitate anymore. She entered the room with trepid steps and stood holding her father's hand.

'Tarini...' Sreedhar Bhattacharya called out.

Both Tarini and Mukund turned towards him. Next to the learned debater stood a woman. She aroused the curiosity of the father-son duo as she stood there draped in a blood-red wedding sari, with her well-formed body and hands the colour of molten gold peeping out from under it.

Tarini asked, curious, 'Who is this girl?'

Desperate to buy time, Sreedhar said a stricken smile, 'Wait a while! Let her pay her respects to you first...'

Sreedhar noticed Gouri shivering. He squeezed her hand to assure her.

'Pay your respects to them.'

Gouri touched Tarini's feet in obeisance.

Mukund said nothing but grew agitated. The girl's step and movements seemed very familiar. Her face was covered by a long veil but he had been familiar with the glow of her body, that molten-gold skin for four years. Who was this girl?

Tarini asked in a jocular vein, 'What is the secret, Sreedhar? Who is this girl? Why are you not telling us?'

Sreedhar did not respond with words. He slowly unveiled the trembling girl. Gouri looked as beautiful as a goddess. Her doe eyes had two streams of crystal flowing from them.

The room could have been struck by a thunderbolt.

'Who!'

Mukund stood up ramrod straight, as if he had been hit by lightning.

'Who is this?' Tarini shrieked.

'We found Gouri.' Sreedhar smiled with strain. 'You had lost your daughter-in-law, Tarini. I found her for you. Welcome her and take her back home, to where she belongs…'

Tarini stared at him for a few seconds, then asked gruffly, 'When did you find her?'

'Some days ago…'

'You rescued her from the Muslims?'

'Yes…'

'What will you do with her now, O learned debater?'

Sreedhar started swaying. His pupils looked disoriented as he said, 'That is an answer you and Mukund will give, Tarini.'

Tarini's face distorted as he roared, 'Mukund is an obedient son. What will he say?'

'Then *you* must answer.'

Mukund felt a momentary shudder.

'There is no answer. There is nothing to say. You must bid us farewell now. Mukund, let's go...'

The women in the verandah started wailing.

'Is this your answer?' Sreedhar cried out.

'Yes.'

'But you just said that if you found her, you would take her home.'

'That was only to console you. If she were a devoted, sacrificing wife, a Sati Lakshmi, she would not have outlived that ordeal...'

'They did not even leave her the option of suicide, Tarini.'

'Can that ever happen?' Tarini added scornfully. 'She could have starved to death! Don't delay, Mukund. We must leave.'

Gouri slumped down on to the floor. Sreedhar was incandescent. He walked up and stood before Tarini, gritted his teeth like a madman, and said, 'Listen, Tarini. Think calmly. According to the scriptures...'

Tarini smiled crookedly. 'The scriptures say many a thing. You ought to know, learned debater, that the Hindu scriptures are many in number. There will be arguments in your favour and there will be those against you. Let us leave those out of this, professor. Scriptures cannot rule the world...'

Tarini took a step forward.

'You are leaving?' Sreedhar's question sounded more like a sob.

'Yes.'

Sreedhar now stood in front of Mukund.

Tarini almost roared, 'He will say nothing! Mukund, come out right now.'

Mukund cast a glance at the figure slumped on the floor, looked at his father-in-law, and ran out of the room. A few teardrops glistened in the eyes of the obedient son.

They left.

Their footsteps died down.

The house turned sepulchral, as if someone in it had died.

The women were weeping on the verandah. Gouri covered her mouth with her saree and wept copiously.

Sreedhar looked at his daughter. She was as beautiful as a goddess, and innocent, like a heavenly nymph. She was crying. Merely eighteen, she had a whole life before her.

Sreedhar's face hardened. His eyes grew wild. Tarini Chakravarty did not accept his daughter-in-law. The soul and the spirit were all lies, then! Only the body was real! Sreedhar started quaking. The Brahmin became a Kshatriya, a warrior, in spirit. He wanted to selectively kill people. If only, like Vishwamitra, the sage warrior, he could create a new world! Today he was forced to find new realities in scriptures, society, righteousness and sins. He rushed out of the room.

That girl he had unjustly ostracized in the village two years ago must have cursed him. That curse had found fulfillment that day. That day the verdict he had doled out as the chief of the panchayat had not spared him. His own weapon had taken no pity on him. But it did not matter. He would not accept defeat. Man, and man's heart, was greater than all scriptures, religions, rules. After all, scriptures and religion are created by men.

He would get Gouri married again.

His clogs sounded *khat-khat-khat* as he hurriedly climbed up to his room. He was back in a few minutes with many books and piles of papers in his hand. He threw them into a corner of the verandah and headed for the kitchen. He returned with a bottle of kerosene and a matchbox.

Dakshayani and his daughters-in-law were still weeping. Gouri was still slumped on the floor. It was like a funeral. No one took note of what Sreedhar was doing. They continued to sob.

Sreedhar poured kerosene on the heap of papers and books and lit a match. A flame leapt up. Sreedhar lowered the lighted matchstick on the books. They caught fire noiselessly. Smoke wafted through the air. There was a mild crackle.

Dakshayani looked up at the sound. She saw what her husband had done from behind a veil of tears. Shocked, she asked, 'What is that? What have you done?'

His eyes bloodshot, Sreedhar straightened his body to stand upright. A satisfied smile played on his lips as he muttered incoherently, 'Om Agni swaha! God of fire, accept my offerings...'

Translated by Mitali Chakravarty

The Path

Madhavrao froze in his tracks. Gunvanti had popped out of the nearby temple without warning, cradling a basketful of flowers. Sandalwood paste sat bright on her brow. Her pale yellow sari, draped tightly, set off her supple form. Her face shone warm in the amber dusk-light.

Madhav could barely breathe. As she neared him with her head lowered, an invisible hand thrummed his heartstrings all at once. For a moment he forgot that he was a teacher in Fatima Devi Primary School and a staid party-worker. He forgot that only a few months ago, he and Gunvanti were in the thick of a scandal in Chincholi. That Gunvanti had returned a month ago as a widow barely two months into her wedding. That the gossip mills, if allowed to buzz again, may damage them forever. Madhav stood arrested by his immediate present. The past and future were unreal trifles. He had not seen her for three months and, now, he was not about to let this opportunity slip away.

Gunvanti stumbled. When she looked up, she felt the blast of Madhav's hot gaze. A mix of bewilderment, shyness and sorrow clouded her face. She veered away. 'How are you, Gunvanti?' he murmured, inching closer.

She gently shook her head.

'I haven't seen you for so long,' Madhav said.

Gunvanti remained silent. She looked up fleetingly, her eyes forlorn.

'Are you okay?' he asked, instantly regretting the inane question.

'Oh I'm fine,' she said. 'I must go. Otherwise…'

An unspoken despair tied them together.

'Yes I know. You must…' he trailed off.

Gunvanti walked away. His eyes followed her receding figure far beyond mere sight. To him, even the gentle twilight took on a baleful cast.

Madhav lived in a house on the rim of Chincholi. His bedsitter occupied the back of a ramshackle structure with a tiled roof. It comprised a bedroom and a makeshift kitchen, for which he paid a rent of 10 rupees. The clerk Tipnis and his family occupied the three rooms in front. Excepting a rare encounter by the well or in some religious function, the neighbours hardly met. After paying the rent and providing for his mother in Pune, Madhav was left with a royal 55 rupees to deal with his monthly expenses. Leading a Spartan life in a world bursting with new luxuries called for some dedication. He had plenty of that.

What he lacked was focus, a noble cause, Madhav reflected. Back then, he had joined the Congress Party as a sixteen-year-old youth who had been swept away by the nationalist movement of the 1940s. He had felt a sense of purpose, an end to his idle wanderings. The conviction that a selfish life was akin to an animalistic existence had hammered home the need for patience.

Soon, India gained her independence in the roll call of history. But Madhav's circumstances did not alter much. He wanted to be more than a teacher. He dreamt of a job that befitted his graduate degree. But Fatima Devi School effectively locked down such dreams. Disillusioned by the native raj of corrupt

Gandhi-topiwallahs, Madhav sought succour in the nascent Leftist movement. So again, a cautious new dream was born, that of equitability.

West of his bedsitter were tall and graceful palm trees, mango trees growing wild, the tang of the backwaters. When the winds howled deep into the evening and the waters took on the hue of a spacy moon-blue, Madhav felt hollow inside, confined. Wracked by loneliness, he could barely sleep. His life seemed puny enough to fit into a page of a palm-sized ledger. It was all too well, serving the nation, following an ideal, but how so? The nation comprised individuals, he reasoned. So, serving the nation should lead to a feeling of personal enrichment. But where was this flat plane leading him?

Then, one evening, he spotted Gunvanti at a Ganesh Chaturthi feast in Tipnis's house. She was the daughter of Hirekar, a widower who worked in a cloth mill and was known for his hearty disposition and love of liquor.

Madhav's angst-driven insomnia melted away. That impactful evening had happened seven years ago. Madhav was twenty-five, with a large salary. Gunvanti was flowering into her teens. They started seeing each other. Conversations led to confidences. They swam in love. The west wind was daunting no more. And, on moonless nights, the stars twinkled just for him.

Numerous trysts and myriad little memories piled up. There was no place for despair in this bright boulevard. The students of Fatima Devi School were mesmerized by their teacher's sudden charisma, Chincholi's denizens discovered a selfless Samaritan.

Meanwhile, the drunken Hirekar got wind of this. He slyly stole up to Madhav one day. In a voice kept menacingly low, he said, 'Sir, I know why you visit my house so often.'

'I love Gunvanti,' Madhav declared.

'We're Brahmins,' Hirekar replied.

'Times have changed, Hirekarji,' he said weakly.

'Keep your high-sounding thoughts to yourself,' Hirekar cut in. 'Listen, I have fixed Gunvanti's marriage. The man is from Dadar. He owns a store in the market. He's rich. So get this straight: you are no longer welcome in my house!'

That was four months ago. The lovers met twice after this encounter. Terrorized, Gunvanti could only stare at Madhav mutely, always in a flood of tears. Madhav did not have the nerve to elope with her. No one in Chincholi, now churning with gossip, could help them. Instead, the twisted looks directed at him drove Madhav further into his shell. Yet again, emptiness filled his tiny ten-rupee room. Phantom life came back to haunt him. The road of exotic possibilities turned out to be ephemeral. It swiftly receded into the moon blue.

That night he bolted his door and clapped his ears shut. Yet the sounds of Gunvanti's wedding revelry leaked in, driving him mad. Madhav's room shook with the groans of a dumb animal in raw pain.

Gunvanti, now in the grasp of an ancient widower deep in Dadar, was lost to Madhav forever. The teacher at Fatima Devi School got tougher on his wards. One of them, emboldened by the movies he watched, scribbled 'Gunvanti' on the blackboard. Madhav saw it, he also saw the impish eyes. He quietly erased the blackboard and resumed his teaching. He felt weary beyond measure. He knew he could not easily erase Gunvanti from the blackboard of his heart.

But he had to get on. Somehow.

He dove back into political work. It felt mechanical, and soon became a grind. He became a shadow of himself, a silent and aloof presence among his friends. He clawed at his dark destiny and, not for the first time, cringed at the pettiness of his existence.

At this point, news filtered in that the grocer of Dadar had died of pneumonia, and her stepchildren had asked Gunvanti to leave. A combative Hirekar had gone to fight it out but had to retreat when his daughter threatened suicide.

Madhav flinched at the image of a widowed Gunvanti in his head, pitiful without her sindoor and mangalsutra. He could not help but weep. At the same time he felt a surge of relief, for which he immediately chided himself. He had to see Gunvanti. He found himself lingering before Hirekar's house on a number of occasions. He also met her various siblings, but there was little beyond small talk. Nor did any vision of the lady herself appear at one of the bay windows above him. Yet he felt an odd sense of peace. She was here in Chincholi. That was all that mattered. If he listened hard enough, he would perhaps hear the rustle of Gunvanti's breath in the evening breeze. He once again became the charming teacher of yore. He rediscovered his political energy. His life was full of promise once more.

She was there, near him. Her image chased him. He had to see her, even if just for a moment.

And now was that moment, in the waning hues of twilight.

Madhav's yearning for Gunvanti fed on itself like wildfire, threatening to consume him. And so it was that his pupils discovered that their teacher's mood had swung once again. He was always preoccupied, dazedly smiling even as they made a merry ruckus. Days flowed by. Then, one day, the face that floated waiflike everywhere, in the stars, the blue seas, in the clouds, was suddenly physically before him. In the vegetable market.

'You!' Madhav yelped.

Gunvanti laughed. 'Viren runs off as soon as he comes home from school, so I have to come to the market. What about you?'

'Well, don't I need my quota of greens?' Madhav smiled playfully.

'You do your own cooking?' she asked.

'Who else will do it for me? Alas, there's no one to save the poor schoolteacher from his lot.'

'Fine. You carry on. I have to go.' She started walking away.

'Gunvanti!' Madhav cried out.

'Yes?'

'Will you meet me by the backwaters tomorrow? I often go there in the evenings.'

'Why?'

'I need to talk to you. How can we talk here, amid vegetable vendors?'

'What is there to talk about, Madhavrao?'

'Maybe nothing earth-shattering. Just a few scraps of conversation. But there's no one else in the world with whom I can share my thoughts, Gunvanti!'

'I should be on my way…'

'What about tomorrow?'

'I don't know,' she said, hurrying away. Almost running away.

Chaos descended. The seas moaned as winds whipped the waves into a blue custard. The palm trees swayed, the coconut trees sighed, surely in empathy. Madhav looked on, piercing the dense darkness around him, lost in contemplation. His heart felt grazed by grief.

He blundered around in school, his maths at sixes and sevens. When the bell rang after tiffin break, he forgot to take a class and was roundly scolded by the headmaster. Then, bang in the middle of the last period, he spied a sliver of light! Gunvanti had not refused his request outright, it struck him. She had only said, 'I don't know.' What did that mean, he wondered, nerves jangling.

He did not waste much time after school, and bounded over to the spot he had fixed for the meeting. Gunvanti was not there. A few bystanders were curious about Madhav's intent. Pointless answers followed pointless questions. Madhav kept sitting, waiting.

Sundown cast its viscous shadows on the sea. The fishing boats in the distance were lost in an aimless haze. The gigantic western sun melted in large blood drops into the saline waters below. The seawater boiled like hot stew, hitting the banks with fury, spreading a million crystal smithereens on the rocks, washing them clean and retreating. But there was still no sign of Gunvanti.

And then she was there. The sound of dainty footsteps sent shockwaves that only he could feel. He looked back.

'Who's there?'

'I,' Gunvanti was barely audible.

'Gunvanti! You actually came!'

She sat down wordlessly.

'What did you tell them at home?'

'I lied to them,' she said.

'Why not the truth, Gunvanti?'

'The truth would have lost its meaning.'

'But the lie itself demeans the truth.' he said.

'It's easy for you to needle me with your big words. But what's the use of all that, Madhav?' she retorted. 'Tell me, aren't you happy to see me?'

'Please don't misunderstand me. I'm not myself. Forgive me,' Madhav added hastily.

Both were silent. Their silhouettes became amorphous in the dimming light.

'I can't see you, Gunvanti.'

'So what if you can't see me... I'm here,' she replied hoarsely.

'Gunvanti!'

'Yes?'

'Why did all this happen?'

'I don't know,' she answered.

'I have lost my way. You have to help me,' Madhav said.

'I just don't know,' she repeated like a robot.

'What will you do, Gunvanti?'

'I have not thought about it,' she said.

'But you have to...think about it.'

'What's the use?'

Madhav was exasperated. 'Do you know what you are saying?'

'I see no other way. I see no point in thinking about my future.' Her voice faded away.

Madhav leaned forward and said, 'Are you crying, Gunvanti?'

'Can't I even cry a bit?' she whimpered.

The fine spray of the waves covered them.

'It feels like my life is in shreds, Gunvanti…'

'Mine as well.'

'There is time… There's a way,' Madhav said.

'Way to?'

'It's up to you.'

'What do you mean?'

'You have to come back to me, Gunvanti.' Madhav finally let it drop.

Gunvanti stood up with a start and said, 'No!'

'But why?' Madhav pleaded. 'Don't you love me?'

She averted her face. 'I loved you.'

'And now?'

'Now I am a widow.'

Agitated, Madhav said, 'You were never married, Gunvanti!'

'Madhavrao!' she said, mortified.

But there was no stopping Madhav. 'Besides, widows are getting remarried these days…'

'How dare you insult me, Madhavrao!' Gunvanti snapped.

'What?'

'What else? Don't you know I'm a Hindu widow?'

'But according to our scriptures…' Madhav soldiered on.

'Don't try to meet me ever again,' Gunvanti said with a sense of finality.

'Gunvanti. Hear me out!'

'Stop hounding me, Madhav. Both your life and my reputation will be destroyed.'

'Gunvanti!' Madhav could only implore her.

'This is our last meeting.' Gunvanti vanished from the scene. Madhav tried to call out after her but his throat had thorns, his body was leaden.

He rose after what seemed like ages. The sea was a monolith of darkness. Thick nimbus clouds had switched off the stars. There were sudden flickers of light in the northeast, followed by distant booms of sound.

Madhavrao started walking away, hating himself. What had come over him, how could he insult Gunvanti? True, Hindu widows believe that life goes on beyond the flesh. But, he reasoned with himself, how was he at fault? It was not like he had fallen in love with the Gunvanti of today, nor was it a one-sided affair. Was it possible that the greed of an alcoholic father and the lust of a senile shopkeeper could kill this love? Besides, the old grocer had died just two months into the marriage. Surely those two months did not leave her with memories to last a lifetime? Madhav's crazed inner soliloquy carried ceaselessly on.

What was the road ahead of him? What was his road to redemption?

That distant booming was getting louder. Madhav strained his ears. It was coming from the direction of the market. It was a loudspeaker. There was a big crowd there. The renowned leader, Kale, was delivering a speech from the verandah of a nearby building. Behind him was a banner with 'Goa Liberation Cooperative Society' emblazoned on it. Madhav listened to him, fascinated.

He spent a sleepless night. He realized all over again that meaningful work could be his only redemption. Personal failures were but a microcosm of the incompleteness of society. So he would work towards building society, a task he had been neglecting. Besides, was his country actually free? Goa, Daman and Diu were yet to be liberated. Nothing good could come out of shirking work, he sternly reminded himself.

The late-night shower cooled his mind somewhat. From now onwards, the unhappy life of the humble teacher of Fatima Devi School would be dedicated to the collective, he decided. Nurturing those budding Madhavraos would be his mission.

Madhavrao felt the tingle of a new excitement. He looked at the faces of the little Shielas, Sushilas, Vikrams and Ajits with fresh eyes. He saw the clutter in their heads, a bewilderment at the crossroads of history. He saw outgrowths of the rot in society in their pliable minds. This insight alarmed him.

He worked feverishly, attending to party matters after school, returning home very late. Goa was the hotbed of action; Bombay, India's political epicentre. Neither rain nor the western wind could snuff out the fire in the air. Madhavrao felt rejuvenated in this climate of unease.

That night, Madhav was walking down a narrow alley on his way home. A man lurched out of one the apartments in front of him. The apartment belonged to a prostituted woman, Shanta. The man stumbled. Madhav rushed to help him. It was Hirekar, his breath reeking of local brew.

'Madhav!' Hirekar hissed out, his antenna sharp.

Madhav strode ahead. But Hirekar bellowed, 'You made my daughter a widow. You still can't leave us alone, eh?'

Madhav stopped. 'You don't know what you are saying...'

Hirekar flapped his arms, trying to balance his body. 'Yes, you murdered my son-in-law with your black magic.'

'Beware, Mr Hirekar!'

'Don't you beware me! If I see you anywhere near my house...'

Madhav did not wait to hear the rest. He rushed home.

Hirekar's depravity shocked him. He felt small thinking about Gunvanti in that house. But why should he feel like this? He had nothing to do with the widow. His lover was the maiden Gunvanti. Why should he agonize over the circumstances of some senile grocer's widow? Rather, he should occupy himself with someone dewy-fresh and exotic, he thought bitterly.

The very person whom he was determined to banish from his brain appeared at his threshold the following morning. Rice pot brewing in his kitchenette, Madhav was deep into the local daily, *Jansatta*. A noise at the door made him look up. And there was Gunvanti, propped against the frame.

'What brings you here?'

She pulled out a rattan stool. 'Well, here I am,' she announced.

Madhav went back to his newspaper. 'But why, pray?'

'I felt like it.'

'What will people say?' He could not help taking a dig.

'Who cares?' she said, looking outside.

Madhav, with an eye on his brewing pot, replied, 'I do care. Last night, your tipsy father warned me to keep out of your neighbourhood.'

'But you never even went there!'

'The fact that you are here, in my private quarters…that should rattle him,' Madhav said.

'My father's up to no good…it's gone beyond the bottle,' Gunvanti said.

Madhav nodded. 'I know.'

All of a sudden, they lost the thread of the conversation. Gunvanti concentrated on the pastoral scene outside: a squirrel was scrambling up the mango tree, a twisty crow cawed and flew away. Madhav busied himself with his rice pot. After the initial airiness, both had become hyper aware of the other's presence. Gunvanti felt cripplingly shy. Madhav was back in his familiar state of ferment.

She tried to make light of it. 'So what are you up to these days, Madhavrao?' she asked archly.

'Well, I teach.'

'And?'

'I'm also into politics…'

'We are a free nation now. So where's the need for politics?'

'Not really. First, the freedom has to be delivered door to

door, and then it has to be nurtured,' he explained.

'What are you doing for yourself, Madhavrao?'

'Well, nothing much for myself. My work shows me the way now,' Madhav said.

Gunvanti sighed softly. 'You have found your path. But I...'

Madhav's pulse quickened. He was struck by a perverse need to hurt Gunvanti. 'Why, you will slave away in your drunken dad's parlour of course,' he spat out.

Gunvanti recoiled.

Madhav was unmoved. 'You came here on your own...after giving me a preachy earful that day. You should be scared!'

'Scared? Why?' she asked softly.

Madhav looked squarely into her eyes. 'What if I suddenly start talking about love?'

'I will leave,' Gunvanti said, brow instantly furrowed.

'What if I stop you physically?'

'That you won't do, Madhav. I know you can never do anything that's wrong.' She smiled desolately.

'Why not? I am quite up to doing wrong things these days!' Madhav said, his voice edgy. 'Besides, your wrong might not be my wrong...'

'I'm off,' Gunvanti headed for the door.

'Wait.'

She stood, just beyond the threshold.

'Well?'

Madhav's eyes flashed. In a measured tone, he said, 'You must never visit me ever again, Gunvanti.'

She managed a mirthless laugh and was gone.

Madhav sat heavily on his bed. How can Gunvanti be so cool, he kept wondering.

The smell of burnt rice filled the room.

These were tiny colonial outposts, a convenient ghetto for pirates, a stronghold of faceless powers. Tax-free liquor, both imported and local, flowed. Sexual licence was rife. Most Goans, used to their easy life, did not want liberation. They preferred to wallow as well-maintained pets rather than face the reality of a free life. But the rest of India could not afford to look away. Satyagraha marches were closing in on Goa.

Sensing the imminent loss of power, the Portuguese police had mercilessly beaten up some Satyagrahis in Banda. It was the same story on the Diu border, in Daman, Vaptey, Castlerock, Patelwadi and in Paliwat, just beyond the Terekhol backwaters. Madhavrao pored over his newspaper, hungry for more details.

Meanwhile, he had trained his students well. They were ready to lay down their little lives for the country.

That day, feeling a bit under the weather, he was home earlier than usual. It started pouring as he sat down with a mug of coffee.

Gunvanti swept in.

'You!' Madhav said, his muscles taut.

Gunvanti laughed. 'Yes. It's brazen old me again.' She sat down. 'Can I have some coffee?'

'Of course.'

Madhav handed her a mug, much to her amusement.

'What's so funny?'

'Oh I'm loving this. Only a full-time cook can appreciate this, the joy of being served for a change,' she laughed.

Madhav hung on to his gravitas and his coffee.

Gunvanti piped up again, 'Can I tell you something?'

'What is it?'

'It's high time you got married.'

Madhav flung his coffee mug at the wall opposite him. She seemed to wilt. Gunvanti finally dared to look up. Madhav's eyes would have stripped her face, foraged her heart, if they could. Her trembling lips could not form any words. The dull, faraway sound of water falling from a height seemed to captivate her.

Madhav was on his feet. She too stood up, slowly. They

stood facing each other, close enough to hear the urgency of their breaths. The sound of the rain was a diaphanous curtain between the lovers. The spell broke suddenly as Madhav sat down with a thud, covering his face, stifled with shame. When he looked up, Gunvanti was gone.

After this encounter, Madhav started returning home very late, preferring to eat outside. His routine comprised leaving at the crack of dawn and diving into his school and party work. He was afraid of himself, of what he had seen when the veils slid off. He would make every possible arrangement to avoid meeting Gunvanti. He also knew that his resolve was a feeble candle in her wind. The two weeks that followed went by with Madhav steeling himself. It left him feeling weak, but no less dogged.

It was almost 11 at night when he returned home that Saturday. He was carrying a garland. Chincholi was in deep slumber. As he switched on the light, someone called out from near the door, 'You are so late.'

Madhav spun around. 'Gunvanti!'

She shut the door behind her.

Madhav was aghast. 'Why are you here so late?'

'Actually I came early in the evening... You're the one who is late.'

'Where were you all this time?'

'By the backwaters.'

'But what will your family say...?'

'I have left my family.' Gunvanti shut him up.

'What do you mean?'

"I will never go back there.'

'Why?'

'Shanta is now the mistress of my home.'

'Shanta?'

'Yes.'

'Where will you go now?'

'I decided to come to you,' Gunvanti responded firmly.

He could not believe this was happening to him. He could not stop devouring Gunvanti with his eyes. 'To me?' he gasped.

'Please let me stay in your home. I have travelled far beyond common conventions.'

'But...'

'I am a woman. I cannot dump customs and conventions in a day like you. Madhav, the sindoor was a curse for me the first time. Only you can make it a symbol of hope,' she said, her voice clear.

Madhav leaned back against the wall for support. His eyes filled with tears.

'You are crying...' she said.

'If only you had come two days ago, Gunvanti!'

'Why?'

'I have enlisted as a Satyagrahi,' Madhav said through his veil of tears. 'I will be travelling to Belgaon day after tomorrow. The next day, that's August 15, I will be crossing the Goa border. Look at this garland. My countrymen gave it to me as a mark of respect.'

Gunvanti paused, absorbing the bombshell. 'Why did you do this, Madhav?'

'My life had become a burden for me, Gunvanti...'

Gunvanti smiled. 'That's fine. I will not stop you.'

'What if I don't come back? They can open fire upon us.'

'No! How can they shoot at unarmed Satyagrahis?'

'They shot down two just a few days ago.'

'No. They can't! They dare not. Madhavrao, don't humiliate me anymore. Let me live...as your wife.'

'I'm leaving very early day after tomorrow, Gunvanti.'

'In that case, we're getting married tomorrow.'

'And today?'

'Today's the eve of our union.'

'What about your father?'

'He won't come, I assure you.'

'What if he does?'

'He won't. Shanta is no novice.'

'But, you won't be happy here…with my tiny salary.'

'I will also earn, Madhav. Don't worry.'

Madhav tenderly placed the garland around Gunvanti's neck. 'Welcome to my life…' he murmured. Frogs added a few original notes to the pitter-patter of rain, as if in celebration. The distant horn of the night train could pass off as the blowing of conch shells. The lovers sat looking deep into each other, like mutual acolytes. The enormity of the following day was slowly sinking in.

They did not wait for the sun to rise. They did not want to risk Hirekar's meanness. It had stopped raining. Chincholi was at peace, bathed in the light of a new beginning. The couple walked on, holding hands.

They boarded a train to Bombay and spent the day strolling around Marine Drive and the Gateway of India. Madhav bought Gunvanti a sari, a mangalsutra and some sindoor, gilded bangles and a hair extension laced with golden thread. Thus equipped, they headed for the Arya Sabha. Then onto the wedding proper, which was over by evening.

They found themselves in the darkness by the sea at Juhu. They sat on the beach, fingers entwined, as if the waves were in their grasp. It started raining. They scampered into a nearby restaurant. After dinner, they walked aimlessly, wrapped in each other. They strolled, spoke utter nonsense; mirth bubbled over for no apparent reason. They stopped under random lampposts on a whim and exchanged lingering looks.

They returned to Chincholi at around 1 a.m., taking a longer route to dodge the inevitable stares. At home, Gunvanti turned dead serious. 'When is your train tomorrow?'

'At 8 a.m.'

She collapsed in a heap on the bed, 'Can't you go a few days later...'

Taken aback, Madhav cried out, 'Come on, Gunvanti!'

Gunvanti could not stop weeping. The common ten-rupee tenement thrilled to the sound of a woman's wails; the magic of the night went up by a few degrees. But Madhav stood in a corner, gritting his teeth.

Gunvanti's sobbing stopped after a while. She dried her tears. 'Forgive me, I do not deserve you. I'm too greedy.'

Madhav sat quietly beside his bride, cupping her face. Gunvanti sprang on him like a small fierce animal. They held each other. The rest was ether. The walls, the stars, the coconut palms evaporated, they were silenced. The sea was finally at peace as a flame glowed softly within them.

The following day, Madhav boarded the train at Victoria Terminus, at 8 o'clock, as scheduled. There were about a hundred Satyagrahis gathered. The members of the Goa Liberation Cooperative Society were in a festive mood, shouting slogans.

Madhav turned to his wife. 'Please, no tears.'

'Don't be upset by my tears,' said Gunvanti. 'I'm crying so that I can feel lighter.' She wiped her face roughly. 'You will come back,' she declared.

'I will. But I wonder what you'll do when I'm not around.'

'Don't worry. My father can't touch me even if he arrives with the police.'

The train whooshed off. Gunvanti's tears washed away the hulking locomotive. The chants rang out extra loud: 'Chalo chalo, Goa chalo!'

It was a hilly route. Madhav's pulse raced in tune with the train. The way everything came together in his life was nothing short of astonishing, he thought.

There were a dozen Satyagrahis in Madhav's compartment. They were from Bengal, Madhya Pradesh and Bombay. Almost three hundred more boarded at Poona. Everyone seemed so familiar with each other, bound by a common cause.

Evening fell. He started chatting with his fellow travellers. They were all from poor or middle-class backgrounds. This journey seemed to be their ultimate moment of validation.

They started discussing the state of affairs in Goa. Both the government and the nation wanted Goa back. But the government was constrained by the hairpin bends of budding diplomatic relations. So it was not officially backing the Satyagraha movement. This gave the Portuguese police a free hand in crushing the rebels, which included use of firepower.

The stations whizzed by: Satara Road, Bhargaon, Bhavani Nagar, Miraj Junction, Pacchapur. They disembarked at Londa junction at around 11 p.m. It was 1.30 a.m. when they reached Castle Rock by bus. There were a few rudimentary huts and tents in an area lit by Petromax lamps. A humble meal was served. Two thousand Satyagrahis had already landed. Madhav's group was 400 strong. They would start their journey at 6.30 the next morning. The date, August 15.

There was something ominous in the air. Goa unfurled like a map of tiny far away fairy lights. The Portuguese were ready, as were the Satyagrahis. Madhav sat by a Petromax lamp. He was caught up in the swell of the previous night's memories. Impulsively, he sat down to write a letter.

My Gunvanti,
I have reached the border safely. I can't stop thinking about you. I do know this will make you even sadder. But I can't help it. Now, as I write this letter, I see your face in this first light of day.

What if we don't meet again? My dear, it's impossible to grasp the gravity of the situation from afar. It is a war out here. Whether weapons are used or not, a war is always a war, a challenge to life. I can hear that loud and clear as I sit here. Gunvanti, please don't be sad if I die. You are with me now, so my road ahead seems smooth. My dear, if your husband followed you around like some lowly animal, it would have debased our love. Of course, I hope to return, but even if I don't, you must not be sad. If I die for my country, the red on your forehead will gleam like the sun.

I will try my best to come back to you, my Gunvanti. Stay safe.

Yours,

Madhav

He wrote 'Mrs Gunvanti Deogirikar' on the envelope before sealing it and tucking it into his pocket. A cool breeze lulled him to sleep. He dreamt that Gunvanti was fanning him as he lay on her lap.

He woke up with a start to the sound of the bugle. It was time to get battle ready! To stand in a queue. The roll calls and instructions from the leader. Madhav was handed a flag. He added his voice to the chorus: 'Goa-Bharat ek hain!'

The letter! It had not been posted, he suddenly remembered.

Someone yelled, 'Salazar, quit Goa!'

Another called out: 'Brothers, on this landmark day, August 15, let us hoist the flag of Mother India on land tainted by the brigands of Vasco da Gama!' The air reverberated with cries of 'Chalo chalo, Goa chalo!'

Who is India? Whose mother is she? Gunvanti's? Of the Shielas and Ajits of Fatima Devi School?

Madhav started marching southwest with a band of fifty.

'Are you ready to go, brothers?' boomed the commander.

'Ready-y—' rose the chorus.

'Forward march!' came the order.

Just behind Commander Ananta Maratha marched Madhav,

the flag-bearer. They marched in rows of three. Someone sang 'Vande Mataram'. The birds joined in with their twitter from the trees. The flags swayed in the morning breeze. Ten minutes later they were on the edge of Goa. The commander hollered: 'Portuguese—!'

'Quit Goa!' the band chorused.

They crossed the border and planted the tricolour on Portuguese soil.

The Satyagrahis proceeded along a narrow, damp path which parted a nondescript field. Suddenly, about ten armed Portuguese soldiers materialized, rifles primed.

'Bharat mata ki jai!' the Satyagrahis shouted.

'Halt!' the soldiers yelled. A minute later they started firing.

Madhavrao was struck on his left ribs by a Portuguese bullet. He crumpled on the tapering path. He felt blood soaking his chest through a haze of pain. His colleagues behind him were charging ahead. He felt his life gushing out of his wound like water from a burst dam. The scenery melted into blackness and morphed into the blackboard of Fatima Devi School. He had not posted his letter to Gunvanti, not in this life.

Gunvanti never received that letter. She read about her husband in the newspaper. Chincholi was electrified with anguish, excitement. The air was ringing with vows of revenge.

Gunvanti sat down, stone-like. Suddenly she stood up. She adorned her forehead with sindoor and braced herself, chanting mantra-like, 'No, I will not be a widow again.'

Her blood came alive, as if a seed had just germinated inside her. It gave her a heady feeling, opened up a luminous road in front of her.

'I have found my path,' Gunvanti told herself.

Translated by Soma Bhattacharya

Possessed

I can't ever forget her.

Society, tradition, customs, rules, bindings, laws—I don't care for any of these. And that is all the more reason why I cannot forget her. Her image haunts me like a ghost, no matter what I am busy doing or not doing. Her memory refuses to die down in my heart like the embers of a fire that has burnt out. She did not love me but I loved her. 'What nonsense is this,' you might be saying to yourself. Believe me, I am only speaking the truth. Almost impossible to believe, most unreal, but true.

Listen to me.

About three years earlier.

One evening in May I was searching for Shekhar's flat in Dadar. Shekhar is my childhood friend. We were separated in Dumka seven years ago when he went away to Calcutta to do his Masters in Art. We corresponded for two or three years and, then, you know how things go…time and distance blur even the strongest love, and pain, and friendship. I had almost forgotten him. I did once hear somewhere that Shekhar was working with a leading advertising firm, but I could not make time to seek him out. As a medical representative of a renowned pharmaceutical company, I was also traveling all over the country. I had tired of my gypsy existence when I finally got a permanent posting in the head office in Bombay; and then a common friend wrote to inform me that Shekhar was living in the same city with his family.

I was having great difficulty in locating his house. These old buildings of the country's financial capital don't care for numbers. Instead, they're identified by their names. Shekhar's building was impressively called 'Amrit Bhavan' and I still could not easily locate it. I might have gone back, but I did not because by then I was determined to seek out the address and the inmates of 'Amrit Bhavan'. Finally, when I did stand before the building, I felt as if I had arrived in seventh heaven.

Shekhar's apartment.

I took out all my frustration on the doorknob. The door opened at once. A lady who looked to be twenty-ish stood on the other side. A slice of light had escaped the room to fall on the threshold. It looked as if a divine light was emanating from the girl. Her features were not perfect, so I can't say she was ravishing. Still, I was charmed by the slight, dusky lady with a mysterious look in her deep, dark eyes.

'Who do you want?'

The minute I mentioned Shekhar she asked, 'Who are you?'

'I am Binoy Dutt, a childhood friend of Shekhar.'

'I know. Come in.'

The corridor led us to a mid-sized room. She ushered me in and pointed out, 'There's Jamai Babu.'

Piles of books and documents, and in their midst sat Shekhar. He lifted his head on hearing the girl introduce him. For a while a bewildered look played on his face as he gazed at me, much like a poet trying to fathom the world. Then he stood up sharply, rushed across the room screaming 'Binoo!', and hugged me.

The unnatural pitch of his voice attracted a married woman

from the next room. She was pretty, poised, and had a pleasing personality.

'Mallika!' Shekhar animatedly addressed her. 'Here's Binoo, our Binoy!"

'Namaskar!' Mallika lifted her hands to welcome me.

She was Shekhar's wife, I understood.

Shekhar wouldn't let go of my hands. 'You must spend the night with us; we will chat away until morning, okay?'

'Okay,' I instantly agreed.

'Wait, I must introduce you to my Soi.'

'Soi? Who's this lady friend?'

'The one who showed you in! Chinmayi alias Chinu aka Saali. She vehemently objects to that last word, because of which I've settled for Soi...'

The lady glanced at Shekhar, then turned towards me and smiled. 'You've saved me by visiting us, Binoy-babu!'

'Saved you? Why do you say so?'

'I won't have to hear about you all the time now. Goodness me! If he happens to be at home, he'll go on and on: Binoo would say so; Binoo would have done this; Binoo once fought with a friend; Binoo once acted in this role; Binoo is stubborn, sensitive, caring... Binoo Binoo Binoo. I had begun to doubt what Binoo's full name was: Binoy or Binodini!'

Both Shekhar and I started to laugh.

'Stop, Chinu!' Mallika chided her.

'Forgive me Binoy-babu, I have a reputation for being garrulous.'

'That's nothing but the truth,' Shekhar reiterated. 'Oh Lady of Truth, if thou wishes to expiate for thy Sin of Garrulity, get busy in the kitchen for the express delivery of chai and samosas for Binoo.'

'Thy wish is our Command, O Worshipper of Truth! Come Didi, we're no longer needed here.'

The sisters went away laughing.

And we got busy chatting. It seemed as if the lively days of Dumka had been blown into the mechanical life of Bombay by a gust of nostalgia. Within seconds, Shekhar forgot all about the papers which were piled up to plan ad campaigns. I forgot all about my Punjabi Dhaba and started rummaging in the dustbin of memories to come up with forgotten incidents, sad or small. The snacks arrived, the tea too. Mallika and Chinmayee came in and sat close to us. Streams of irrelevant and inconsequential words started to crisscross the room.

Shekhar asked me in the middle of a sentence, 'Have you married?'

'No.' I shook my head. 'I'm waiting for a desirable bride.'

'What rubbish is this?'

'You know that my taste is somewhat unorthodox. Pardon me, Boudi, the exterior is not the key factor for me. I am yet to come across a woman who touches my soul.'

Chinu laughed out loud.

'You find my words funny?'

'I do,' Chinu replied. 'Pardon my garrulity, Binoy-babu, I could not arrest my laughter since you sound like a dejected poet.'

'Aey Chinu!' Mallika chided her sister.

I was piqued by Chinu's sharp words. I looked anew at her. 'Keep an eye on this Goddess of Garrulity,' said a part of me. 'Your quest for Ms Right might just end in those deep, dark eyes.'

'Amen,' I said to my heart.

But at that point it was urgent to steer the conversation in another direction. So I asked Shekhar, 'When did you marry? And where is Boudi from?'

'Calcutta.'

'Originally from Dhaka,' Chinu chipped in. 'Calcutta after Partition.'

'She is the daughter of a Brahmin, you know.'

'Oh!'

'Beware, Chinu,' Mallika piped in, 'these non-Brahmins will now derive mean pleasure by hunting down the once glorious Brahmins!'

'Shame on these non-Brahmins!' Chinu got up. 'Come Didi, let's go to the kitchen to cook up some poison for these conceited upstarts.'

'Let's do that.'

Once they were out of the room, Shekhar recounted the story of his marriage with Mallika.

Her father was a friend of Shekhar's father. When Shekhar left for his MA in Calcutta, he wanted to earn his own upkeep in order to spare his father any further burden beyond providing for his large family. He managed to secure a tuition. When Mallika's father came to know of this, he vested Shekhar with the responsibility of teaching his motherless daughters. Mallika, then seventeen, was completing her IA; Chinmayee, thirteen, was already in Class VIII. The studies went smoothly. To his father's friend, Shekhar was not merely a private tutor, he was more like a family member. Going by the social order, Shekhar and Mallika were guru-shishyaa, but the two broke the sanctity of that relationship and fell in love. Shekhar had deciphered the involved hieroglyphics of a young woman's heart even as he was decoding the intricacies of the arts. And his student, Mallika, came to the conclusion that Shekhar was Mr Perfect for whom she could risk the rejection of her family and friends, social sanctions and caste demarcations.

But they revealed this mutual affection when Shekhar had completed his MA and was looking for a job, and Mallika had completed her IA. Meanwhile, their love was already announcing itself to the world. Love, they say, is like murder: it can't be hidden from the world no matter how hard you try. Thus, Shekhar's life as a teacher and Mallika's as a student came to an abrupt halt.

Shekhar asked for Mallika's hand in marriage. Her angry father cabled his friend to 'Come Sharp'. Shekhar's father came down, he heard everything and felt betrayed by his son. He admonished Shekhar and forbade him to step into Mallika's house.

But neither Shekhar nor Mallika were to be cowed down by any restriction. They went on meeting secretly, and in this, Chinu was their ally. By now she had reached the fulsome age of seventeen. On the other hand, preparations to marry off Mallika—now a full-grown twenty-one—were going on in full swing. Nothing to worry about, Mallika assured Shekhar, since there was no dearth of kerosene or of rat poison in Bengal. Shekhar became desperate to land a job and succeeded in securing one with the Ajanta Ad Agency in Bombay.

Mallika left home as soon as he got his appointment letter. With their respective friends as witnesses, they got married in a private ceremony conducted by a Brahmin priest and, a day later, the newlyweds left for Bombay. The following morning, Mallika's father received a letter from his runaway daughter. She'd written that she had come of age, and had married the person of her choice, of her own free will. So, instead of filing any police case against Shekhar, she desired that he bless them both. Needless to say, that stopped her father from visiting the thana, but the blessings did not come as he could not forget the assault on his 'dignity' and forgive the 'errants'.

It wasn't a cakewalk for Shekhar to establish himself in his profession. But Mallika was not disheartened in the least. With a smile on her lips, she shared every worry, every concern of her husband. When love is your inspiration, nothing is impossible. Naturally, they won. They found a good apartment to live in, there was a rise in his career and their social standing. Regular money orders eased his father's sense of hurt.

But Mallika's father? There was not an iota of softening on his part. He nurtured his anger, his sense of betrayal, his sense of insult, and his ageing body did not take kindly to it all. He fell ill in no time and breathed his last within three years. That was the first time since their marriage that Shekhar visited his in-laws with Mallika. His father-in-law had left no savings, and his younger brother, who now headed the flock, was neither welcoming nor blunt. Once the rituals were over, and it was time for them to return to Bombay, Chinu said in no uncertain terms that she would not stay behind and Mallika would have to take her along with them.

So true! Nobody had given a thought to Chinu or how she would survive in her uncle's household. In the absence of any assurance from her Kaka, Mallika thought it prudent to bring Chinu along. Since then, she had been a part of their household. She gave up studies midway, at the IA level. They were now keen to marry her off to a suitable boy.

'You are still a bachelor,' Shekhar whispered to me. 'Why don't you try to see if she touches your heart?'

I smiled. 'I pray to you, Shekhar, don't let these words fall on their ears! It might block my path to your house. I have traced one childhood friend in this heartless city with a lot of effort. I'm not overly keen to reassign him as a co-brother just yet!'

'All right, all right. I won't utter these words again.' Shekhar smiled.

He stuck to his words; not once did he repeat the request to me.

But no matter where the seed blows in from, if it finds fertile soil, it will grow into a tree. Those words germinated within me, and gave birth to the sapling of attraction and the plant of love. That is why every subsequent evening found me bridging the distance between Jogeshwari and Dadar. I was trying to unravel the enigma that is the heart of a loquacious, witty, sharp-tongued, sweet-faced young lady. I can't say I was particularly successful. Chinu would smile at me, engage in banter, but I could see no tidings of love. 'It won't be easy to win Ladylove over,' I thought to myself. You may blast your way into a rocky fortress but how do you drill through flesh and blood? So I advised my heart, 'Don't be impatient.'

Whether or not I could plumb the depths of Chinu's heart, I did not stop going to Dadar. Besides, there were other attractions in that house: Shekhar's friendship and Mallika's filial affection. Every visit to the family suffused me with contentment.

Days rolled by. I got accustomed to Bombay with its Arabian Sea, Juhu Beach, Malabar Hills, Elephanta Caves et al. I got acclimatized to its severe sun and I learnt to wade through its relentless rains. Shekhar's wife was with child. And through all this, I realized, Chinu had come to hold my heart with an invisible harness.

When I finally decided to confide this to Shekhar, I arrived at their apartment and was jolted by a sudden shock. I had not visited them for just one day—the previous day—and that was when Chinu had gone back to Calcutta.

'Suddenly?' I was curious. 'When will she be back?'

Shekhar did not speak.

Mallika said quickly. 'She will be back. She was here for a long time; Kaka had also written asking her to go back. She's of a marriageable age, we can't just wait for a groom to arrive at our doorstep, right?'

'Is there someone in mind?'

'Yes.'

I kept silent. The words died at the tip of my tongue. I was not as young as I used to be; the fear of rejection, of my dignity being hurt, forced me to cloak myself in nonchalance. Life might drain out of me before I freely expressed myself, so my heart's desire with regard to Chinu stayed bottled up inside me. 'Later,' I said to myself. Patience and forbearance, I consider these to be two pillars of my persona. The pride in these two qualities helped me hold my peace.

But I noticed a difference in Mallika after Chinu's departure. She wasn't quite herself. She'd gaze at her husband with such intensity as though Shekhar would melt into air if she so much as turned her eyes away from him. She would sit right beside him, as if someone would step in between them. If I asked for a glass of water, or tea, I'd get it—but by the servant's hand. Mallika wouldn't budge from Shekhar's side, not for a moment. Shekhar could interpret the mute query in my eyes but wasn't annoyed by it. On the contrary, whenever he would turn his eyes towards his wife, they would overflow with pure love.

I couldn't make head or tail of it. Did pregnant women become so possessive about their husbands? Or perhaps Mallika's love for her husband was such. How else could she leave her family, friends and city overnight to make a home with Shekhar?

I would bring Chinu up in our conversations now and then. What news of her? Had they found a match for her? Should I join their quest for Mr Right? Shekhar would only laugh and Mallika would come up with a cursory reply. It was as if she wanted to hastily move away from the topic. In fact, her replies were so vague that they gave rise to plenty more questions in my mind.

My Dadar visits grew less frequent. I discovered that Shekhar's friendship and Mallika's affection were not my main attraction. Even when I dropped by, it wasn't so much for them as for some news of Chinu, about her return.

Eventually even those rare visits diminished. I joined an amateur theatre group in Parel and became busy rehearsing to play Dildar in the Bengali classic, *Shahjahan*. Two months were nothing to prepare for a stage show. Shekhar was a busy professional; even at home he remained immersed neck-deep in paper. Naturally, he had no time to seek me out. 'All for the good,' I thought to myself. This would help erase the memories and my longing for Chinu. 'Too much trouble!' I tried to convince myself.

'The day the animal inside my body awakes, I'll go shopping for flesh!'

But Shekhar sought me out one August evening when a downpour threatened to wipe out the sky. The vacant look in his eyes was scary. He'd withered down to skin and bone. His uncared-for hair was sparkling with crystal raindrops. His restless eyes had a wild look in them.

He flopped into a chair and said, 'Can you get me tea, Binoo?'

I sent the servant out to get tea and asked him, 'What's wrong with you, Shekhar?'

His eyes filled up with tears as he said, 'Mallika is gone, Binoo!'

'Where? What happened? Did you have a fight?'

'She died at childbirth.' Shekhar covered his face with his hands.

I could not think of a single word that could console Shekhar. He shuddered as he tried to stop the tears. The downpour outside seemed to keep pace with them. The music from the radio playing in the restaurant not far off seemed to heighten the sadness in the air.

I did not know what to make of this. I was speechless at the thought of how I had neglected Shekhar over the last two months. How could I wrong him so! To avoid my friend in his hour of need!

When Shekhar got a grip over his pent-up sorrow, he brought me up to date on all that had transpired. Mallika had been gone for about a month now. The child—Mallika's final gift—was alive. A son. He had taken after his mother. A nurse looked after him for a few days. Then Chinu got the news, and returned.

Chinu! I felt a sudden upheaval in my heartbeat. I was not sorry about my happiness even sitting in front of a mourning friend. I said, 'I have failed you. I should have visited you many days ago but why didn't *you* send for me?'

'What was the hurry, Binoo?' Shekhar replied. 'Do you mean to say you'd have shared my grief? That, no one can.'

I kept quiet. How could I deny the truth of his statement? 'Do you know why I'm here today?' Shekhar continued. 'I am facing a problem.'

'What's it?'

'Mallika comes to me every day.'

'Comes!' I was startled. 'What do you mean?'

'It's been happening for the past few days. She comes to possess Chinu. Chinu passes out; then, when she comes around, she is a different person. She's almost Mallika.'

'Impossible!' I reacted rudely.

'It'd have been better had this been impossible.' Shekhar shook his head.

'How many times a day does this happen?'

'Twice today. So far, once a day...'

'What does Chinu say when she's possessed?'

Shekhar said, 'Chinu doesn't speak then, Mallika does. She says that she has come for the child. She hasn't experienced life as both wife and mother. She also tells me, "Besides, I don't want you to fall sick worrying over me. You must eat proper meals, go to bed at regular hours, care for yourself. I'm still yours. I'll linger around."'

'Hard to believe?' Shekhar must have seen skepticism in my eyes. 'All right, you take leave from work and be with me tomorrow.'

I agreed.

I went to bed after Shekhar left but could not catch a wink of sleep. I was raging against the spirit of Mallika. I did not doubt her deep love for her husband, but why torment Chinu over it? Mallika's death, Chinu's return, her being possessed; all of this had overtaken me with such suddenness and in such rapid succession that they seemed unnatural. It was surreal. I lay tossing and turning, simply unable to sleep.

The following day I went over to Shekhar's.

Once again, Chinu opened the door. She'd lost weight. She smiled wanly.

'How are you, Chinu?'

I felt sheepish the minute I uttered those words. But Chinu spared me further embarrassment. 'Come in,' is all she said.

As I walked in, I said, 'I have scores of issues to settle with you, Chinu.'

'Why?'

'You did not even bid me goodbye when you left!'

'So what? Here we meet again. You go over to that room. I'll get you tea.'

I went to Shekhar's room. The morning passed, the afternoon was upon us. I had lunch with them. But…Chinu looked quite normal! Shekhar asked me to stay on until late night. I was willing. The evening set in. As it wore on, the weather turned stormy. Lightning struck repeatedly. The roll of the thunder and the force of the gale threatened to blow away the doors and windows. Chinu walked in with tea and pakoras. Shekhar and I started chatting. Chinu left the moment she heard the faint cry of the infant in the next room. She returned a while later, having comforted the child back to sleep.

This was when I noticed a restlessness in Chinu, as if something was bothering her. Shekhar looked awfully tired. His attention would wander off mid-sentence. Judging the state of his mind, I made an attempt to divert him with entertaining anecdotes. Shekhar smiled and relaxed somewhat. One of my jokes made even Chinu laugh.

I looked at Chinu. She cast a spell when she laughed. But my enchantment metamorphosed into amazement within a split second. All at once, Chinu stopped laughing. A mere breath can snuff out a candle and plunge the room into darkness; likewise, Chinu's smiling lips curved into an arch of pain. A faint groan escaped her as she momentarily looked at us, uncomprehending, before collapsing on the sofa.

Thunder struck somewhere in the distance.

'She's here.' Shekhar sprang to his feet.

I stood up alongside him.

I noticed that Chinu's teeth were on edge and her fingers were rolled into a fist. Some water sprinkled on her face brought her around. She opened her eyes. She wore the same bewildered look for a fleeting second, then she gathered herself, sat up, straightened the pleats of her sari and drew the pallu over her head—just the way Mallika used to.

The wind was whistling away as if a thousand witches were howling outside the window.

'Mallika!' Shekhar whispered.

Chinu looked at Shekhar. Her lips moved, 'I have been here for quite a while, dear; but I dared not enter the room in Binoo-bhaiyya's presence.' Chinu looked at me just the way Mallika would and said with a clipped smile, 'Unbelievable, isn't it, Binoo-babu?'

I tried to speak up but couldn't. The whole thing was so incredible, I couldn't muster the right words for the moment.

Chinu said, 'Fear not, Binoo-babu, I've left the babe behind, that's why I come down again and again. Besides, no one knows my husband better than I do. I'm pained to see him suffer. I'll sort things out and then leave for good.'

By this time I'd regained myself. 'If you keep returning thus, won't it traumatize Chinu?'

Chinu, now Mallika, retorted, 'Chinu is my sister, why should I torment her? Okay, you to keep chatting, I'll go see the baby.'

Chinu left for the adjacent room, walking just like Mallika used to. I was astounded. All this while Chinu was speaking exactly like Mallika. The choice of words, their articulation, the vocal meter, the underpinning of laughter, the glances... everything was Mallika's.

The moment Chinu left, Shekhar was up on his feet to follow her, entranced.

'Shekhar!' I called out.

He stopped, but kept looking towards the other room. 'Mallika…'

'Sit down, Shekhar.' I placed a hand upon his shoulder to restrain him. 'There are things to discuss.'

Shekhar snapped out of his trance. He sat down.

'How long does this last?' I asked.

'Half an hour…an hour…there's no certainty,' he said with his head bowed.

'Does Chinu lose consciousness again after that?'

'Yes. She remembers nothing when she returns to her senses. Only, she sleeps for some time. I haven't said anything to her. I've also forbidden the servants to talk about this.'

'You should consult a doctor.'

Shekhar was surprised to hear this. 'You think this is an illness?'

'It could be. Chinu adored her sister, this could be a fallout of that.'

'But…a reflection of Mallika!'

I grew impatient. 'So won't you get her treated?'

'No no,' Shekhar fumbled, 'I don't mean to say that! Why don't you find us a good doctor?'

'I'll organize that.'

I checked around and, two days later, I took a physician along. Chinu was astounded.

'What's wrong with me?'

'You've not been keeping well,' I said gently, 'so Shekhar wanted to call in a doctor.'

'This is so unfair, Jijaji.' Chinu was angry. 'I'm quite all right.'

The doctor echoed her words. 'Everything seems normal,' he said as he left.

'It's not an illness, in all likelihood...' Shekhar muttered.

'Impossible,' I asserted. 'She needs to see a specialist.'

'But the patient is not willing, Binoo.'

Right then the servant ran up to say Chinu had fallen unconscious in the bedroom.

Both of us rushed there. Chinu had just finished feeding the baby when she collapsed. She exhibited the same symptoms as she did earlier. A sprinkling of water brought her around. The same momentarily befuddled look. Then she sat up and drew the pallu over her head.

'You!'

'Yes,' Chinu said softly, 'it's me, Mallika.'

To my surprise, this brought a strange look of assurance on Shekhar's visage.

Chinu patted the baby's head for a while. Then she looked at me and said, 'The universe is full of mysteries, Binoo-bhaiyya; can a doctor solve them all?'

All at once I lost my cool. Why was this spirit tormenting Chinu in the name of love? 'I accept what you're saying, but please, I beseech you, do not torment Chinu in this manner. Your love is now trauma for your family!'

'Binoo!' Shekhar reacted sharply.

Chinu smiled, just like Mallika. Then she fixed her gaze upon me and said, 'Chinu is my sister but she's nobody to you, Binoo-babu.'

I could have said that I loved Chinu, that I wanted to marry her. But it seemed rather melodramatic to give an explanation to a disembodied spirit. So I said, 'I'm a friend of this family...'

Chinu smiled just like earlier. 'Does being a friend give you the right to interfere in our lives?' she asked.

'Shekhar!' I looked towards him.

Shekhar had eyes only for Chinu, and his gaze was not quite normal. I realized that he was impassioned by the appearance of his departed wife.

'Shekhar,' I repeated.

Shekhar looked at me.

'Li-ss-en!' Chinu called out.

Shekhar looked at her.

Chinu sounded just like Mallika as she said, 'Binoo-bhaiyya has no credence in all this, right? It is better if he stays away for some days.'

'Shekhar,' I cautioned him, 'this might mean danger!'

'How many days am I here for, dear?' Chinu chimed in. 'In a matter of days, I'll go away forever, into eternity. You can't bear separation from your friend for these few days? Tell me, just tell me.'

'Shekhar,' I called out again.

'Tell me, my dear!' Chinu raised the pitch of her voice.

Shekhar looked at me helplessly. 'Binoo, my friend, I think we should respect Mallika's wishes.'

'So I shouldn't come.'

'Mallika is my love, Binoo!'

I left forthwith. May the spirit win! Let the man mourning the untimely demise of his wife do as he pleases. As I stepped on the road, it felt as if I'd emerge from the Kingdom of the Dead and back to life. I breathed deeply and chanted to myself, 'Chinu is nobody to me, I'll never return to that unhealthy environment.'

I did not go back. A year and more passed. The Pujas came and went by. I put on greasepaint to play Arjun under the cool autumn sky. Then came Vijaya Dashami, the festival of meeting and greeting. Suddenly, I felt a stab of sadness. Should I go on nursing my grievance against Shekhar? And what would have happened to Chinu?

I went over. Darkness had descended with dusk, just as it had on that very first day. I was nonplussed to find that a new set of tenants had replaced Shekhar in that apartment. A Maharashtrian family. They had moved in about two months earlier.

So where had Shekhar moved to?

The following day I went to his office. He was still with the same office but had been on sick leave for the last two days. I got his new address from the office.

The same evening I traced him to his new apartment in Bandra.

Chinu opened the door once again. But who was this Chinu? The acuity and vibrancy that had once lent a glow to her face were gone. She was dull and overcome by ennui. Only the intriguing gleam in her deep dark eyes was intact.

'Chinu!' A screech escaped me as I scanned her. She had vermilion in the parting of her hair. Was it my blood?

'Come in, Binoo-babu.'

'But what's this, Chinu,' I said quickly as I tried to get a grip on myself, 'I didn't even get a message!'

'It wasn't anything to tom-tom about, Binoo-babu. Come in.'

She shut the front door and pointed to another across the hall. 'Go in there.'

She walked off towards the kitchen.

'Is it Binoo?' Shekhar's voice floated over. 'Come, come.'

I entered the room. Wrapped in a shawl, Shekhar was reading a book. He stood up as I entered. He had lost weight. There were dark circles around his dreamy eyes. His hair had been cropped really short.

'Sit,' he said once we'd greeted each other with the traditional embrace of 'Kola-kuli' that marks Vijaya greetings. But his smile had no joy.

I started bombarding him with questions. Why did he move house? Why had he shifted to Bandra? When did Chinu get married? Where was she married? Why wasn't I invited?

The air in the room was still and heavy. An ayah left the room with Shekhar's baby.

Since I'd received no reply to any of my questions, I prodded him, 'So tell me Shekhar, when did Chinu get married?'

Shekar folded the book in his hand, put it aside and said in a tired voice, 'Two months ago.'

'What does her husband do? Where do they live?'

He said with a sour smile, 'I have married Chinu.'

I froze. The electric siren of a distant train rent the air.

Shekhar looked at the ceiling and spoke in a low voice. 'One night, when she was possessed, she came to me as Mallika. I moved to this house and married her to safeguard her honour.'

My body shuddered with rage; my whole being revolted in distaste. At that very moment Chinu walked in with tea and samosas. There was no trace of emotion on her face.

'Have some tea.'

'No,' I replied, 'I've stopped drinking tea.'

'Then have some snacks.'

'No, I've eaten.'

Chinu looked at me with curious eyes. Shameless creature! I turned my face away.

Chinu picked up the tray and left the room.

I was silent for a while, then I wanted to know.

'Does Boudi still come?'

Shekhar looked out of the window as he spoke. 'She does, but not as frequently. Maybe once in four days. Now it pains her to come, it seems.'

'What else is new?'

'All good.'

'Does your father know about this marriage? And her uncle?'

'I haven't informed them. Besides, I didn't have the time to inform Baba. He passed away suddenly, right after this marriage.'

'So you're doing fine?' I could not help but inject a little bit of venom into my words.

Now Shekhar looked at me. He spoke as if into space, 'Yes, I'm doing fine...'

'I learnt in your office that you have fever.'

'Not much. Nothing to worry about. I should be fine with a day's rest.'

'Well then. I'll say goodbye.'

'Won't you have dinner?'

'No.'

I didn't look back, as though I was running from hell itself. As soon as I stepped out, I spotted a taxi. I hailed it down, got in and said, 'Drive!

'Where to?'

'Straight on. And fast. Let me think of a place where I want to go and I'll tell you.'

Then I erased them from my mind. At that point, that's what I thought.

I don't know how many days had passed. Fifteen, maybe twenty days.

That evening, I started as if I'd seen a ghost. Chinu was at my doorstep.

'Binoo-babu, there's deep trouble.'

All at once I had this crude impulse to be ruthless. I put aside every trace of gentility and mocked her, 'But who are you? Is it Mallika Boudi speaking or Chinu?'

She looked at me with wide-open eyes and said, 'It's your childhood friend's second wife'

There was something in the way she spoke; I stopped short.

Chinu said, 'Your friend is extremely unwell. Pneumonia. Both his lungs are congested. He's not responding to any treatment.'

My grievances evaporated instantly. 'Why didn't you tell me earlier?' I chided her.

'He had forbidden me. He sensed your contempt for him the other day.'

I walked out with Chinu without uttering another syllable.

Shekhar grew misty-eyed as soon as I entered. 'Sit,' he said weakly.

I sat next to his bed.

The night went by. Came morning and his condition deteriorated.

Doctors came, doctors left. I consulted top specialists. There was no improvement. On the third day, his condition turned grave. The hours went by without offering any hope. The sun set. Darkness enveloped the ocean. An unusual fog hid the starry sky. Shekhar ceased to speak.

Abruptly, Chinu fell into a heap. She sat up as Mallika. She strode up to Shekhar, bent over him, shook him by his hands and said, 'You must live, dear.'

Shekhar opened his dull eyes, smiled faintly, and mumbled, 'Malli... I'm coming...'

'No my dear, no, *no*! I'll live with you through Chinu. You must live!'

Shekhar shut his sunken eyes.

I pulled Chinu by her arm and drew her away from him, towards the door. 'Why this haste to steal your husband, Boudi? Leave, go elsewhere.'

Chinu looked at me, just like Mallika would, and then exited the room.

The night wore on. A servant and I were keeping vigil. I soon dozed off. All of a sudden I was stirred awake by Shekhar trying to say something.

'What Shekhar? What's it?'

Shekhar made to say something, he looked around as if to see something, then shut his eyes.

'*Chinu!*' I shrieked.

She ran into the room. At that point she was Chinu. Mallika had left with her husband.

Two days passed by in a haze. I took more leave from work. I had to assist Chinu through the rituals until everything settled down.

Two days later I said, 'We must inform Shekhar's brothers.'

'I've done it.'

'When will they come?'

'I've told them not to come.'

'Why?'

'What purpose will they serve?'

'Meaning? Will you stay on alone?'

'Yes. A widow gets scant respect in a Hindu household, Binoo-babu. Whatever he has left behind will suffice. I'll also find something to do. And then, ultimately, everyone is alone in this universe.'

This philosophizing raised my gall. 'Do as you please,' was all I could say.

'You had to suffer so much because of us!'

'Thanks,' I said. 'I suffered only to earn this bouquet from you!' At this, Chinu blanched.

Thereafter, I would look her up now and then; only for the sake of my friendship with Shekhar. Such a lovely life—gone!

But Chinu was stoic. She wanted no help from me, she hardly spoke, nor was she vexed by my presence. I'd go, sit for a while, be dejected by the snow-white purity of the widow, and come away. This became my routine once again. And frequenting her fanned my attraction once more. I started sprinkling the colours of my desire on the unblemished white of her mourning.

One evening, I found Chinu putting the child to bed. She smiled at me. 'Khokan is getting naughtier by the day.'

She tucked him in, then came and sat by me.

'Chinu,' I asked, 'Does Boudi still visit you?'

She was startled. 'No, Didi doesn't come anymore.'

'So has she left along with Shekhar?'

Chinu turned towards me with that mysterious look in her deep dark eyes and smiled. 'You are too inquisitive, Binoo-babu!'

'Yes Chinu, I want to know more about you.'

'Then listen,' she said with no trace of hesitation. 'Didi never came, nor did she go away, since she died. My evocation has come to an end since he passed away.'

Was the room swaying? I stared, dumbstruck. The suspicion that had been gnawing at my mind all these days had proven true. Still, I was dumbfounded.

'Let me tell you all,' Chinu continued. 'I can't be at peace until I've confessed to someone. You might detest me for this. Do so, by all means. There is no other soul on this planet who would listen to this tale. Don't think of me as a shameless hussy. A woman who can pull off this performance has the courage to confess too.'

I turned away my face and said, 'Speak, Chinu.'

She started her monologue. 'I have loved him since the time he would come home to coach Didi. But he didn't love me. He loved Didi. With his heart and soul. My love seemed too petty in front of his love for Didi; my desire seemed too mean. So I admonished myself, tortured my soul and helped them. When the whole world had ganged up against them, I helped Didi to run away from home because of my love for him. She got married. She got a home. Had Baba not died so early, this unnatural love of mine might have lost its way in the dreary routine of some loveless middle-class home. But that was not to be. Baba died. Becoming a burden on my Kaka paved the way for me to join Didi in her household.

'I was happy to see Didi's household. Didi's happiness. But was there no trace of jealousy? There was. If I don't admit that I was jealous, there would be no point in this long confession. So I must be honest enough to own up to you that their happiness was like a tiny fish-bone stuck in my throat that I could neither swallow nor spit out.

'Love sharpens a woman's sense of belonging. That's why Didi became aware of my attachment. She wrote to Kaka on the pretext of my marriage and sent me back to Calcutta overnight.

All for my good, I thought to myself. For I could have taken on my own sister for my love; but if the man in question did not reciprocate my love, how could I win?

'No, he did not love me. Not one bit. He was a sage, no sin had ever touched him, there was no blemish on his soul. So I distanced myself. But that only intensified my longing. On the other hand, no proposal for me worked out. How could it? I would reject any match that came for me, find fault and threaten to poison myself if I were forced into a marriage.

'Kaka got desperate; and he might have worked something out but, before he could, Didi died. I did not want that. God Almighty had planned this obnoxious role for me; that was why I was back in Bombay. I hugged the baby to my bosom. But I found my love rapt in thoughts of Didi, like a pensive Shiva. Just watching him like that, so immersed in her memories, made my inner being revolt. I thought he was being pretentious. That he was putting on an act. I felt like testing his dedication, and the force of my sexuality. Who could that harm anyway? I wanted him and I had no shame in admitting that. As long as Didi was alive, I had fulfilled my duty as her younger sister, and also lived within the limits of civil existence. I did not for a moment betray Didi. But now? Where was the need for restraint?

'Because I loved him, I had the right to seduce him. So I started dressing up. I used every weapon that a woman has in her armoury to captivate a person. But he was more austere than the meditating Shiva. He was unmoved. No, he wasn't putting on an act. He was so wrapped up in memories of Didi that he did not even notice my attempts to draw his attention. I was his Soi, his lady friend, that's all.

'I realized that Didi had retained her hold on him even after death. I could see only one way to loosen her grip and make him mine: impersonation. A very difficult path to tread, but there was no other way left for me. That's why, one evening,

Didi "possessed" me. And Shiva came out of his penance at once! But though he was drawn to me, he panicked; and so he went and shared everything with you. You came, and I read doubt in your eyes. I realized that I had an adversary in you. I had to stop you from coming to our house.

'Your friend was fully taken in by my impersonation. Mallika, back from the dead, fully possessed him. He was enchanted by Mallika, and I became desperate. I realized that my best effort to get him to love Chinu had failed. One day I, as Mallika, asked him to marry Chinu. He broke into tears and said, "Don't add to my agony with such words Malli…"

'My cleverness had borne no result. By now I was ferocious like a wounded tiger who's tasted blood. I pulled out the last arrow in my archery. I went up to him as Mallika and deceived him into union. He initially drew me to his bosom in a tight embrace. This was what Chinu wanted, but only Mallika enjoyed it. But was there any joy in it for me? I suffered only mortification. I'd lost to Didi in every possible way! And still I plodded ahead with the play-acting. If a lie was the only way to him, so be it. I became one with Didi in order to taste his love.

'The result was corrosive. He could not bear to look at me when I was myself. A sense of guilt was wearing him down. All of a sudden he decided to move house. He shifted here and said, "Chinu, I want to marry you." I gave my consent with trepidation. We had an Arya Samaj marriage. I got to show off the sindoor gifted by the very man I loved! But he stayed away at night. I became Mallika and entered his room, to assure him that he had made the right decision, but he folded his hands and kept muttering, "Forgive me Malli. Please, please forgive me…"

'Thereafter he never once touched me. Since I legally became his wife, even Mallika could not sway him. Then I scaled down Mallika's appearance in our midst. I thought perhaps this might ease his sense of guilt. I remained Chinu and licked my wounds. One night he came to my room and called out my name, "Chinu." I joyously opened my arms and he returned my embrace. A union with Chinu! The blood he'd tasted that one night was now forcing him to climb down to Chinu's ground. I won! But only for that one night. As soon as the heat of the moment ebbed in his veins, he fled my bed. After that, he simply stayed away from me.

'I felt abhorred, scorned. Nor could I bear to look at his guilt-ridden face. I'd pray for his well-being and return to normalcy; I returned as Mallika to admonish him for his neglect of himself. He held my hand and pleaded, "Malli please take me with you, please!"

'Our relationship only worsened. He started staying away from home. He would roam the streets and return late at night. One day he had a slight temperature. The next day you had come. After you left, he abruptly went out. The whole night he stayed out in the open and came home with a raging fever...'

Chinu could speak no more. She fell silent. I looked at her. No, her eyes were dry. Instead of tears there was a fire. They were burning like a spectre's.

I discovered Chinu anew that day; as an unusually alluring woman. I was entranced. I kept staring at her. At the same time I felt aggrieved and indignant.

'What are you thinking?' she asked me.

'Do you have the spunk to hear it?'

'Yes, tell me,' she nodded.

'You are a sinner.'

'Binoo-babu,' Chinu turned her deep dark eyes with their mysterious look towards me and said, 'You have no idea of this phenomenon called love. Love is neither a sin nor a holy act.'

I stood up to go. No, I could not win over this sinner.

'Leaving?'

I paused before replying, 'Yes.'

I looked at her. The snow-white purity of the widow once again coloured my longing for her.

'Chinu,' I recklessly called out her name.

'Go on.'

'Aren't you afraid to carry on alone, all by yourself?'

'No. I'm not a normal being, Binoo-babu! Besides, with two children, how can I be alone?' She cast a glance at me, then turned her face away as she said, 'Your friend's second child is growing within me.'

That was why she had this newly acquired glow upon her face!

'Can I share something with you, Chinu?'

'Tell me.'

'I, too, am not an average person. I'm not afraid.'

'Of whom?'

'Of society. Of norms. Of traditions.'

Chinu smiled at me. 'I understand what you're saying, Binoo-babu. For days now I have known your feelings for me. But that's not possible.'

'Why not?'

'I no longer live in this world!'

'But I will wait,' I said, gritting my teeth, 'just as you waited for Shekhar.'

'There's no use, Binoo-babu.' Chinu turned away. There was a ring of finality in her words. I had no vocabulary to respond to her with.

'So, then, should I leave?'

Chinu bowed her head and nodded. 'Go.'

'I'll come again.'

'No,' she said in a clear voice, 'don't come again.'

I had to hold on to the wall and grope for the door even in broad daylight.

I have not visited her since. But I have not given up on her. Everything that is born on this planet must also die. Love too. Won't Chinu's love for Shekhar come to an end some day? I'll live to see that day.

Translated by Ratnottama Sengupta

The Story of Fatima

It is 1 a.m. now. Mariam, my housekeeper, is fast asleep in the next room. But I am wide awake. Lying in bed, I play the video of my past and watch it with my mind's eye.

My abbajaan, Dr Sadiq-ul-Hosain, is a professor of Economics. Ever since I gathered my wits, I remember him going to Presidency College every morning. Abba is not only handsome, he is a man of character too; spiritually inclined and intellectually alive in equal measure. Education, to him, is the be all and end all of human existence. A man deprived of education is, for him, a living being who doesn't deserve to be included among humans. Muslims, Abbu maintains, have fallen behind because they do not invest in education. Since I was a child Abbu would encourage me to study. Toys, books, sketch books, colouring pens—they would all be mine if I did well in studies! On my part, I never disappointed him.

Ammi was the love of Abba's life. Every husband loves his wife, so what's new, you might ask. But in most cases the physical relationship gets primacy, not mental compatibility. There is almost no longing or restlessness to be merely in the company of their wives. Abbu had that. Once, when Ammi had gone to visit her parents in Kaliachak in Malda district, she got held up because her father was taken seriously ill. I was about seven. I clearly remember that Ammi was to return on a Tuesday, perhaps the 9th or 10th of March. A day before she was to arrive, Abba got a telegram saying Ammi would arrive on the 12th. That day, he was up at the crack of dawn. He spruced up his beard and took care to dress well before he left for Sealdah. The train was delayed by an hour. All the passengers alighted, they emptied the platform and left for their homes—but there was no sign of Ammi. Abbajaan was not to be defeated. 'She must have taken a later train,' he thought to himself, 'or she must have had to change at some station.' So he kept waiting at the platform, checking every long-distance arrival from New Jalpaiguri. At about 1 in the afternoon he gave up his watch and returned home by 2 p.m. This was his routine for three days in a row. Every morning he would leave for Sealdah and return after 2 p.m., missing college as a result. On the fourth day, Ammi alighted from the first train arriving in the morning. Nana, my grandfather, had suddenly taken a turn for the worse, and Ammi hadn't been able to return until there was some improvement. There was no one she could ask to send a telegram, nor was she in a condition to go out herself. The moment she got off the train, she knelt before Abba and sought forgiveness in a tearful voice. Abba had clasped her hand in his and said, 'Tehmina, don't make me guilty!'

Yes, my mother was called Tehmina. Fair-complexioned, tall and pleasant, she was a college graduate. Abbajaan had stood second in the BA exams of Calcutta University; and so, although he was from a modest background, my wealthy nana, Hamidul Chowdhury, had personally approached him with the marriage proposal for his daughter. Lady Luck smiled on Abba after their marriage. He followed up his brilliant result in MA with a doctorate, and that got him the lectureship in Presidency College.

No wonder Abba would keep repeating in his conversations with almost everybody: 'My life would not have got its shine had Tehmina not come into it. She's my inspiration!'

And what kind of attachment did Ammi have for Abba? From the bed-tea in the morning until his supper, from the suit he would wear to college to the pyjama-kurta he would wear at home or the sherwani he should wear to a dinner invitation, from the slippers to the shoes, from the perfume to the ittar; she would look after, plan, and fulfil all his needs. Every evening, soon as the clock struck 5, Ammi would keep glancing out of the drawing-room window of our second-floor apartment, keeping her ears glued to the door for his triple knock...

I was nine then. One evening, Abbajaan did not return at his usual hour. Ammi anxiously paced in and out of the drawing room. The sky was overcast with rain clouds, the followers of the devil Iblees were growling in the form of thunder. At 7 p.m. Ammi called up the college. After several insistent rings the chowkidar answered the phone. The office closed at 6 and no one's around, he told Ammi. She called up a few other friends and relatives. Hafiz Khan, Sanjib Chowdhury, Ammi's elder sister Roksana-bibi, Ammi's first cousin Amina-khala... No, Abba was not with any of them.

In desperation, Ammi called one of his colleagues, Anadi Sen, who told her that, as usual, Abba had left at 5 p.m., even before Mr Sen did. But where did he go? At this very moment it started to pour, and the sky was repeatedly fractured by 1600-watt lightning. But Ammi was unstoppable; she set out for the thana with Mumtaz in tow. Mumtaz? She was a seven-year-old Moin girl whom Ammi had taken her under her wings. She would assist Ammi in all her domestic dealings. By this time she was a dusky nineteen-year-old enchantress with attractive eyes, who not only had full command of the household routine, but was also a fine cook and very careful with the household expenses.

Ammi left for the police station with this Mumtaz in tow. I was left in the care of our ancient retainer Afzal Chacha. He had calmed Ammi saying, 'Do not worry Amma, Saheb is blessed by Allah Almighty, no harm will befall him.' But the rain gathered greater force at this point and pelted down relentlessly for an hour and more. Meanwhile Abba returned, drenched to his bones. The minute he heard Ammi had gone out in search of him, he made an about turn and headed for the thana. Fortunately, before he could leave, Ammi had lodged the FIR and entered through the gate, her eyes red from crying.

That evening it was Abbajaan's turn to kneel before Ammi and seek her forgiveness. 'After long years I ran into my college friend Aminul Haque, IAS, no sooner than I stepped out of college. He forcibly took me to his home. His telephone was dead, so I could not inform you. I'm so sorry! Please forgive me for causing you so much worry...'

Ammi knelt beside him and said, 'Please don't add to my burden of guilt. What to do Mian, I'm born a woman, I cannot but worry!'

The day I turned ten quite a few people had been invited to partake of the birthday cake. Abbu's friend, Hafiz Chacha, his begum, both their daughters, Mehtab, fourteen, and Mariam, sixteen, were there. Sanjeev Chowdhury and his wife, Farzana Chowdhury; Khala, my maternal aunt and her sons, Shaukat-bhai, twenty-four years old, and the twenty-year-old Hasrat-bhai; Ammi's first cousin, Khala Amina Begum and her son, fifteen-year-old Aslam; my paternal aunt, Nargis Begum and her husband, Phufa Asghar Hosain; about thirty people in all. Mumtaz, an expert chef by this time, seemed to have put her heart into the biryani; its scent pervaded every room and nobody could wait for their share. I was preening in my dress with its layers of lace—it must have cost a fortune even then—my pearl necklace, eardrops and gold bracelets. We—Mehtab, Mariam, Aslam and I—spent more time chatting than playing games. The ladies were in the 'zenana mahal'—our bedroom—while in the living room men raised storms in their teacups, over politics, economics and social trends.

In due course, everyone joined in the chorus of 'Happy Birthday to You'. The ten candles required two breaths to blow out and the cake from Flury's was passed around. Then it was time for dinner with the much-awaited biryani and kebabs. Everybody had only praises on their lips—for the food, the cake, the company—as they departed. Then, as Mumtaz ripped open the wraps off the gifts I had received that evening, Ammi got up from the bed to go to the washroom. That's when it happened, in a flash.

'Ahh!' she cried out in pain, clutching at her heart, swayed a little and fell to the ground. Abbajaan rushed to pick her up. Even as he lifted her in his arms, her head fell backwards at an alarming angle. 'Hai Allah!' was all he could utter as he lay her flat on the floor and started pumping her heart. He continued to do so for a couple of minutes but it brought no change in Ammi's condition. Then he put Mumtaz in charge of Ammi and dashed off to dial our family physician Dr Sen. 'Please Doctor, please please rush to our house, Tehmina seems to have suffered a heart attack...' he shouted in an abnormally high-pitched voice.

Dr Sen arrived in a quarter of an hour and headed straight for Ammi. By then, Abbu and Mumtaz had managed to lay her on the bed. Dr Sen felt her pulse for what seemed like an endless hour, then quietly put her hand by her side. Softly he said, 'Massive heart attack. Mrs Hosain is in God's care, Dr Hosain.'

'Hai Allah!' Abbajaan uttered once more in a quivering voice. Mumtaz collapsed next to Ammi. A strange fear gripped me. I embraced Ammi and started howling. 'Ammi! Oh Ammi jaan!' I kept repeating. I was feeling guilty; did the stress of the birthday evening bring this upon her? Abbu staggered up to us, slumped down on the bed and froze into vacant silence. 'You'll have to get a hold of yourself, Dr Hosain,' Dr Sen rested his hand on Abba's shoulder. 'If you lose your calm, it will badly affect your child.'

It did. For months after Ammi passed away I could not laugh. And every few seconds Abba would look at me to plumb the depth of my grief.

Time, they say, is the biggest healer. But two years passed and I still could not smile. One day Abba made me sit next to him, took my hands in his and said: 'Beti, anyone who is born on this earth has to die, and the only power that rules our birth and death is Allah. He speaks thus through the Prophet in the Surah-e-Sajda chapter of the Quran: "Oh Mohammed, you tell your people, even those of you who have been sent to care for people, Death will reap even their lives and you will return to your Creator." In plainer words, even prophets are mortal; and, dear girl, death has returned your mother to Khuda. Why did she have to leave before so many of us? There's only one reply to that: "It is God's will." So don't bleed your heart for her, my darling daughter. Learn to face the truth and put your heart into your studies, okay?'

That somehow calmed me down. My dear Ammi is in heaven, at the feet of Allah! She feels no pain or sadness, she's submerged in bliss! From that night on, I would recite the Munajat prayers for her before going to bed.

After Ammi's demise, Mumtaz devotedly cared for me and protected me from any and every harm. As for Abbajaan, she took as much or even greater care of him than Ammi even did. For, with her native intelligence, she had realized that both Abba and I had become rudderless with Ammi's death. She steadily became an elder sister to me; my aapa, Mumtaz-aapa.

In keeping with Abba's wishes I immersed myself in my studies. I started securing the highest marks in my class. 'Excellent,' everyone would say, 'Fatima is bound to come out with flying colours. After all, she is Dr Sadiqul Hosain's daughter!' Year on year I would stand first in the exams. I finished school and reached college. I joined the college where Abba was teaching: Presidency College! By now he was the vice principal. I graduated in History honours with a first class first. Abba's happiness knew no bounds. His eyes were glistening with pride. 'Allah Meherban! Allah be praised for his mercy!' he kept repeating as he knelt on the ground and performed a sajda. 'Oh Rasul! I have no words to praise your grace!'

'Beti Fatima,' Abbu called out, his voice quivering with emotion, 'now my heart desires only one thing: that I hand you over to a groom worthy of you in every respect. A match who is a man of character: righteous and educated. I dream of a highly qualified match for you.' Abbu laid so much stress on the words 'highly qualified' that I felt uneasy. I shall disclose the reason for my uneasiness in good time.

Abbajaan kept urging me to enrol for a doctorate. I also felt that I was the only person, boy or girl, to carry forward the legacy of Dr Sadiqul Hosain; so what if I was a daughter, if I finished my doctorate, it would enhance the status of the family. Eventually I embarked on a dissertation titled 'Islam's Contribution to India'. Abba got enthusiastically involved in this and offered to support me.

Meanwhile someone arrested my attention: Mumtaz-aapa. I suddenly became aware that she was dressing up more than necessary. She was tiptop even when she was cooking in the kitchen or washing utensils. Always attired in a well-fitted salwar-kameez or a cheerful sari, she was, these days. Her curly hair was well-groomed and so plaited as if she would step out of the house at any minute. If you so much as went past her you could not miss the whiff of perfume. The nails on her fingers and toes were always shimmering with a fresh coat of polish. Aapa's biggest asset—her dreamy eyes—would now sport surma or kajal. I seemed to rediscover Mumtaz-aapa, I came alive to her attractiveness, I noticed she was flushed with excitement. What's going on? Who is she trying to entice? Who's the person she's decked up for? I kept an eye on all the men who were coming into our house or who were gazing into our house from the neighbour's window or terrace. After a few days of playing the detective, I found the man. Rather, I realized that Mumtaz-aapa's target was Abbajaan. But my abba had no eyes for anybody and cast no longing glances at any woman who would make him go weak in the knees. He worshipped Ammi like a Hindu and would garland her photograph everyday.

I felt a surge of anger against Aapa, as if she were a fallen woman out to desecrate the sanctity of Abba's marriage. I stopped addressing her as 'Aapa' and would simply call her 'Mumtaz'. The first time I did so, she was taken aback and looked at me with questioning eyes. The next moment they expressed hurt. I could read her feelings, but they failed to soften me. On the contrary, I took a perverse pleasure in humiliating her. I would be rude to her for no reason. I would use harsh language and be curt with her on any pretext. Soon, my full-time preoccupation was to guard her, or Abbajaan, as long as he was at home. By and by, Mumtaz caught on; she gradually stopped dressing up and, before long, she was wilting.

One night I was up late, studying. Needing a break, I wanted to munch on something. Without switching on the light in the passage, I walked past her tiny room to go to the kitchen. I came to a sudden halt when I heard the muffled sound of someone crying in a low voice. It was Mumtaz, of course. I stood in the dark as seconds ticked by, listening to the anguished outpouring. Then, soundlessly, I returned to my room and lay down in my bed.

But sleep evaded me for a long time. There was a tug-of-war in my mind. On the one hand was the stately, supercilious, haughty daughter of Dr Sadiqul Hosain, proud of her sophisticated upbringing; on the other was my educated, cultured self with its natural empathy for a woman. The woman in me said, 'Mumtaz, in all her life, has never misbehaved or ill-treated anybody. She has not so much as cast a glance at any man, let alone fall in love with one. The only man she has nurtured in her heart since Ammi passed away is Abbajaan. She has worshipped this man only in her heart and has allowed it to blossom only when Ammi is no more. So what should I do? Should I throw her out or should I pardon her? At this moment she is struggling to forego what is seemingly an impossible dream. Besides, Abbu is wrapped in the memory of Ammi, daily counting the rosary beads in her name. So I should let her be. She is unlikely to articulate her love henceforth.' So, after much thought, I accepted her back in my life and the next day onwards I went back to addressing her as 'Mumtaz-aapa'. She gave me another startled look, then wistfully smiled.

One evening, after he returned from college, Abbajaan sat down at the table with me and a pot of tea. 'Today a proposal had come for you, Fatima,' he said, taking a sip. 'Haji Murshed Khan was my classmate in school. Now he is the owner of a steel factory with millions in his bank account. He showed up at college without notice. "Do you recognize me?" he asked. "How can I forget the boy who made it his business to flee the class everyday through the window?" After chit-chatting for awhile he came to the point. 'Praise be Allah, you are now the vice principal of Presidency College! Someone mentioned this yesterday that your daughter too is mighty good at studies, and I immediately rushed to you. We are meeting after many many years; why not transform our friendship into kinship?" "How?" "By marrying your only daughter to my only son." It sounded good to me, so Murshed took out a photograph from his wallet. The son is a tall, healthy, good-looking guy. He has taken up the reins of his father's business and is doing well financially. But the moment I got to know about his education I turned down Murshed's request. Ershad has not gone beyond Class IX.'

Abbajaan laughed out loud. 'Murshed must have thought that currency counts more than degrees...' he paused. Then, thoughtfully, he added, 'Your husband will be highly educated and highly placed, Inshallah!'

I spoke not a single word. Because, now I don't believe that my shohar has to be highly educated. Let me be frank about why it was so. In the last few months I had fallen in love with a person who did not have much formal education to boast of. This person was Aslam, Ammi's first cousin Amina-khala's son, whom I had known and grown up with since childhood. I enjoyed chatting with Aslam—an ever-smiling, ever-ready-to-oblige-everyone, witty, handsome, pleasant, dashing young man. When she got widowed, Amina-khala would visit Ammi at least every other month. This stopped after Ammi's untimely death. Aslam kept it up, visiting us on Sundays and on festive occasions. Abbu was very fond of him for his exultation of spirit although, behind his back, he would comment, 'Such a lovable fellow, why did he give up his studies after ISc? So unfortunate!'

Fact is, Aslam had to give up his studies after his father's death in order to pick up the reins of their family business. He had expanded his small button-manufacturing unit into a medium-sized enterprise and then started exporting the product. His turnover had gone up and his profit margin was no less than 25,000 rupees every month. But for Abbajaan none of this compensated for the lack of formal degrees in higher education. A poor but well-educated man was more acceptable; he respected such a man far more. So, if Aslam stopped by, he would exchange mere pleasantries and then leave the scene on some pretext or the other. Aslam could see through these pretexts and yet he would visit us, he would talk to me on various topics, have some snacks and leave.

A year on, I finished my dissertation and was ready to add 'Dr' before my name. My mug was in the papers, my work came in for fulsome praise by academics. I became a lecturer in History at Lady Brabourne College almost effortlessly. I was set for life; Abbu's happiness was beyond description.

But there was a dark lining to this silver cloud. I became aware that Aslam had not visited us for the past four months. Why? I rang him up. Amina-khala said he was out of town on business. A whole month went by and there was still no sign of Aslam. I was furious. One day, on my way back from college, I stopped by at Amina-khala's. She wasn't home. The domestic help said Aslam was in his room. I went in. As soon as I entered Aslam stood up, alarmed.

Before he could utter a word I asked with furrowed brow, 'Aslam-bhai, have I erred in any way? Has there been some lapse in my conduct?'

'Fatima,' Aslam lingered on name as if caressing it, 'you cannot do anything wrong. You are an angel from the heavens...'

Now I could smile. 'Then why are you inviting the ire of the angel from the heavens? Why have you made yourself scarce?'

'Workload, Fatima...' Aslam was evasive. 'It's rising...'

'But your tenor belies you. Aslam-bhai.' I walked right up to him, took his hand in mine and placed it on my crown. 'Now tell me the truth.'

Aslam lowered his head. 'Truth is...' He paused, then said softly, 'I have sinned in my thoughts, Fatima.'

'Sin!' I could not quite comprehend what he was saying.

'Yes, Fatima.' Aslam looked straight into my eyes. 'I have been entertaining impossible thoughts about you.'

'What's impossible?'

'One fine morning I woke up to the realization that I was dreaming of being by your side all through life. I pondered over it and came to the conclusion that I must curb this desire. And the only way to do that is to stay away from you.'

Wonderstruck, I gaped at Aslam. And I flushed as I became aware of the deep longing in my heart to be by his side through life. Yes, the same desire was spreading its fragrance: I wanted to be Aslam's wife.

'Aslam,' I mumbled. 'I'm a sinner too.'

'Meaning?'

'Fathom it for yourself!'

Aslam stepped towards me. He held my face in his hands and said, 'Fatima, I am not a scholar.'

'I don't care Aslam…' My voice was tremulous. 'And I don't think you are unscholarly. You possess the magnanimity and catholicism that education bestows upon us.' With these words I held up my parched lips towards him and put my arms around his neck. Aslam kissed me gently. After a while of savouring this bliss, Aslam asked, 'What do we do now? Go to Ammi? Meet Mousaji?'

'Nothing in haste,' I responded. 'We won't… Abbu will not give his consent right away. We must wait for an opportune moment.'

'Sure, we will.'

We decided to speak with Abbu when I would be alone with him. That would save Aslam the ignominy of an outright rejection.

I approached Abbu on at least four different occasions in the next two months but could not muster enough courage to open my heart. After all, he nurtured the dream of giving away his only daughter to a highly qualified groom! How could I selfishly crush that dream?

One Friday, like any other day, I came home at 5. Abbajaan would normally come back by 6 or 6.30, but that evening it was past 7.30 by the time he returned. When I enquired what had delayed him he called out, 'Mumtaz! Quick, get me my tea and something special to go with it. I have good news to share.'

'Ji, right away,' Mumtaz-aapa replied.

'What's the news Abbu?' I wanted to know.

'Na-na.' Abbu smiled. 'Not until I have had my tea!'

Abbajaan went into the washroom, refreshed himself and returned to the table. These fifteen minutes were enough for Mumtaz-aapa to whip up a platter of nimkis and a pastry to go with the steaming tea. He popped a piece of nimki into his mouth and sipped tea before speaking. 'Mohammed Idris is the name. Aged about thirty-two. Doctor of Physics. An American citizen. Here's his photograph.'

He plucked out of his pocket a postcard-sized colour photograph with a flourish and placed it on the table. Mumtaz-aapa came forward to take a look.

I looked too. Medium built. 'Intellectual' stamped over his face. Bright eyes. Good-looking. An endearing smile playing on his lips. The photograph hinted at a life of wealth, luxury, comfort. Abbu explained the rest: 'Idris has come to India on a three-month leave. He will go back with a wife. He is an American citizen, so his wife will also get citizenship. He wishes to marry you. I have given my consent.'

I hung my head and made no reply. I felt Mumtaz-aapa's eyes on me, and Abbu waiting to hear something from me. He ruptured the silence: 'Nothing to be worried about, Beti. You are highly educated; it would break my heart if I had to give you away to an unequal match. It is God's grace that this proposal has come to me. Say yes to him.'

But my lips had tasted of Aslam. I slowly raised my head to say, 'Abbu I will not go to America.'

'Why Fatima? Everyone else…'

I didn't let him complete the sentence. 'Is your daughter like everyone else?'

'Fatima, life does not throw up such good offers again and again.'

'Abbu, if God wills it so, we will get....

Abbu was as devout as he was knowledgeable. So he fell silent.

'Please pardon me, Abbu,' I said as I tried to lighten my discomfort, 'but I will not live abroad.'

That put an end to the conversation. Abbajaan wasn't one to impose his will on his only child. And ever since Ammi's death, Abbu had lived only to see his daughter happy.

The following day I met Aslam at Science City. We sought out a solitary corner and sat on a bench next to each other. I picked up his hand in mine and told him all about The American Citizen. I finished by asserting that I would not become an American nor live away from India.

'Listen to me, jaan, say yes to this man. It will make your father happy and you will also lead a happy life.'

'You're right about Abbu,' I told Aslam, 'but no, I will not be happy. I might have been if I were not in love with you.'

'But Fatima,' he tried to explain, 'we have to find a way forward. We must face your Abbajaan...'

'No,' I was firm, 'it will break his heart to marry his daughter off to a non-doctorate groom. How can I subject him to that fate?'

'I understand, but how can we marry then?'

'I can't think of a way out,' I despaired. 'It might be better that you get married to someone else.'

Aslam was hurt. 'I'm not faithless, Fatima. I cannot marry anyone when my heart is with someone else.'

'Then you might be in for a long wait, Aslam.'

'So be it.'

'What if I grow into an old maiden by then?'

'Then I will be an old man.'

'Aslam! Aslam!'

'Yes Fatima, my love, my life!' He folded me into his arms. Our heartbeats became one.

Months went by thus. Two years rolled by. I was now reputed as a professor par excellence. Every day, after I returned home, I would immerse myself in the pages of History books, discuss doubts with Abbu, and then settle down to write my book. I had already found a publisher. Silently and wholeheartedly, Mumtaz-aapa would look after every need, articulated or not, of Abbajaan and mine.

By and by, Abbajaan turned sixty and retired. His dream of becoming the principal of Presidency College remained unfulfilled. But he nursed no regret. The change of routine saw him regularly read the Quran Sharif, say his prayers five times a day, and advertise in the matrimonial columns of *The Statesman* and *Bartaman* for a suitable groom for me. He would get many replies to the advertisements but none were to his liking. One day he was chatting with his friend in the living room. I could hear Hafiz Chacha say, 'Sadiq, we respect educated girls but avoid them as brides for our sons, because most of us still have to claim those peaks.' I moved away from the words.

Days rolled on. I would meet Aslam once every week. Sometimes on the banks of the Ganges. Sometimes in a restaurant. Once in a while, Aslam would go mad. 'Let's book a room in a hotel,' he'd insist. I would have to calm him down. He would respect my wishes. The only liberty we took was to kiss each other now and then in some dark corner. Aslam was now doing extremely well in his business. He had diversified from manufacturing buttons to exporting ready-made garments, he owned the dealership of five petrol pumps, and he was venturing into motor parts. From a millionaire he had turned into a billionaire. He was still counting the days to be united with me, and I was counting the hours to meet him.

Then I turned thirty-four. I opposed the cutting of the cake and the singing of 'Happy Birthday to You'. Abba agreed to a quiet Munajat. At the end of it he distributed sweets to me, Mumtaz-aapa and Afzal Chacha.

Six days later, I returned from college to find Abbajaan and Mumtaz-aapa missing from home. They'd gone out together in the car, Afzal Chacha said. Abbu had left instructions for me: 'Don't worry even if we are late.' He had to take Mumtaz-aapa with him for some important work. I was up till very late at night. Abbu wasn't back even at 3 a.m. I don't know at what point I fell asleep.

It was late the following morning when I got out of bed. I had my morning cup of tea, finished my bath and was getting dressed to leave for college when I heard the familiar honking of the car at the gate. I opened the door. Abbu stood there, dressed in a finely embroidered kurta-pyjama. By his side stood Mumtaz-aapa, in a brocade salwar-kameez, sporting a zaridar odhni, and dazzling in all kinds of jewellery. I had to blink to recognize her; she had become a beauty queen overnight.

Amazement must have been writ all over me. For, Abbajaan started to give an explanation. 'Beti Fatima.' His voice was grave. 'I could no longer carry on alone. So last night I married Mumtaz. She is a gift of Tehmina, your Ammijaan. She's been caring for you almost like a mother. Now I have formally given her that status. It is my request to you; please accept her in that role.'

I could say nothing for a while. Then I said, 'Yes Abbu, from this day I will think of Mumtaz-aapa as my mother.'

Mumtaz-aapa raced to draw me to her heart. As she did so, she burst into tears that washed away her suppressed anger, grouses, humiliations, indignations… Standing next to Abbajaan she looked like his daughter. Still, I could not but take comfort in the fact that Mumtaz-aapa's mute love had emerged triumphant; she had finally united with the man she had loved all her life.

But me? What about me? If Abbajaan could marry the unlettered Mumtaz, I had also earned the right to marry a less educated Aslam.

A little later, I set out from home the way I always do for

college. I directly headed for Aslam's office. There, I learnt that three days earlier he had gone off to Puri for his honeymoon.

Honeymoon?

Honeymoon!

Disconcerted, I spent the rest of the day roaming the streets. I lost count of the hours. When my legs refused to take one more step, I hailed a cab and returned home.

I shut myself up with my books and my writing. My concentration was not helped by the intermittent call of 'Mumtaz!' from my Just-married Abbajaan or the eager response of 'Ji huzoor!' and 'Right away…' in her voice. That's when the courier brought in the letter.

A letter from Aslam.

Very brief.

'Dear Fatima, at the instance of my mother, on her deathbed I was forced to marry. I lost my love. I lost out to you. I am at a loss for words. Forgive me if you can. Stay well—Aslam'.

I left home on some silly pretext. I contacted a Mr Guha, a property agent, to find me a decent apartment. Then, a few days later, I approved of a south-facing self-contained flat in New Alipore. The monthly rent was 5,000 rupees but an unusually hefty advance payment was to be made because I was entering a three-year lease. Of course, the sum would be partly adjusted against the rent every month.

Another week went by in paying the advance and signing the lease agreement with the landlord. Three days after that, I packed three large cases saying that I was going out of town on official work. With my most essential books, papers and some clothing, I left home to move into the apartment. I didn't want to leave my address for Abbu. I would tell him in good time that I wanted to live all by myself. I desired nothing from him except his blessings. Right, I also stealthily brought away with me the enlarged portrait of Ammi. I did not want Abbu to suffer any pangs of conscience.

And I had not broken his heart.

In my apartment, kneeled down on the bare floor and said in thanksgiving: 'Oh Allah, my Lord! Oh Rasul, the almighty! From this day you are my all: my Abba-Ammi, my brother and sister, my friend and confidante, my offspring too. Now, as long as I live, I want only you in my life.'

Translated by Ratnottama Sengupta

The Fifth Raga

I met Saadiq Hossain, again, out of the blue.

We were stuck in a little railway station called Fatehpur. We, meaning Ranbir Singh, Manuel Dias and I. A branch line was being constructed twenty-five miles down to the village of Neemgarh, and we had just returned after checking the progress of the work. On returning to Fatehpur we learnt that the 8 p.m. train that evening would probably turn up at 2 a.m. because a freight train had derailed en route, near a place called Shivnagar. Since it looked like we were stuck for the night, I went to the 'Hindu Restaurant' outside and ordered food for the three of us. Salivating a little from the fragrance wafting from the restaurant, I wandered up the station, and ran into Saadiq Hossain. After ten long years.

He laughed and broke into a sher by Mirza Ghalib:

'Zindagi yoon bhi guzar hi jaati
Kyun tera rahguzar yaad aaya!'

'Meaning?' I asked, confessing my unfamiliarity with Urdu even as I grabbed hold of his affectionately proffered hand.

'Meaning,' Saadiq Hossain said: 'life would have carried on somehow, why then did we have to meet again thus...'

As the surprise of seeing Saadiq Hossain after a decade wore off, I noticed that the hair which used to be as black as a bumble-bee was now almost entirely the colour of a wild goose. He was then thirty years old, and now he was forty. Most of us had greyed a little by the big 'four oh', but none quite to this extent. When I asked him about this, Saadiq Hossain smiled enigmatically and said, 'Having been around a bit, and seeing the various colours of life, has provoked the chromatic change that you notice, Ashok.'

I introduced Saadiq Hossain to my colleagues. The nostalgic memories of our friendship from the ittar-perfumed days in the alleyways of Lucknow brought about a tightness within my chest. Now, he lived in Hyderabad, and I in Nagpur. He was on his way back home from Jamshedpur. The Saadiq Hossain of Lucknow had been poor, but there was now a glow in his appearance that indicated wealth. The pride in the blood of the ancient nawabs that coursed through his veins had, for some thirty years, prevented him from ruining his elaborately elegant kurta with sweat. But all of a sudden he had decided to go on a tour of India, and something had inexorably changed within him. He had ended up in South Africa, where fortune had smiled on him and, in these five years, he had been the owner of a mill. The story of his fortune made me immensely happy. As we celebrated the success of my benevolent, humorous friend rather boisterously in the restaurant, the weather gods decided to bless our rather ill-fated journey with a thunderstorm.

By the time we had filled our gullets to the brim with Banwari Thakur's pooris and other delicious side dishes, and gotten sodden in the rain on our way to the tiny 'waiting room' on the platform, it was 10 p.m.

In the waiting room, Saadiq Hossain opened his suitcase and brought out a half-bottle of whisky. 'Let's make this meeting after all these years really colourful,' he said. 'Let's celebrate, friends!'

'Saadiq Hossain zindabad!' we cheered together.

The bearer brought us some soda. We divided up the whisky among the four of us. As the warmth of the whisky slowly spread its conviviality of spirit within us, our discussion touched upon numerous topics. Soon, aided by the gradually gathering fumes of our cigarettes, we ended up talking about love. The question was: What is love?

I said love is a disease.

Ranbir Singh said love is what makes life worthwhile.

Manuel said love is the 'romantic' name given to a biological hunger within us.

We all decided to tell a story each to defend our points of view. In the whisky-tinted heat of our arguments, Saadiq Hossain maintained an attentive silence as a serious listener of our various tales. There we were, amidst the tumult of the wind and torrential rain outside, sitting in a tiny waiting room in an unknown little railway station beneath a dim lamp, discoursing on how someone's life was destroyed at the whim of a doe-eyed damsel's mischievous glance. How someone else gave up the respectability of rank and set tongues wagging in his quest for the hibiscus lips of a lady. How another committed suicide when frustrated in his pursuit of the sylphlike body of a woman.

'Love is purely an attraction to external beauty,' I summed up at the end of my story.

'No, beauty is an external quality,' Ranbir Singh protested, 'but it is merely a basis. Real love may be provoked by a voluptuous glance, or by the lightning of an arched brow, or the taut excitement of a well-endowed female body. But it ends in the deeply felt camaraderie of souls, where they discover their soulmates.'

'What rot!' Manuel remarked. 'Love is like a flame of desire which is surrounded by blind moths desperate to immolate themselves in it! Take it from me; that is the last word on it.'

'No, sahib, no!'

We collectively looked up in surprise. Saadiq Hossain had broken his silence, and there was a wild glint in his eyes.

'All that you have all said so far may all be true, but none of it is the last word on love,' he said. 'It is also possible that love is like the sound of Lord Krishna's flute, as you Hindus say; the moment it is heard, one loses all care for every social mores. It might also be that love is like the perfume of a flower freshly bloomed at nightfall that makes one go mad with yearning. Might one then not lose sight of caste or rank or upbringing when these other senses are involved? Maybe one doesn't need to see surma-bedecked eyes, or lips the colour of Basra roses, to fall madly in love. One can be enamoured even without setting eyes on the object of one's love.'

'Saadiq Hossain!' I said derisively.

He raised a hand to silence me. 'Don't think I'm mad, Ashok. Don't even laugh, thinking that two drinks have inebriated me. I am fully "compos mentis" and aware of what I'm saying to you. And to explain further, I will tell you all a story of true love. Place: The city of Lucknow. Time: About six or seven years ago. Subjects: All well known to me. Principal character: Nawab Akbar Ali.'

I do not wish to trouble your sense of geography by telling you which tiny state he was the nawab of. Suffice it to say that he was a nawab by his inherited title only; in reality, he was bankrupt. The British, in the heydays of the Raj, had conspired to annex the state that had long been consigned to a dusty grave in the pages of history. All the inheritance they had left the family with was the worthless title of nawab. As the dust of forgetfulness has gathered on history, the number of such nawabs have kept multiplying. Like the broken-down remnants of empty havelis and mansions scattered through our towns and villages, there are so many nawabs wandering around! Some are businessmen like me, some are government servants, some are gangsters, and, some, bidi-shop owners. They no longer live in palaces or marble edifices washed by rosewater, nor in the myriad reflections of Sheesh Mahals laden with the intoxicating smell of ittar. No durbar hall echoes to the sound of supplicants. But even now, there are many infamous roads and unlit alleyways where people with the title of 'nawab' live off the memory of the days long gone with the chime of the clock. In their mind's eye, they can clearly see those resplendent palaces in spotless marble and, when they put their hands to their hips, they can almost feel the daggers in gold-covered scabbards sporting the emblems of their power!

That was the kind of nawab Akbar Ali was. His father, Sajjid Ali, was a sub-deputy magistrate. When he died, Akbar Ali was twenty-four years old. Sajjid Ali's wife had died before he did. Sajjid Ali's hard-earned savings acted as a catalyst in bringing out the undisciplined nawab that lay dormant in Akbar Ali's dissolute blood while his father lived. All the money grew wings and flew off within two or three years. The whirling ghagras of the nautch girl Kanis Begum and the frowns of the surma-bedecked songstress Feroza Bai led, initially, to the mortgaging of the family mansion and, eventually, its auction.

All that was left was the two-storeyed house that had been rented out. The tenants were asked to vacate it and Nawab Akbar Ali moved in. By now, his various relatives and friends had forsaken the sinking ship. In spite of it all, when the uncaring nawab knocked on the doors of Kanis Begum, they remained shut. And Feroza Bai smiled a vacant smile of half-recognition as she passed by him in the arms of businessman Imam Baksh. Looking daggers drawn at the brazenness of it all, Nawab Akbar Ali had to remind himself, in despair, that he was in the British Raj. The days of nawabi rule were long gone and he couldn't punish the betrayal as he might have wanted to.

Akbar Ali felt mortally hurt. He bought a bottle of White Horse to take home and drown his sorrows in. And when the hangover wore off, he was overcome by a sense of stoicism. In that spirit he decided, one day, to get married.

Into the landless, palaceless house of the 'nawab' arrived Roshanara Begum, the daughter of another poor aristocrat, and noticed the dark shadow of poverty in every room of her very limited domain, with Sakina as her only servant in the house. All the retainers who had served for generations had disappeared along with the wealth. Not only that, many of them were financially far better off than Nawab Akbar Ali. What was a cause of greater shame was that the magnificent building right next door, which elicited gasps of admiration from every passer-by, belonged to Khansaheb Mohammed Yusuf, whose great-grandfather had been the favourite slave of the then all powerful Nawab Asadullah, Akbar Ali's great-grandfather. But such were the changed times! In this way Khuda-ta'Allah turns the wheels of fortune, so those who were once underneath rise to the top and those that were at the top descend to the depths, at his mercy. Akbar Ali bore these indignities with fortitude, but made sure never to walk by the side of Yusuf-mian's house.

For the time being, Akbar Ali focused attention on his new begum. Days and nights passed. Once the excitement of novelty wore off, it occurred to him that Roshanara Begum was cold in her ardency. That she was too civilized, too composed. She simply did not sing on the same scale, in tune with him. She could not keep pace with his hot-blooded needs; her glances did not have the glint of Khorasani daggers as Kanis Begum did; nor did her lips curve with the promise of cruelty as did Feroza Bai's. That she wasn't 'an angel in the house and a whore in bed' irritated him like a persistent thorn in his flesh.

On the other hand, the household's daily requirements of rations and the blankets for winter began to take precedence over his perfumed bottles of ittar and requisitions of imported liquor. When the warm slumber in 'Never-Never Land' was invaded by the cold winds of reality, Nawab Akbar Ali realized he had to get a job and earn a living. He became an insurance broker, got a few commissions on the basis of people he'd known in the past and, of course, earned some easy money. As soon as he was paid, he extracted the thorn from his flesh and turned it into a whip to lash the pent-up Arab stallion within him to the door of Kanis Begum.

Perhaps there is a smell to easy money that spreads out ahead of it, which explains why Kanis opened the door herself. Seeing her at the door, Akbar Ali rained a fistful of currency notes across the plinth of the door and recited a sher:

'Shola-e-ishq! Laga aag na dil mein mere,
Yeh Allah ka ghar hai, kisi dushman ka nahin.'

(O spark of love, why set fire within my heart!
This heart is the abode of Allah, not that of an enemy.)

Kanis smiled sweetly, glancing at the notes on the floor, and said, 'You are so lively, Nawab-sahib! Tashrif laiye, please come in.'

Roshanara Begum came to know of what had happened, and fully recognized her husband. But she said nothing and made no comment. And indeed what could she, a poor man's uneducated daughter, say in anger to a nawab! The nawab also realized that his begum was aware of what had passed. But he felt no need to justify himself. And if he did feel any regret, he kept it to himself. Only, occasionally, he'd needlessly draw his wife to his breast and silently attempt to expiate his fault—in vain. Then, drawing back, he'd once more think how cold, unexciting and distant Roshanara was.

Slowly, an invisible wall seemed to grow between them.

By now, the insurance work had dried up. In dire poverty,

Akbar Ali started to drink locally produced cheap spirits. In the end, even that became a luxury. Helplessly, after much trying, he got a position through Haji Nizamuddin, a friend of his father's, in his import-export business and set off for South Africa. He was to stay there for about a year. Roshanara was to stay back with the servant Sakina and an aged, distantly related maternal uncle, Rahmat Khan, an opium addict. In the end, Akbar Ali was forced to swallow his pride and request the rich Mohammed Yusuf—once a family servant—to keep an eye on his household.

He wrote a letter as soon as he reached South Africa. In a foreign land, bereft of family, and lonely, the tone of piteous supplication in the exiled nawab's letter touched Roshanara. While she managed to get the letter read to her by Khan-sahib's wife, writing a reply became a serious problem—an uneducated, poor man's daughter that she was. Mohammed Yusuf's wife was somewhat snooty, and put on airs, as if she was determined to eradicate the generations-long servitude of her husband's family to the nawabs in one fell swoop, all by herself. So Roshanara did not feel inclined to seek her help. On the other hand, she had been brought up in strict purdah, and kept away from all contact with men other than her closest family. Who could she possibly approach for help in this situation?

Roshanara called on old Sakina for counsel. She explained the need for a circumspect, dependable scribe.

'Hai Allah,' Sakina said, 'how on earth would I know of such a person?'

Roshanara exhorted her, 'If I had any idea of whose help I should seek, do you think I'd seek yours in this embarrassing matter?'

'All right, Begum-sahiba, I'll ask around.' She came back after a couple of hours and said, 'I've found someone, Begum-sahiba.'

'Who?'

'Solayman-mian. He stays as a dependent in Khan-sahib's

house next door. He is very poor, but a good man. He passed the university entrance exam too!'

'What does he do for a living?'

'He works in Khan-sahib's brother's stationery shop.'

'Okay, ask him to come across in the evening.'

Solayman arrived soon after sunset and waited in the outer room. He was a quiet, polite man approaching thirty.

Sakina informed Roshanara of his arrival.

'Give him a pen and some paper,' Roshanara said. 'I'll be down in a moment.'

Sakina obeyed her directions.

After a few moments, there was the soft tinkling of bangles behind the heavy saffron-coloured curtain of the inner quarter.

'Begum-sahiba is here, Mian,' Sakina said sweetly.

'Aadaab bajata hoon!' Solayman bent forward slightly and offered his respects to Begum-sahiba.

'Aadaab!' Begum's voice floated back. Solayman-mian glanced momentarily in the direction of the curtain, then his polite, subdued voice said, 'At your service, Huzoorain! What is your command?'

'I'm obliged to you for your kindness, Mian-sahib. Would you write a letter for me?'

'Sure! Please proceed...'

Roshanara dictated and Solayman started to write her words down in an orderly fashion. It was a very simple letter. There was anxiety for an emigrant husband, reassuring him not to worry on her behalf; there was news of the well-being of every member of his family; and prayers for the husband's welfare, etcetera. What more could she have dictated to a man who was unrelated to her? Therefore, the letter had no mention of superlatives such as 'Dearest', 'Darling', 'The Light of My Eyes'. Nor did it reflect any of her frustrations and deprivations, or the emptiness of her existence in this state of enforced estrangement. It did not end in 'Yours Forever', nor with the smudge of tears shed. It ended with just 'Your Servant, Khadima Roshanara'.

'Ji, the letter is written,' said Solayman hesitantly, looking at the curtain. 'Is there any other command for me?'

'No Sir. Many thanks to you,' Roshanara replied. 'But I do have a request. If you could occasionally come and write a letter in this fashion, I'd be most grateful...'

'Your servant will always be ready to serve you,' Solayman said, bending forward in a salaam. 'Whenever you need me, Begum-sahiba, just send for me. Aadaab.'

'Aadaab.'

A strange, intense feeling seemed to overcome Solayman-mian as he left the room.

'Quite a decent sort, isn't he, Bibi-sahiba?' Sakina observed.

Roshanara nodded in assent. 'From the way he spoke, he sounded like a good person.'

'Yes Bibi, he's a good sort but he's always too serious, and doesn't mix with other folks.'

'Why?'

'God alone knows why!' Sakina pulled a face. 'Maybe that's his nature.'

'Let everyone be according to their nature,' Roshanara responded. 'How does it matter to us?'

'Yes, of course. What concern is it of ours?'

A slight cough was heard outside the room at that moment. Old Rahmat Khan was at the door. 'I need some wherewithal for me, child.'

Rahmat Khan needed six annas worth of opium every day. He went to the shop twice a month. His supplies were probably running low, hence this reminder to Roshanara. As she counted out the money, Roshanara smiled to herself. 'What an inappropriate guardian Akbar Ali has appointed!' she thought. If Rahmat Khan was just a little lettered, she need not have invited strangers into the house to read and write letters. What use was a man who stayed under the influence of opium for the better part of a day?

Two letters started arriving every week. Living amongst people of different colours and cultures in Africa, Nawab Akbar Ali seemed to rediscover Roshanara Begum and explore her in his memory. He seemed to fall in love with his begum for the first time from thousands of miles away. It wasn't feasible to openly display this love in his letters, as he realized that a stranger would read them out to his wife. What he could not express in so many words, he seemed to make up for in sheer numbers. And, with every letter, he would exhort her to reply soon.

Naturally, Solayman-mian was called in quite frequently. And, in the course of reading and writing those letters, he penned a strange story. That strange flower which no magical spell of seasons can force open, suddenly blossomed in the heart of Solayman-mian. The aroma of that flower was more intoxicating than the most potent opium; and it engulfed him. He became infatuated, enamoured, impassioned—he went mad. He discovered a mysterious message in the mellow voice that reached him from the other side of the saffron curtain. That dulcet voice distracted him, just as Krishna's silken flute would affect the gopinis in your Krishna lore. It robbed him of his faculties, he was utterly destroyed.

'What shall I write, Begum-sahiba?'

'Write that Nawab-sahib should not fret about me at all. Uncle Rahmat Khan is looking after me quite ably.'

Roshanara would keep dictating, Solayman-mian would keep writing. The evening sun would peep through the window on the west and cast a mellow shadow on the walls. Its mysterious effect on the minds was sharpened by the soft courting of the pigeons on the cornices outside. The exhilarating mellifluousness of Roshanara Begum's voice was laced with the rejuvenating freshness of spring air. Listening to that voice, the saffron-coloured curtain would seem to transform into transparent muslin; and on it would be the impress of a beautiful woman. The muted beauty he had idolized in his heart through the travails of his poverty-stricken adolescence seemed to come alive in the words from the other side of the saffron screen he sat in front of.

'What else shall I write, Begum-sahiba?'

'Write, Nawab-sahib should take particular care of his health. It will never do to fall ill in a distant land!'

Solayman-mian writes on. As he writes, he keeps listening to Begum-sahiba's voice, and as he listens, he seems to see the play of inky clouds in the jet-black tresses of the unseen lady, her brows arched like the wings of a hawk, her lips red as a rose, her body soft as the narcissus, covered in zari-decorated peshwaz and churidar, and a long tinselled odhni kissing her hennaed feet.

The trance wears off all at once. 'Your servant, Khadima Roshanara Begum!'

The letter is finished. Solayman-mian offers his obeisance and departs.

Seated on a cotton carpet spread on the platform outside the door, Rahmat Khan puffs on his bidi as he fixes Solayman with a reptilian stare. 'Finished the letter, then?' he says through an opiated smile. 'Good, good. But listen Mian, the next time you write to Akbar, will you urge him on my behalf to bring a big supply of opium, if it's cheaper over there? Do write that, won't you?'

Solayman nods in assent and leaves.

Then a day passes. Two days pass. Solayman gets restless. When will she send for him? When will he hear that magical voice again?

He is summoned again on the third day. He rushes over.

'Order me, Begum-sahiba…'

'Will you read this letter to me? It just arrived.'

Solayman reads out the letter, then starts writing a reply.

'Write that we are worried to hear about Nawab-sahib's ill health. That we pray to Allah day and night and seek His blessings for his continued good health. Would he kindly see a good doctor and get himself well very quickly?' Solayman writes slowly on purpose. What he might have written in ten minutes now takes fifteen minutes, then twenty minutes, and, finally, half an hour.

'Have you finished writing?'

'Nearly there... Seeking His blessings. I beg your pardon, what next?'

'That he should arrange for good treatment...'

'Yes Huzoorain...'

Solayman was late returning to the shop. Khan-sahib's brother Altaf became cross with him and issued a warning. Solayman remained silent. The voice, as dulcet as a cuckoo's call, was still ringing in his ears. Its sweet memory haunted him through the night and the following day. He began to yearn for the music of that voice again. He was like Rahmat Khan without his timely dose of opium. Solayman-mian pined and thirsted for the soothing flow of that ringing voice.

He suddenly turned up at the house without being summoned and asked Sakina if he could speak to the begum.

'Why? Tell me what you need.'

'No, I must speak with Begum-sahiba.'

Sakina went off within to inform her mistress. The sound of velvety footsteps ended on the other side of the gently swaying saffron curtain. Solayman's heart quaked in anticipation.

'What do you want?'

'Is there a letter you want read?'

'No letter has arrived today.'

'Oh. But don't you want to dictate one?'

'We just sent off a letter day before yesterday! When we receive another letter, then...'

'Oh.'

There was disappointment in Solayman's monosyllable. As he stood there speaking to her, he sipped the wine that was her voice. In it he found the playfulness of swaying daisies, the headiness of a kiss, the potency of a tender touch. The voice was an invisible fire flickering its way through his veins.

But Sakina's brows were knitted in anxiety. She had noted a strange light in Solayman-mian's eyes, and in the way he stood in front of that curtain.

Old Rahmat Khan saw Solayman on his way out.

'Hello Mian, what news of my nephew?'

'There was no letter today.'

'So what did you write?'

'I didn't write any letter today,'

'Then?'

'I had just come to enquire...'

A shadow of doubt crept into the Rahmat Khan's opiated, watery eyes. 'Oh! So you'd come to enquire? Well, well, that's good!'

But Solayman no longer lived in the flesh-and-blood world around him. So he did not notice the fierce frown on Sakina's brow, nor did he perceive anything abnormal in the way Rahmat Khan looked at him. He now breathed in the world of sound, and it consisted of only one tune—that female voice.

Slowly, ever so slowly, Solayman went out of his lonely, introverted mind. The clothing of quiet politeness with which he'd covered up his soul to save it from life's hammer blows was suddenly discarded and it took wing. He started making mistakes in adding up accounts, he couldn't hear what the customers were saying. He was not worried anymore by Altaf's threats, and he felt no shame. His perception of days and nights had gone awry. He'd write a letter now and the next moment get an intense yearning to start writing another one. He wanted nothing: in the pariah dog's life that he otherwise led, he just sought a magic wand using which he could sit in front of that saffron curtain and immerse himself in the waterfall of that resonant voice. Or, in reverse, be immolated by the flame of that voice.

On the other hand, many eyes now cast sidelong glances at Solayman, many a brow furrowed on looking at him. There were some who would whisper under their breath and some would giggle, pointing at Altaf's shop and the house of Nawab Akbar Ali.

Solayman-mian was oblivious to all of this. He was past noticing worldly goings on.

He wrote a letter one morning and turned up again the same afternoon.

Sakina looked surprised. 'What do you want, Mian-sahib?'

'I've come to read the letter.'

Sakina flared up. 'Are you going out of your mind? You were here only this morning.'

'Never mind that, will you inform Begum-sahiba that I'm here.'

'No, would you kindly leave now?'

'Please, just inform her once.'

'No!'

Solayman looked at her helplessly for a moment, then suddenly raised his voice, 'Begum-sahiba!'

Sakina shouted, 'Solayman-mian!'

Nonetheless, Roshanara Begum had heard the voice. Her footfalls rushed down to stop on the other side of the curtain.

Sakina said, 'Solayman-mian has turned up needlessly. I asked him to go away but he won't.'

'Why Sakina, what's happened?'

Solayman took one step forward and spoke timidly, as if some slave were addressing the Empress of Hindustan: 'Is there no other letter to be read today, Begum-sahiba?'

There was a moment of silence.

'No.'

'Is there any letter to write?'

'No.'

There was an unusual agitation in Solayman's voice as he said, 'But Begum-sahiba, have you considered the faraway land where Nawab-sahib is spending his days in abject loneliness, amidst jungles and strangers? Should you not send him a letter every day to dissipate the pangs of his loneliness?'

Roshanara Begum's voice rang with firmness as she said, 'Mian-sahib, I'm well aware of what I should or should not do.'

'Pardon?'

'You may leave now.'

'Right Begum-sahiba. My respects...'

'Aadaab. And please note, return only when you are needed.'

'Ji Begum sahiba. Aadaab.'

Solayman lowered his head and walked away slowly.

Rahmat Khan arrived on the scene as silent as a cat. He had just had his last fix of opium. He smiled, and said, 'Did you send another letter this afternoon, Sakina?'

'No sir.' Sakina shook her head.

'Oh!' Rahmat Khan wandered out, a curious smile spreading over his bearded face.

Pushing the saffron curtain aside, Sakina entered the room to find Roshanara standing still. The light from the evening sun was fading away. The open window was covered by a chick sunblind, but traces of the red sky showed through the slats. The pigeons were at their post on the cornices, their 'bak-bakumm' presaging the arrival of dusk.

'Begum-sahiba,' Sakina said, 'I don't think you should call in Solayman-mian again.'

'Why?' Roshanara Begum was startled.

'Why?' Sakina paused for a moment, then looked up and said: 'If you pardon me for saying this...'

'Go on.'

'Solayman-mian has fallen in love with you.'

'What!' Roshanara seemed to shiver. Her eyes were ablaze, her nostrils were flared up, and a contemptuous smile flickered on her lips. 'He loves me?' she repeated quietly.

'Yes. Haven't you noticed the way he's behaving? I've been thinking of telling you this for a few days, now that folks in the mohalla are whispering. Everyone has noticed Solayman-mian's distraught behaviour.'

Roshanara silently heard all that Sakina had to say. At the end of it she said, 'In that case never let Solayman-mian into this house again.'

Thereafter things started to happen in rapid progression. Solayman lost his job at Altaf's shop, and Mohammed Yusuf drove him out of his house. He wasn't paying attention to any matter at hand. Khan-sahib heard the whispers in the neighbourhood and was enraged.

Solayman came down to the footpath. He would sit under the portico of Lala Kishanlal's house and stare for hours at Nawab Akbar Ali's house.

Sakina informed her mistress of this.

'Really?' Roshanara could not but be surprised.

'Yes.'

'Hai Allah!'

'The man must have been a few pennies short to start with, and now he's gone and lost it all…'

All of a sudden there was a loud knock on the outer door.

Sakina opened the door, to shut it almost immediately.

'Who's it?' Roshanara asked from her room. Sakina didn't answer.

Right then Solayman's voice floated in: 'Has a letter arrived, Begum-sahiba? A letter?'

Roshanara heard him.

'No, there are no letters,' Sakina shouted. 'You may go.'
There was no sound after that.

Old Rahmat Khan popped out of his room for a bit, looked around, then returned to his room. He chuckled to himself, reciting a verse:

> *'Kya kahoon, kuch kaha nahin jaay?*
> *Hai, chup raha bhi na jaay!'*

(What shall I say when I dare not speak?
But, oh dear, neither can I stay quiet!)

Solayman-mian became stark raving mad. Nobody knew where he ate. He'd lie on the footpath. Everyone's eyes were upon him every day. Dust would fly about, rain would pour upon him, the sun would blaze down, yet the madman would take no note. Occasionally, he'd wander around Akbar Ali's house. If only he could hear some stray words of conversation! Then, as if struck by a thought, he would suddenly go to the front door, knock on it and shout, 'Don't you want to write a letter? A letter?'

Morning, evening, night. Days passed by. The door remained closed, and Roshanara Begum would silently listen to the shouts of the madman and sit still as stone. Then it became a routine occurrence and she got used to it. The sun would rise and set every day, the horse-drawn carriages would pass by, the hawkers would go by announcing their wares, the siren of the oil mill would screech three times a day, and along with it all, the madman's shouts... Just another day.

Except that people found different interpretations to the story every day. New juicy bits of gossip to elaborate it with. They looked at the madman, and who knows what imaginary tales went through their minds. Once in a while the young lads would creep up behind him and shout, 'Would you write a letter, Mian? A letter?'

Startled, Solayman would look up, then gently smile. Then

he'd lose all interest and, instead, listen intently for something. Was there a dulcet voice floating down upon the wind?

Akbar Ali returned home after ten months. Now he need not go back to Africa. He'd work at the Lucknow office of the firm, and his salary had increased.

He pulled Roshanara to his chest during the afternoon siesta. A voice floated up, 'Would you have a letter written, Begum-sahiba? A letter?' Hearing that voice, Sakina took fright, Rahmat Khan laughed, and Roshanara Begum looked startled.

Akbar Ali asked, 'Who's this?'

Roshanara replied quietly, 'A local madman.'

'Madman! Why is he ranting about letter-writing?'

Roshanara smiled weakly. 'Who knows what madmen mean in what they say?'

'That's true.' Akbar Ali smiled. Then he looked at his begum again. There were slight dark circles underneath her eyes, and her cheeks lacked their rosy hue. Had Roshanara lain awake at nights thinking of him, as he'd sometimes done, thinking of her?

He said, 'Roshanara, I realized your true worth only after going so far away. Every day I'd impatiently await with trepidation in my heart for your letter. You know, when Wajid Ali Shah was exiled to Calcutta, not all his begums went with him. Badr Alam Begum stayed back in Lucknow. My extreme distress was similar to hers; on receiving a letter from Wajid Ali, she wrote:

Tumhare khat ko jab dekha
Tan-e-murda mein jaan aaya
Hua saabit ki hai tahrir mein
Izazay Masihaayi
Bala-e-hizr mein jabse phansi hoon
Main angaron ke upar lot ti hoon...

When I received your letter, I too felt as if my dying body was revived. And at that moment, I would believe in God. Believe me Roshanara, the day we parted, I too felt as if I was sleeping on burning embers!'

Roshanara smiled a wan smile again.

'Who did you get to write the letters for you? Khan-sahib's wife?'

Roshanara freed herself from her husband's embrace to say, 'No.'

'Who then?'

'Solayman-mian from their house.'

'Oh yes, he works in Altaf's shop. He does have rather nice calligraphy.'

The discussion ended there.

Akbar Ali went out for a walk in the evening. He noticed that all the people on the road, in the neighbourhood, were looking at him in a strange way. Why? Possibly because he had returned after all that time abroad. The people from Khan-sahib's house were also looking at him in that same strange way. Why?

Akbar Ali headed home as the evening darkened. Passing by Lala Kishanlal's carport he came to a startled halt.

Solayman was babbling away to himself, 'Don't you want me to write a letter for you, Begum-sahiba? A letter?'

Akbar Ali recognized him. The madman. He recognized Solayman-mian as the local madman.

The madman was laughing as he recited these lines:

'Mohabbat mein nahin hai farq
Jeene aur marne mein,
Usiko dekh kar jeete hain
Jis kaafir pe dum nikle...'

By the time he got home, a storm was raging in Nawab Akbar Ali's mind. He could guess who the madman was asking about writing letters. But why did he recite that poem? When in love, there's no difference between life and death. You live by the sight of that very person, on whom you would sacrifice your last breath… Was that poem a key to the madness of Solayman-mian?

As soon as he stepped into the courtyard, he went straight to Rahmat Khan's room. The usual tablet of opium had dissolved in the old man's stomach by then. He smiled benignly. 'Come in, son, come in.'

'Mamu-ji, can you tell me…'

'Yes, of course.'

'What made Solayman mad?'

Rahmat Khan looked at him, then smiled and said, 'Why not leave that for now? You'll learn in due course…'

'No, you tell me now!'

Rahmat Khan smiled again. 'In that case, sit yourself down, son. Do you have a cigarette? Give me one. Since you insist, I must tell you.'

Akbar Ali retired to his bedroom after a considerable length of time. His eyes were bloodshot. He went straight to bed.

Roshanara came up to him and said, 'Why are you lying in bed now? The food is going cold…'

Akbar Ali sat up. Casting a piercing look at his begum, he said, 'You lied to me.'

'Why?' Roshanara looked squarely in the eyes.

'You did not make clear to me what Solayman-mian's "have a letter written" meant.'

Smiling a sad smile, Roshanara asked, 'So you've heard all about it?'

'Yes, why not? Everyone else seems to know.'

'The thought of telling you revolted me. It was no fault of mine!'

'Hmm…'

Silence enveloped the room. Akbar Ali lay down again. Sakina had decorated the chamber with strands of beli flowers; their fragrance filled the room. But they failed to win Akbar Ali's attention.

Roshanara stood by silently.

After a long while she asked softly, 'Won't you have dinner?'

'No,' Akbar Ali's reply was almost inaudible.

Roshanara woke up with a start around midnight and found Akbar Ali gazing intently at her. The light was on. As Roshanara made to sit up, Akbar Ali drew her to himself. Folding her in a fiercely passionate embrace, as if to unite her body with his, he said, 'All these days I've never quite seen you properly, Roshanara! I've wilfully neglected you...' But even in the passion of the moment, that old feeling came back to Akbar Ali: Roshanara was too beautiful, and frigid.

Tonight, though, he did not recall Kanis Begum and Feroza Bai. He just felt determined to infuse the unquenchable wildfire of passion coursing through him into Roshanara and to bring her ever closer to him.

But the ghostly calls would chase him. 'Would you have a letter written, Begum Sahiba? A letter?' Those words were like whiplashes to Akbar Ali, they made his blood boil in impotent fury.

Whenever he went out, he'd notice Solayman. The madman would be babbling to himself, and casting an occasional glance at his house. An inexplicable agitation held Akbar Ali in its thrall.

A few days later, the sunset sky was overshadowed with rain clouds. As it grew dark, a thunderstorm started to brew. The duet of stormy winds and heavy downpour ran equally hard. And still Akbar Ali did not return from office.

'Nawab-sahib is probably stuck because of the thunderstorm,' Sakina surmised.

'I suppose so,' Roshanara responded.

The thunderstorm let up a short while later. The wind blew off. The skies cleared and even the moon came out. The giant bell at the thana rang 9 o'clock, then all way through to 1 in the morning. That's when Akbar Ali arrived, rather drunk and singing softly.

Sakina opened the door and stood to one side.

Entering his room he stood facing Roshanara, and stopped singing.

'What are you looking at, Begum?'

'You have been drinking.'

'I have.'

'Suddenly?'

'Suddenly. Everything happens suddenly, Begum-sahiba! Man is born suddenly, dies suddenly, so this too was sudden!' Saying this, Akbar Ali guffawed loudly, and recited:

'Hansi aati hai apney roney par
Aur rona hai jug hunsai ka...'

'Meaning?'

'Meaning?' Akbar Ali went up to his begum, gathered her in his arms, and said, 'Does everything have a meaning? Do the ramblings of a drunk have meaning? Roshanara, I'm so happy today.'

'Why?'

'I don't know. Roshanara, your pupils have such a depth of darkness! They're mesmerizing!'

'Why do you tell me these endearments in this drunken state? I'm not Kanis Begum.'

Akbar Ali tried to look squarely at her. 'I know,' he said in a twisted voice, then added: 'I never think of Kanis Begum anymore, Roshanara Begum! I value you far, far more now.'

Roshanara shut her eyes. With her eyes closed, she listened to the hyperbolic endearments of the drunken nawab until Akbar Ali started snoring. Then she rose, switched off the light, pulled the chik blind off the window and looked out. The rain-washed sky was not besmirched by a single dark cloud. The light of the waxing moon on its thirteenth night moulded the whole city in silver foil. Looking at the moon, Roshanara Begum started weeping. No one heard her cry save the moon.

The following day everyone noticed something. Pagla Solayman had disappeared. His shouts were missing from all the noise and hullabaloo of life in the neighbourhood. At the end of the day, Roshanara too realized that. She felt like calling Sakina to enquire, but couldn't bring herself to do it.

In the end it was Sakina who cornered her to say, 'That unpleasant man's gone, Begum-sahiba!'

'Who?'

'Who else? That madman.'

'Where has he gone off to?'

'No one knows.'

'Hunh.'

That evening, Akbar Ali returned with a bottle of spirits under his arm. He started drinking openly in the house. Roshanara said nothing. But she watched him desperately trying to suppress an intense upheaval within him.

He looked up at his wife all at once. 'What are you gawking at?'

'You.'

'Why?'

'For the same reason you look at me.'

'I do. I try to look inside you.'

'And what do you see?' Roshanara asked gently.

'Just blood and flesh.'

'I, too, see the same.'

'Is that all? What about my heart? Don't you see that?' Akbar Ali leaned towards her.

'I haven't managed to plumb the depths of your heart yet.'

'Did you ever want to?'

Roshanara laughed. 'It's not much fun playing a one-sided game, Nawab-sahib.'

'I understand.'

That day passed. A few more thereafter. The same routine

followed. Every day, after work, Akbar Ali would sit at home and drink while Roshanara would sit and watch him.

One day, as he was pouring his drink, Roshanara pushed forward a glass. Akbar Ali smiled. 'What's this all of a sudden, Begum?'

'I want to call a truce with my co-wife.'

'Good, good.' Draining his glass in one breath, Akbar Ali laughed admiringly and said, 'Well said, Begum!'

Roshanara asked all at once, 'Have you got the news?'

'What?'

'That unpleasant person has left the neighbourhood.'

'Who?'

'That madman.'

Akbar Ali looked at her through drowsy eyes. Roshanara continued, 'It would be a relief if he doesn't show up again.'

'Why, Begum?' Akbar Ali asked, placing his hand over Roshanara's.

'Why! Do I need to explain that to you?'

Akbar Ali laughed drunkenly. 'That fakir will never return,' he said in a hushed voice.

'Why? How do you know that?'

'Shush... Quiet!' Akbar Ali replied in the same hushed voice, 'I've sent him to hell, Roshanara.'

'Meaning what?' Roshanara too used the same voice as her husband.

'Meaning, I've finished him off.'

Roshanara groaned in distress, 'No! No! No!'

'Yes.'

'But why?'

'Why not? Was I to listen to his shouts every day, to see him, and that sly smile on people's faces? I cannot live shorn of respect, Begum!'

Roshanara fell silent for a while. Then she said, 'What you did was for the best... But with what did you...?'

'Very simple! I pushed him off the bridge into the Gomti.'

Roshanara stood up. 'Come Nawab-sahib, let's say the Fatiha prayers.'

Akbar Ali looked up at Roshanara in amazement. 'What are you saying!'

'Yes, I'll have no peace if the prayer for mercy is not recited.'

'You're needlessly scared.'

'No, I must go. However strong your rationale, in God's judgement this is still murder...'

'I committed the murder for you, Begum,' Nawab-sahib spoke through gritted teeth. 'If need be, I'll commit more murders.'

'But murder is just that, murder. Moreover, the man caused us no harm, Nawab-sahib.'

'Caused no harm!'

'Tell me, what harm has he done us?'

'His madness turned us into the laughing stock of the mohalla. It was an insult to you and me!'

'But people would have forgotten it all in time. Who remembers a madman's ranting? Besides, the only one harmed was him; he became insane. Khuda himself punished him!'

Akbar Ali said nothing in reply, but beads of sweat appeared on his forehead. His eyes lost their spark. A dispirited look spread over his face. He mumbled, 'Since that night there's been no peace in my heart, Roshanara Begum...'

'Then let's recite the Surah Fatiha. You'll get back your peace of mind.'

'Will I be at peace again? Well, then, let's go.'

Akbar Ali poured himself some more whisky, drank it all in one go and stood up.

'Can you walk straight?' Roshanara asked.

'I can, but the bridge on the Gomti is far away. Let's take a tonga.'

'Yes.'

Roshanara donned her burqa and followed the nawab out of the house.

By now well under the spell of opium, Rahmat Khan asked from the outside room, without opening his eyes, 'Who's that, son?'

Nawab and Begum made no response. Rahmat Khan returned to his dream world.

They got into a tonga and proceeded in silence. It was nearly 11 in the night, and there were few people around. The tonga proceeded to an even quieter area on the city limits.

The moon shone brightly upon the world. The strain of a qawwali floated out of a house. The words of the unseen singer reached them over the beats of the horse's hoofs.

Iss ishq ne ruswa kiya,
Main kya bataoon kya kiya!
Aah-e-dil naashadne
Aur aasman paida kiya…

(This love has besmirched my name,
What has it not done!
These cries from the shards of my heart
Have created more heavens!)

Nawab Akbar Ali heard the lyrics and glanced at his begum. Roshanara was looking the other way.

As they neared the bridge, Akbar Ali called out, 'Halt!'

He paid off the tonga and turned to his wife, 'Come.'

They walked up to the bridge and then upon it. Everything looked strange in the moonlight. The water in the Gomti glinted like molten silver, the soft susurrus of its gentle flow was a sweet accompaniment to the rustling breeze. It seemed to deepen the nawab's intoxication.

'Begum, we've never walked together like this before,' Akbar Ali remarked.

'No.'

Akbar Ali staggered slightly and, with his voice laden with emotion, he said, 'Khuda's world is so full of beauty, Begum...'

'Hmm...'

'But why are humans so vile?'

'Hunh.'

'Begum...'

'Unh?'

'There's no other soul upon this bridge. Why don't you lift your veil so I might see your face in this divine moonshine?'

Roshanara stopped, and lifted her veil. Nawab Akbar Ali's started to breathe hard. Was he seeing Roshanara for the first time in his life?

'What are you looking at?' Roshanara asked.

'You.'

Roshanara smiled. 'I'm merely flesh and blood.'

'No, Begum, today I feel that's not all,' Akbar Ali's voice quivered as he said this.

'It's the moonlight that makes you say so, Nawab-sahib!' Roshanara walked on. 'Let's go.'

Akbar Ali took a few steps and stopped abruptly. 'Here...' he said.

'What's here?'

Akbar Ali looked around surreptitiously, steadied himself, and lowered his voice to a whisper. 'This is where he was waiting.'

'Who?' Roshanara's voice was disinterested.

That irritated the nawab. 'That... That madman!'

That roused Roshanara's interest. 'But how did he arrive here?' she asked. 'And why was he here?'

Leaning on the bridge, Akbar Ali said, 'I asked him to come here. I told him, "She by whose orders you used to write the letters, for whose voice you've become distraught, do you wish to hear her again? Do you want to see her once?" He

looked at me in astonishment and said, "Yes, I'll listen to her, and
see her…" I asked him, "What will you do when you see her?"
He laughed and said, "I'll only look at her, and listen to her
speak."

Roshanara stood still as a stone as she listened.

Akbar Ali carried on. 'I said to him, "That won't be possible
at home, people will say evil things. It will be better for you
come to the Gomti bridge at 11 in the night. Then you can
see Begum-sahiba to your heart's content." He consented. "I'll
be on the bridge at 11 o'clock." When I arrived, punctually, I
found him waiting…'

'Where?' Roshanara asked feebly.

'There, at that stop.' Akbar Ali pointed out the place.

'Then I said to him, "Begum is here, but you must look the
other way because she's feeling shy. You will turn around when
I ask you to." "Yes yes, I'll do as you say," he muttered under
his breath and turned around at once to face the river. I strode
towards him then, halfway, I took off my shoes and tip-toed up
to him. He never felt my presence, he never looked back. He
was steadily staring at the Gomti, as if focused on a thought,
and muttering to himself. I looked in every direction to ensure
no one was around; then I quickly lifted him up and shoved
him over.'

As Akbar Ali finished talking, a sudden blast of wind blew
up, as if from the depths of the river, threw dust in Akbar Ali's
eyes and blew off Roshanara's burqa. It rustled the papers and
dry leaves scattered on the bridge and whizzed by like the
batting of a hawk's wings, as an unknown bird cried out in the
darkness. It almost sounded human; as if Solayman-mian had
cried out from the other world, 'Would you have a letter written,
Begum-sahiba? A letter?'

Akbar Ali trembled as the whining of the wind petered off.
As everything went still, the soft susurrus of the Gomti sounded

like moaning. This complex world of longings and desire dreamed on in the surreal glow of the moon

'Where was the madman standing, Nawab-sahib?' Roshanara Begum wanted to know.

Akbar Ali pointed out the spot without uttering a word. Roshanara went there and leaned forward to look at the river below. The fractured moonbeams shimmered upon the flowing water like countless shards of broken glass.

Roshanara said, 'I shall recite the Fatiha now. Please close your eyes and pray to Allah, Nawab-sahib, that the Munificent Almighty forgive your sin.'

Akbar Ali closed his eyes.

Roshanara raised her palms in supplication and started to recite the Fatiha. It was an indescribable, sad, yet spellbinding voice. 'Ya Khuda, we are immersed up to our necks in sin, please forgive us… O Benevolent Rahim, O Munificent Karim! Bless the ones whose thirst was not quenched in this life, whose dreams remained dreams… Bless that they be fulfilled now. Victory to you, O Allah…'

The voice stopped unexpectedly. There was a scraping sound. Akbar Ali opened his eyes to a fleeting view of Roshanara Begum jumping off the bridge.

A split second. But in that split second Akbar Ali turned to stone and shook free. In that split second Akbar Ali became intimately acquainted with death. In that split second he saw Roshanara with her arms flailing through the air like some fabled fairy, and then, like a body carved out of stone, she descended to the river and hit the waters with a resounding splash. Momentarily. Then the cold, bottomless flow of the Gomti claimed Begum-sahiba forever.

Like a man possessed, Akbar Ali bent over the parapet and shouted in despair, 'Ro-sh-an-arra-aa.'

Gomti mockingly echoed his cry: 'Ro-sh-an-arra-aa–'

Akbar Ali fell silent. Roshanara's death cleared up the mystery. The truth was revealed. And the truth was as frightening as death...

Saadiq Hossain stopped. Beads of sweat spread on his forehead. Utter silence engulfed the waiting room. The thunderstorm outside had ceased. The wristwatch stood at one minute past midnight.

'But what happened to Nawab-sahib after that?' Ranbir Singh wanted to know.

Saadiq Hossain drained the last bit of whisky from the bottle into his glass and wanly smiled. 'But that's not the real story,' he said. 'Even the conclusion is not the purpose of our story.'

'But Roshanara Begum?' I was curious. 'Do you mean to say...'

Saadiq Hossain smiled again but said in a tired, lonely voice. 'If you dissect art too much, Ashok, it loses its essence, its rasa. Yes, unnatural though it may've been, Roshanara Begum too had fallen in love with Solayman-mian—only by listening to his voice! Standing on either side of the diaphanous curtain, both had been maddened by the call of the same magic flute. One could guess what Solayman-mian went through, but no one could guess what was in Roshanara's heart. It is possible that she believed these words of Daag; it is possible too that the shayar describes the nature of all women!

Apne dil ko bhi bataaun na thikana tera
Sabne jaana, jo pata ek ne jaana tera...

(I won't reveal your address even to my own heart,
If even one soul knows, the world will get wind of it...)'

Cooo-ooo-ooo... The plaintive whistle of a train's engine was heard in the distance. It somehow sounded like Akbar Ali's despairing cry: 'Ro-sh-an-arra-aa-'

Ignoring the grating sound of the engine, I looked once more at Saadiq Hossain. All at once, I had the intuition that Nawab Saadiq Hossain and Nawab Akbar Ali were one and the same.

Translated by Dipankar Ghosh

Editor's Note

A Pen That Loved Man

Time and again, the strange ironies and mysteries of History have lit up your questioning mind. At the centre of history is Man. History is the conveyor belt that leads man from past to present, sometimes with affection, mostly through rough and tumble. History never stands still; it makes its way ahead through conflicting turns of events. You found a way to still Time in your pages. In *Daak Diye Jaai*, published in *Prabhati* from Patna, Bengalis discovered the language anew. It indicated the dawn of a new chapter.

Through the 1940s, your writings reflected your progressive thought that confronted the brutality of imperialist activities. Your world of letters brought home to Bengali readers your pain, your anger, your desire to free Mother India of her chains. With the mind-set of a historian, you portrayed the ugly face of communalism unleashed by Independence. It revealed to the populace the many walls that fragmented our land. A worshipper of humanity, you waged relentless battles against this compartmentalization of our identities, in the name of caste, creed, colour and class. Love for Man is your signature tune.

—Citation from the Bangiya Sahitya Parishad Award

I am truly privileged to write this note as the editor of this collection of stories penned by my father, Nabendu Ghosh (1917-2007). *That Bird Called Happiness* is the first anthology of stories to take Baba to an English-speaking readership. Before this, *Me and I*—translated by the author's grandson Devottam Sengupta—presented him to young adults through a volume of space-travel fiction that blends scientific theories about cosmic life with tenets of faith—a racy adventure that perhaps only Nabendu Ghosh could imagine, being adept at writing screenplays in Bollywood for six decades and more. Other than that, a single story, 'Market Price', appeared in English as part of *River of Flesh: The Prostituted Woman in Indian Short Fiction*. Published by Speaking Tiger, that anthology effectively set off this one.

Baba was very keen that his literary self should reach readers outside Bengal. That is where he spent a major part of his life—growing up in Patna, making a living in Bombay, teaching students at the Film and Television Institute of India (FTII), Pune, receiving national awards in the rajdhani, Delhi, leading delegations to Kerala, spending a rare family holiday in Goa, going on a pilgrimage to the Himalayas... His writings reflect all of this India: the Quit India movement, the Bengal famine, communal riots, the Partition that bled Independence, the industrialization of the '50s, the political unrest of the '60s, Mukti Juddha—the Bangladesh Liberation War—and the nuclear tests. His writing was also influenced by historical India, by the days when Buddha walked upon this soil. For, the Prophet of Ahimsa was as integral a part of his life as was the Vaishnav principle of love for life even in a blade of grass.

Born in Dhaka to Suniti Bala and Nabadweep Chandra, Nabendu Ghosh had their love for letters coursing through him. In his pre-teens, he was so charmed by Bankim Chandra's Durgesh Nandini that he stayed up nights to create a Nawab Nandini. The copycat act was interrupted by his father, who advised him: 'Learn from those you admire, but write from life around you.' The budding writer did just that, even as he wrote for the school's hand-written magazine, and grew up to become the voice of the 1940s. When he sent his stories to established literary magazines in Kolkata, he kept their attention riveted and had no problem being published. So, in 1945, after losing two government jobs for 'seditious writing', he shifted to Calcutta to live by the dint of his pen.

A house on Pataldanga Street near College Street—Boi Para—became his home. The same house had another tenant, Narayan Gangopadhyay, a professor who is immortalized by his creation of 'Tennyda'. Not far off lived Narendranath Mitra, the author of *Ras* which provided the basis for the Amitabh-Nutan starrer, *Saudagar*. These three 'N's were the Young Turks of Bengali literature after the three Bandopadhyays—Tarashankar, Bibhuti Bhushan and Manik—who had effected a stylistic break from the towering personality of Tagore.

Another 'N'—poet Nirendranath Chakraborty—was their contemporary and a close friend of Nabendu. Of course, his friends included the 'S's too: Samaresh Bose, Sushil Jana, Santosh Kumar Ghosh, and the poet Subhash Mukhopadhyay. It was a clime he would not dream of giving up. Yet, before the dawn of 1950s, he had to follow the route Saradindu Bandyopadhyay—creator of the fictional detective Byomkesh Bakshi—had taken, to Bombay. Here's why: After Partition, when Urdu was declared the official language of the newly founded state of Pakistan—although 95 per cent of the population spoke only Bengali—books from West Bengal were banned in erstwhile East Bengal. Cinema too was grappling with the economic crisis unleashed by the halving of viewers. It was a massive setback for the Calcutta-based literary and film market. In a way it was this political division that prompted Nabendu Ghosh to join Bimal Roy when he left New Theatres—then reeling under the loss of its studio in Lahore—to make films for Bombay Talkies.

With Bimal Roy, Nabendu Ghosh shared a rare bonding. From 1951, when they left to make *Maa*, to 1964, when *Bandini* was awarded at the Karlovy Vary film festival in the Czech Republic, the writer was by the side of the director, creating classics that include *Parineeta, Baap Beti, Naukri, Biraj Bahu, Devdas, Yahudi* and *Sujata*. What made their creative association work was the common binding of love for humanity—the film-guru's expressed on celluloid, the writer's through his pen. Through the '50s and the '60s, Baba also lent his talent to the cinematic geniuses of Guru Dutt, Vijay Bhatt, Phani Majumdar, Gyan Mukherjee, Satyen Bose, Asit Sen, Sushil Majumdar, Raj Khosla, Lekh Tandon, Shakti Samanta, Prakash Mehra, Mohan Segal, and Dulal Guha, not to mention his 'gurubhais' Hrishikesh Mukherjee and Basu Bhattacharya. This turned him into a legend in screen-writing; but at no point did he stop penning the novels and stories which kept winning him the many literary honours awarded in Bengal: Amrit Puraskar, Bimal Mitra Puraskar, Bibhuti Bhushan Arghya, Bangiya Sahitya Puraskar, and the Bankim Puraskar awarded by the state government.

The thirty novels and fifteen anthologies that bear his name are marked by his distinct attitude towards life. His literary efforts are, to quote him, 'pointing fingers'. Literature was, for him, an instrument to tackle all that is sordid and destructive in life, the society or the state. What endeared him to readers was the simple, direct structure of his dialogues. The paragraphs were short, and his uncomplicated writing made even complex thoughts easy to comprehend. The multi-hued variety, deep empathy with human emotions, layers of meanings that add to the depth of the spoken words, subtle symbolism, and flights in the limitless sky of imagination—through it all speaks his love for Everyman. This man can, at times, be empty and loathsome; at other times he is supernatural. But no matter how unbearable his reality, Nabendu Ghosh's pen is rich with absorbed meditation.

Being productive until the age of ninety gave him the opportunity to write for several generations of readers. And, being unique, his themes continue to retain their charm. Sample some of them: In *Nayak O Lekhak* (Writer the Hero), a poor writer, sick of the reality around him, creates a hero who will head a revolution that'll change the world. In *Daak Diye Jaai* (The Clarion Call), a militant, a nationalist, a communist and a writer dream that all parties will unite to force the British to Quit India. *Dweep* is an allegory of love set in an island scorched by communal conflagration. A pious Muslim lays down his life in *Phears Lane* to save a Hindu family during the 1946 riots. *Prithibi Sabar* (This Earth Is Ours) recounts a movement, mounted by tribals in North Bengal, to win back their rights to fish in a lagoon. *Ajab Nagarer Kahini* (In a Curious Land), another allegorical novel about life, society and politics, is still considered unparalleled by scholars, writers and readers in Bengal and Bangladesh.

But, through the decades, these watershed creations have remained outside the curriculum of schools and colleges, because Baba was also scripting films that today constitute much of our celluloid classics. *Devdas* (1955), *Baadbaan* (1953), *Sujata* (1959), *Insaan Jaag Utha* (1958), *Aar-Paar* (1954), *Bandini* (1963), *Teesri Kasam* (1966), *Abhimaan* (1975), *Lal Patthar* (1971), *Do Anjaane* (1976), *Trishagni* (1989)—these are just a few on the list. Note that here, too, effectively Nabendu Ghosh was retelling stories penned by literary greats, be they Sarat Chandra, Subodh Ghosh, Saradindu Bandyopadhyay, or Manik Bandopadhyay, Bibhuti Bhushan and Phaniswar Nath Renu. For, he maintained, 'every writer is the product of the land and the clime he is born into. As such, each has his individual "window" to assess the world. This is what brings freshness into the eternal emotions tying men and men, men and women.'

Perhaps writing for cinema equipped Nabendu Ghosh with

the ability to imagine situations and incidents as if they were unfolding before his eyes. Or perhaps this quality already existed in his writings even before Bimal Roy asked him to join his team as a screenplay-writer. At any rate, we find the writer assuming the position of a viewer with an over-arching presence. Most of his stories are, then, narrated by a witness who was present when it happened. Sometimes it is a persona in the drama who is looking back; at other times it is a friend, an acquaintance, a crow, a monkey, a ghost, or the moon—the only constant through waxing and waning centuries—as in *Chaand Dekhechhilo* (Witness: The Moon) which fetched him the Bankim Puraskar in 2006.

Nabendu Ghosh carried his love for literature to the FTII, where he was a guest lecturer for a full twenty-five years, from 1966 to 1991. Among those who acknowledge him as a master who trained them for life are Kumar Shahani, Jaya Bachchan, Vikas Desai, Aruna Raje, Girish Kasaravalli, Vidhu Vinod Chopra, Syed Mirza, Ketan Mehta, Sanjay Leela Bhansali, Kundan Shah, his son Subhankar Ghosh, Ashoke Viswanathan and Shyamal Sengupta. Almost all of them went on to win National Awards for their work, and every one of them have acknowledged 'Sir's' role in their growth, by rekindling a lost love for literature which, he always stressed, was essential even for film-writing.

In particular, those who attended FTII in the 1980s were heavily into image-building—they thought writing 'a rather unnecessary pre-condition'. Nabendu Ghosh brought them back to the value of writing in cinema. 'In his classes he dinned screen-writing foundations into the students through an engaging emphasis on the value of plot-making, of strong characterization, and above all, the supreme value of social contexts,' says Shyamal Sengupta, who scripted the National Award-winners *Antaheen* and *Anuranan*. To unfold the truth, to make even the unexperienced a part of our realization, is the obligation of literature. And Baba dedicated his life to this.

My thanks to Anurag Basnet of Speaking Tiger for having made possible this befitting finale to the Nabendu Ghosh Birth Centenary. I am grateful to my elder brother, Dr Dipankar Ghosh, for setting out on the onerous task of translating Baba's stories while he was still alive. I say 'Thank you, Bubun-di' to Aparajita Sinha for her labour of love. And I shower affection on my 'sisters' Mitali Chakravarty and Shoma Bhattacharjee, student, former colleagues—you have made the journey possible. And Dilip Rangachari; I thank god for giving me a friend who made time to read, iron out angularities, and inspire with appreciation.

May *That Bird Called Happiness* be everybody's!

April 2018 RATNOTTAMA SENGUPTA

Notes on the Translators

Born to pioneer filmmaker Bimal Roy and Manobina Roy, one of India's earliest women photographers, **Aparajita Sinha** has grown up with an abiding love for the arts. She founded Sanskar to nurture the performing arts, and Moving Images to promote love for cinema. A freelance journalist who subtitled films for the National Film Development Corporation, she made two documentaries for Doordarshan and Channel 4, UK.

Dipankar Ghosh qualified as a physician from Calcutta in 1969 and worked as a surgical specialist after he emigrated to the UK. There he joined the Royal Army Medical Corp and retired as a Colonel in 2006. But, being the son of Nabendu Ghosh, he has always nursed his literary side and, after retirement, is pursuing his interest in translation.

Mitali Chakravarty writes essays, short stories, poetry and reviews. Her bylines have appeared in *The Times of India, Pioneer, Statesman* and *Hindustan Times.* Her poetry has been included in two anthologies, *In Reverie* (2016) and *An Anthology of Indian Poetry in English* (1984). She has also authored a book, *In the Land of Dragons.* She also writes for kitaab.org and blogs at 432m.wordpress.com.

Ratnottama Sengupta, formerly Arts Editor of *The Times of India,* writes for newspapers and journals, teaches mass communication and film appreciation, curates film festivals and art exhibitions, and writes books. The daughter of Nabendu Ghosh, she has written *Krishna's Cosmos,* a biography of the pioneer printmaker Krishna Reddy, and also entries on Hindi films for *Encyclopedia Britannica.* She has been a member of the Central Board of Film Certification, served on the jury of the National Film Awards, and has herself won a National Film Award. In 2017, she directed *And They Made Classics,* a documentary about Nabendu Ghosh.

Shoma Bhattacharjee has fourteen years of experience with leading media houses. She currently writes commissioned articles on art, translates from Bengali to English, and edits journals. A freelance instructional designer with TIS, she makes time to pursue two passions: photography and travel.